IT'S OUR PROM

(SO DEAL WITH IT)

IT'S OUR PROM

(SO DEAL WITH IT)

A NOVEL BY
JULIE ANNE PETERS

Megan Tingley Books
Little, Brown and Company
New York   Boston

ALSO BY JULIE ANNE PETERS:

Between Mom and Jo

Define "Normal"

grl2grl

Keeping You a Secret

Luna

Pretend You Love Me

She Loves You, She Loves You Not…

Copyright © 2012 by Julie Anne Peters
Questions for Discussion copyright © 2012 by Little, Brown and Company

Little, Brown and Company

Hachette Book Group
237 Park Avenue, New York, NY 10017
Visit our website at www.lb-teens.com

Little, Brown and Company is a division of Hachette Book Group, Inc.
The Little, Brown name and logo are trademarks of Hachette Book Group, Inc.

The publisher is not responsible for websites (or their content) that are not owned by the publisher.

First Paperback Edition: April 2013
First published in hardcover in April 2012 by Little, Brown and Company

Library of Congress Cataloging-in-Publication Data

Peters, Julie Anne.
It's our prom (so deal with it) : a novel / by Julie Anne Peters. — 1st ed.
p. cm.
"Megan Tingley Books."
Summary: Told in separate voices, Azure, who is a lesbian, and Luke, who is bisexual, help plan an inclusive senior prom while Luke is writing and producing a musical about his life, both are working through the crush they have on their friend Radhika, and all three are dealing with problems at home.
ISBN 978-0-316-13158-2 (hc) / ISBN 978-0-316-13144-5 (pb)
[1. Proms—Fiction. 2. Interpersonal relations—Fiction. 3. Lesbians—Fiction. 4. Bisexuality—Fiction. 5. High schools—Fiction. 6. Schools—Fiction. 7. Family problems—Fiction. 8. Popularity—Fiction.]
I. Title. II. Title: It is our prom, so deal with it.
PZ7.P44158It 2012
[Fic]—dc23   2011031756

10 9 8 7 6 5 4 3 2 1

RRD-C

Printed in the United States of America

To the JAP Mafia,
the most loyal and loving fans in the world

AZURE

There must be an epidemic of flu or cold virus going around, because when I walk into my last class I see Mr. What's-His-Sub, the same guy I had in third period. He says, "Your teacher didn't leave any lesson plans, so you can use this time as a study hour." Good idea. I pull out my cell and scroll through my pics from Friday night.

We made our usual entrance to the theater, walking down the side aisle all the way to the front. As we crossed the curtain, Luke and I waved to people in the audience, while Radhika shielded her eyes as if she didn't know us. People turned to see who we were waving to, which was hilarious because we didn't know anyone. Then the three of us climbed the steps to the back row and scooted in with our tub of popcorn and supersized Icee to share. Luke plopped down next to Radhika, so I stepped over them to sit on the other side of her. I still remember the first whiff of her jasmine-scented shampoo, and how my breath caught.

Luke started pitching popcorn in the air and catching it in his mouth. "Radhika," he said, tossing a kernel to her. She stuck out her tongue, but missed. Luke grabbed a fistful of popcorn and threw it high in the air, all of us opening our mouths like hungry chicks, and laughing when most of the popcorn landed on our laps or the floor. I picked out a kernel from Radhika's hair and ate it. She turned and smiled.

That's the first picture I snapped on my cell. I study it and imagine her lips on mine. Shiver.

The next pics are a series with the three of us, heads together, making silly faces, or sipping from the Icee. Me, Radhika, and Luke.

How long had it been since the three of us had gone out together to a movie? Too long. I missed "us."

I'm so engrossed in scrolling through the pictures over and over that when the bell buzzes, I'm startled back to the present.

"Get a lot of homework done, did you?" the sub says to me on my way out.

I turn slowly. "Yeah," I go. "I read *War and Peace* on my iPhone."

"I've been waiting for you." Mr. Gerardi, the principal, ambushes me as I shut my locker door. "Follow me." He turns and lumbers down the hall of doom toward his office.

I grimace. Last week Luke and I had the bright idea to superglue UNISEX over the faculty restroom sign. It seemed only right; the Diversity Club has been campaigning for a unisex bathroom for the last three years. Now we have one.

We get to his office and Mr. Gerardi says, "Sit down, please," as he circles his desk. He folds his hands on top and smiles one of those smiles that looks like it hurts every muscle in his face. "I have a proposition, Azure," he says.

Uh-oh. When my dad says that, it means do or die.

"Is this going to take long?" I ask. "Because my ride's waiting."

"It might," he answers. "Do you have another way home?"

"Let me make a call." My heart thrums in my chest as I text Luke:

In deep shit. Go ahead w/out me. Blame you later.

After I drop my cell in my bag, Mr. Gerardi says, "Do you remember how last year you circulated the petition to eliminate prom?"

"It wasn't just me."

"But you started it."

Did I? Luke was the one who got all the signatures. I'm about as popular as herpes.

"If I recall correctly, your complaint was that prom wasn't inclusive."

"Because it's not," I say.

His smile is stuck in place and it's creeping me out. "Apparently, one of the board members got hold of the petition and agrees with you. Prom should be an event for

3

every student in school. Although I don't see how it's not inclusive—"

"It's elitist." I edge forward in my chair. "It's so expensive only the richie rich can afford it, then the populars are the only people who go, so they can be seen. You have to take a date or you're labeled a loser."

Mr. Gerardi's smile fades from his face. He doesn't respond, so I go on.

"The tickets are seventy-five dollars, then you have to buy a dress and shoes you'll probably only wear once, or rent a tux. There's the cost of the limo, and probably dinner before or after." Not that I'd know. I've never been to prom. "I bet it comes to three hundred dollars. I'd have to work for fifty years to make that much money. Even then, I wouldn't go because right now I don't have a girlfriend."

I choke. TMI.

Mr. Gerardi must space my last comment because he asks, "If it was cheaper, would you go?"

"Not the way it is. I mean, the geeks, freaks, and uniques, like me, don't feel welcome at prom. It's a dance, but it could be so much more."

"Like what?"

"Like...I don't know. I haven't thought about it. Because nothing will ever change."

He plasters on that fakey smile again. "What if I gave you a chance to make a change? Would you consider serving on the prom planning committee so the event would be more inclusive?"

"Are you serious?"

"It was suggested by the board. You don't have to—"

"I'll do it."

He fidgets with a paper clip on his desk. "Your biggest problem is time. You're going to have to organize this thing fast. It's already January, and the prom's in April. Mrs. Flacco, who usually sponsors the committee, has... dropped out. But I did manage to persuade another teacher to be the sponsor."

He makes it sound like he had to beg, bribe, or torture a teacher to volunteer. "Who?" I ask.

"Mr. Rosen."

My eyes light up. Mr. Rosen is cool. He's young and has a ponytail, and from what I've heard all the girls are gaga for him. But not only the girls—Luke signed up for Mr. Rosen's Life Skills class, even though Luke's basically been living on his own for the past eight months.

"Can I ask people to be on the committee with me?"

"That's up to Mr. Rosen. I'm not sure who's already signed on." Mr. Gerardi stands, brushes by me, and holds open the door.

"Thanks, Mr. Gerardi." I head out. "Really. It's going to be great. You won't regret this."

His smile is kind of jagged. Behind me, I hear him mutter, "I think I already do."

Slipping into the unisex restroom, I text Radhika and Luke:

Guess what? They want us to be on the prom planning committee. Can you believe it? We're going to PIMP THE PROM.

5

* * *

I catch the bus home, and by the time I get there, I haven't heard back from either Radhika or Luke. Radhika, I can understand. She leaves right after sixth period and has to turn her cell off at home to study. But Luke? I call him as I'm traipsing up the drive to my house. "Didn't you get my text?"

"Yeah, I did," he says. "I just don't know if I can handle another commitment. I have my play, you know."

"Luke, this is what we've always wanted! Our prom. An alternative prom. The way we envisioned it, with everyone having a reason to come."

He sighs. "I know. I'm just really busy. I haven't even written all the music."

"Did I mention Mr. Rosen is the committee sponsor?"

I picture Luke's jaw dropping and drool sliding down his chin. "When do we meet?" he asks.

"I have to talk to Mr. Rosen first, but I'll let you know."

Dad's getting ready to leave as I open the door and slip out of my leather jacket. "Do you need a ride to work?" he asks. "I'm going your way."

"Going where?" I ask him.

He shoulders his holster, which means he's going to the shooting range. He blasts human targets to work off stress. I hate that he's a cop. Couldn't he find a safer job, like Ponzi schemer?

"I don't need to be there for another couple of hours," I tell him. "I'll catch the light-rail." It stops three blocks from the thrift store near Exempla Hospital in Denver.

"Oh, and I downloaded the police scanner, so I'll know if there's an officer down."

He tousles my hair before shutting the door behind him. I wonder if there is a police-scanner app. I'm always afraid that one night I'll get the call, or the doorbell will ring, and the officer on the porch will inform me: "I'm sorry. He died doing what he loved."

What does it matter if you die doing what you love or hate? Especially if the daughter you leave behind has to go live with her psycho mother?

I crank up my nano as loud as possible without my eardrums exploding. For English, we're supposed to choose our favorite opening line from a list we got in class of the one hundred best first lines in literature. So far I have it whittled down to "Call me Ishmael." Brilliant.

"I was born twice: first, as a baby girl, on a remarkably smogless Detroit day in January of 1960; and then again, as a teenage boy, in an emergency room near Petoskey, Michigan, in August of 1974." That's from *Middlesex*, which I actually read and loved. Or, "Lolita, light of my life, fire of my loins." My mind drifts and I think about prom. About what could make it the most magical night of my life. One word: *Radhika*.

How do you tell your best friend you're in love with her without ruining the friendship? Or making it awkward, or scaring her to death because you know, you're absolutely sure, she couldn't possibly feel the same way about you? At the thought of her my palms sweat and all my pores swell. I can't remember the last time I felt this way. It's been a while. Whenever Radhika's near, I want to take her in my arms, kiss her until we're both gasping for breath, then know — *know* — she feels the crush of passion I do. Even though she doesn't, and she can't, and she never will, because Radhika Dal isn't gay or bi or even curious. She loves me as a friend, and it'll never be anything more than that.

I see my cell light up and Radhika's ID appear. My stomach vaults and I toss my homework aside. I have a voice mail, too. How did I miss that?

"Tell me about pimping the prom," Radhika says.

I glance at my clock. Yikes. Time flies when you're fanning the fire in your loins. I fill her in on Mr. Gerardi asking if we'll plan an alternative prom as I sling my pack over my shoulder and rush out the door for work. "You'll help, won't you?"

She says, "What does it involve?"

"I don't know yet. I've never planned a prom, not to mention an alt one."

Radhika hesitates.

"Please. You have to. I can't do this alone."

"Can we talk about it tomorrow?" she asks.

"Sure." I don't want her to hang up, so as I'm sprinting down the drive, I say, "What are you doing?"

"Nothing. I finished my homework a while ago and now I'm just waiting for Mom and Dad to go to bed so I can Netflix a movie."

"Wish I could be there to watch it with you."

The silence stretches, which is unusual between us. "What's going on, Radhika?"

She expels an audible breath. "Mom and I had a fight."

"Over what?" Radhika and her mom never fight. Unlike other mothers and daughters who can't be together five minutes before they start screaming at each other.

"I want to cut my hair short like yours, and she won't let me."

"No!" I blurt out. Radhika can't cut her hair. It's gorgeous. Long and black and sleek as silk. "I'm still trying to grow mine out from the last time I butchered it," I say.

"You didn't. It looks..."

Hideous. I hear the train in the distance and start trotting. "I think you should think about it." Long and hard.

"It's my hair," Radhika says. "I should be able to do anything I want."

She's right. But still.

Radhika says, "My mother's so controlling. I thought I'd have more freedom now that I'm eighteen. You know?"

I send her a mental plea: *Please, please don't cut your hair.*

"I left you a message," Radhika says. "You can just delete it. I'll see you tomorrow."

"Wait!" But the line's already gone dead. The light-rail screeches to a stop and passengers surge out. I hop on board, grab a seat in back, and listen to Radhika's message. "You didn't tell me what your self-affirmation was for today."

My self-affirmation. I forgot. I pull out the calendar

page and reread it: "Undertaking endeavors that seem beyond reach will grow you as a person from the inside out."

Radhika gave me this daily self-affirmations calendar for Christmas. I love it. I'd love it even if I didn't love it just because she picked it out for me.

Undertaking endeavors beyond my reach…That could be anything. That could be prom. That could be Radhika.

When did she leave this message on my cell? I listen again for the time. Right about when she would've gotten home from school. Which means she was thinking about me at the same time I was texting her. Karma? I save her message, the way I do all her messages, to play at night so hers is the last voice I hear before falling asleep.

LUKE

"Wonker. Fill up the munchie bowl," Dobbs calls from the dining area where he's playing poker with my brother, Owen, and their crew. Of course Dobbs is referring to me. Does he care that I'm comfy on the sofa? That I'm fine-tuning my script on my netbook and watching a *Top Chef* marathon? Does he realize his cursing and throwing cards down and crushing cans under his foot is driving me to digital distraction? "Hey! You deaf?" he goes.

I look at Owen. He doesn't glance up, doesn't shut Dobbs down.

I set my computer on the coffee table and unfurl my legs. As I kick through a pile of crushed cans to retrieve a bag of mustard pretzels (those things are nasty), Dobbs goes, "Get me a Coke while you're up, faggot."

The tips of my ears burn. I wait for Owen to throw himself across the table and smash a fist into Dobbs's face, beat him to a bloody pulp. Instead, Owen deadpans, "He prefers to be called 'maggot.'"

Owen's crew snickers. I pretend I can't find the Coke, even though there are cases of it in the fridge.

Dobbs says, "Any day, zitwit."

I dump the pretzels into the bowl. Crumpling the bag, I fling it to the floor, knowing full well I'll be the one cleaning up. Accidentally on purpose, I overturn the bowl of pretzels into Dobbs's lap.

He stands and pushes me against the wall. His beefy hand clenches my neck.

Owen says, "Cool it, Dobbs. He's just a spaz."

Eyes shooting sparks, Dobbs lets me know who's in charge. He releases me with a shove.

Owen shuffles the deck of cards nonchalantly as Dobbs resumes his seat. "Don't call him 'faggot,'" Owen tells Dobbs. "He's bisexual."

Owen's crew "oohs" like a bunch of owls in heat. Dobbs curls a lip at me.

Cram it, I think. I head back to the sofa.

"Luke," Owen says, "he's sorry he didn't know you swing both ways. Tell him you're sorry, Dobbs."

Dobbs isn't Owen's lackey, the way I am. The look he gives me is: *If we ever meet in a dark alley, only the ugly one is coming out alive.*

"And if I don't?" Dobbs says.

Owen deals the cards. "I'll give you the cougar run next weekend." Everyone laughs.

Cougars are like the Real Housewives, but single and slutty. They pick up these boy toys in bars and party all night, then trash Owen's limos. Owen owns and operates a gypsy transport company, sort of a rogue limo and sedan service. He's never been one to work for The Man. He *is* The Man. He keeps telling me that: Don't forget who's *The Man.*

Even though Owen's drivers are supposed to return their vehicles in immaculate condition, guess who ends up scrubbing cougar vomit? Not Dobbs.

Dobbs breaks a pretzel in half and goes, "Soooooooooooo sorry."

Soooooooooooo insincerely. You can always judge a person by his taste in friends. Owen's palate is putrid.

When I first moved into Owen's house, after Mom and Dad got stationed overseas in Stuttgart, I thought my brother and I would hang out. Go to sporting events and concerts together. I thought I might even get Owen to take in a play or musical with me once in a while, seeing as how he could use some culture shock.

Futile fantasy. Owen's ten years older, and he's been on his own for a while. He bought this house in Lakewood that had horse property and converted the stable to a garage. I guess I had this idealized version of him in my head. Bachelor. Entrepreneur. Since the day I moved in, he's treated me like horseshit.

Some days, like today, I wish I had gone to Germany. But I really wanted to graduate with my friends. And when

Miss Wells, the theater director, came to me and asked if I'd expand this skit I wrote into a full-blown musical for the whole school, the deal was sealed.

The phone rings and Owen slides back his chair to take it. His loser pals groan. "It's an airport run," he says. "Who wants it?"

His employees stare down at their cards. A beat passes.

"I could take it," I say.

Owen just looks at me. He sighs. "I'll go. Sorry to break up the game, dudes."

Dobbs tosses his cards on the table harder than necessary. No doubt he blames me for the buzz kill. What he doesn't know is that Owen wouldn't let me take a fare if I begged, pleaded, or bribed him.

Another reason I moved in was I thought I could help out with Owen's business. I even got my chauffeur's license and taxi driver's permit. But not once has he asked me to pick up a client. The most I get to do is wash and wax, then equip the cars with magazines and water bottles, which any moron could do. Occasionally he lets me park the cars in the garage. Whoop-de-doo with a cherry on top.

Oh, and let's not forget scooping out cougar chunks.

It's not about the money, either. I could give Owen every dime from the fares and he still wouldn't let me represent his firm by driving an actual customer. It's me. I disgust him. He hates what I am.

Dobbs makes a point of yanking the pillow out from under my head on his way out.

Turd.

Everyone leaves and I have the bachelor pad to myself. I log on to Facebook IM and she's there. My pulse races. The only girl in the world who can turn me into butter with a smile. I think I'm in love with her. Take that back. I *know* I am. I type:

Sup, Radhika?

On the way to school Azure prattles on about all the awesome things we could do for prom. My head spins. I can't process one thought as fast as that girl can talk.

"I didn't get to ask Mr. Rosen about meeting times because he was out sick yesterday," she says, finally taking a breath.

"Tell me about it. We had Flacco for a sub. Her only life skill is living to a hundred and eighty." I stick out my tongue in disgust and Azure whaps my thigh. "Flacco actually taught us how to scrub toilets, like I haven't been doing that since I moved in with Owen. I was seriously considering stabbing a pencil in my eye to get a pass to the nurse." Azure laughs. Wistfully, I add, "I wish Radhika hadn't dropped the class."

"She dropped it? When?" Azure asks.

"After the first day."

"Why?"

"Something about it not being approved by her parents as intellectually challenging enough."

"It's only an elective. Can't she take one class for fun?"

"Apparently not."

"Why didn't she tell me?" Azure says. "She tells me everything."

She probably just forgot. Or Azure didn't give her a chance. Anyway, Radhika could blow off this entire semester and still graduate with straight As. She'd win Miss Congeniality, too. I've known her since the first day of junior high, and she's never said an unkind word about anyone. Smart and nice—a killer combo. Oh, and did I mention drop-to-your-knees-and-beg-for-mercy gorgeous?

"About the prom," Azure says. "I was thinking we could go all black. Black decorations, black clothes, black lights…"

I tune her out. Not that I don't care what she's saying, but now I'm thinking back on junior high. Azure, Radhika, and I were lab partners in biology. We just clicked. Seventh grade is hell anyway, and having Azure and Radhika for friends got me through. Even after I confided my sexuality to them, they weren't shocked or appalled. Azure because she had her own confession to make, and Radhika because she's a guardian angel. I think we were treated with more respect in school because of Radhika's acceptance and support.

Azure goes, "I hope Mr. Rosen's back today, because we need to get started ASAP."

I plug back in to her channel. I hate to tell her that my real fear about prom is that no matter what kind of event we put on, it won't be my vision of perfection unless I can go with my dream date.

"Who are you thinking of asking to prom?" I say to Azure as we pull into the parking lot.

She gets out and hikes her backpack over her shoulder. She must not hear, so I repeat, "Who are you going to ask —"

"We have a few minutes before the bell. Why don't we go to the teachers' lounge to see if Mr. Rosen's there?"

I have to hurry to keep up. The room's almost empty, but Azure knocks on the doorjamb and sticks her head in. "Mr. Rosen?"

He wanders over from the coffee area. "Hi, Azure. Luke." At the sound of my name, I melt.

"Did you get my note?" Azure asks.

"I did. The committee meeting is at two thirty today, if you can make it. Sorry for the short notice." His voice sounds nasally and he sneezes into his arm. He glances at me and says to Azure, "We already have five people. The bigger the group, the harder it is to come to a consensus. Sorry, Luke."

I thought it was a done deal that I was on the committee. I kick Azure's shin.

"But we need more people from the Diversity Club," Azure says, kicking me back. "Is everyone in favor of an alternative-type prom? Do they even know what it is? Do they care about making it happen? If it's just me against the world, we don't have a chance in hell of changing anything."

Mr. Rosen looks from Azure to me. "You're right. You're welcome to join, Luke. You'll be a great addition."

I feel my cheeks flame.

The bell blares and Mr. Rosen says, "We better bust it." He saunters over to a table to grab his backpack. Pivoting, he adds, "The meeting is in Art Studio 2B. If you're going my way, I'll walk with you, Luke."

We head down the corridor together, arms almost touching, and I swivel my head around, mouthing to Azure, *Oh. My. God.*

Her eyes roll back in her head.

AZURE

Radhika slides across from me at lunch, immediately stimulating all my senses. She's wearing a yellow cashmere sweater, which looks luscious against her dark skin and black hair. "Thank God you didn't cut your hair," I say. I want to clap a hand over my diarrhea mouth.

"I was this close" — she spaces her fingers a quarter inch apart — "and I couldn't do it. Don't ask me why."

"There's a reason for everything. Oh, wait. Someone told me that once." It was Radhika, when my girlfriend Ami dumped me. Best thing that ever happened.

Radhika smiles and my stomach breeds butterflies.

"Have you had a chance to think about joining the prom planning committee with me and Luke?" I ask her. *Please, please say you will.* We need a leader. Luke's good for support and all, but he's not an organizer or a chief, and neither am I.

Radhika takes a bite of salad, not glancing up.

"I know you're busy with your college prep stuff. This'll be fun, though. It's our senior year, and we can really make a difference by putting on a prom that includes everyone."

She still doesn't answer. I wish Luke had the same lunch hour as us because he's better than me at begging without it coming off as...well, begging.

"I was thinking we'd go all black. Black clothes, black lights. Or if that's too one-note, maybe rainbows. Rainbows represent diversity, which this is all about. What do you think?"

Radhika finally looks up. "Whatever you do will be amazing." She takes a gulp of Snapple.

Not me. Us. "Will you join the committee, though? I really need you. I mean, *we* do." I mean, *I* do.

Radhika pokes at her salad, and I'm getting this weird vibe from her. "Radhika...?"

"I can't. Mom and Dad would never let me do something so frivolous."

"It's not frivolous! It's important."

Radhika grabs her tray and stands.

"You could ask them, at least."

She casts her eyes down on me with a fierceness I've never seen before. It actually makes me flinch. There's something going on with Radhika that she's not telling me—beyond dropping a class, or cutting her hair. We've always shared everything. Why is she holding back?

I watch her dump her half-eaten salad in the trash and

think, *This is so not Radhika.* She's always happy, or at least content. Rarely emo. She keeps me grounded.

At the exit, she doesn't even turn around and wave or smile. This horrible feeling comes over me that everything I've known is about to change, and there's nothing I can do to stop it.

I'm startled when the final bell blares. My mind's been on Radhika all afternoon, on how I shouldn't have challenged her. Her parents have always been strict, and it's not my place to force a stupid issue like the prom com. I know she's under a lot of pressure to get good grades, and what she needs from me is encouragement. Encouragement and friendship.

I call Radhika as I'm packing my gear at my locker after school, but she doesn't answer. I can only hope it's because she's studying and not because she sees it's me on caller ID.

As I arrive in Studio 2B, Luke's already there, working on his netbook. He's alone in the room. "Mr. Rosen did tell us Studio 2B, right? At two thirty? Today?" I sit beside him.

Luke says, "That's what I heard." He clicks away on his keyboard.

Art classes must be doing pottery because the air smells like wet mud. I look at the vases and sculptures in various states of completion, feeling awed. Jealous. I wish I had an ounce of artistic ability. Luke got it all. He can draw, paint, sing, dance, produce, direct. "You're so damn greedy," I tell him.

He looks at me. "Huh?"

I point to a shelf. "Did you make that?" It's a miniature sculpture of a nude buff guy. I guess that's where the term *sculpted abs* comes from.

"No," Luke says. "But I plan to steal it."

A pair of giggling girls bounces into the room, interrupting our conversation. The Zeligman twins, Mollie and Haley. I'm not in their social orbit, but Luke is. Or was. Haley was his girlfriend for all of three weeks until she dumped him for Gabe Hightower. It took Radhika and me three banana splits to pull him out of his funk.

"Hey, Luke," Mollie says. They both dump their junk on the floor, ignoring me. "We're having a prom committee meeting in here."

Luke shuts his netbook. "We're on it."

They widen their eyes at each other. "Suh-weet," Mollie says. "It's going to be so super awesome." They take seats opposite us.

Mr. Rosen hurries in. "Sorry I'm late." He sets a folder on the table and blows his nose. "We're not all here yet." He opens the folder. "We're missing three people."

Haley goes, "Gabe decided he had other priorities."

She sounds pissed, but I see Luke's shoulders relax.

The last person swaggers in as if out of *GQ* magazine, and Luke gasps. It's Connor Spears, aka Fabio. Not only because his bleach-blond hair is long and wavy, but also because he's a gorgeous specimen, as Luke would say. If I were into guys…

Mollie says in a singsong, "Hi, Connor."

"Hey," he says in his deep voice. Luke literally hyperventilates. Connor scans the room and decides to sit on the twins' side of the table. Which is for the best, because if he'd pulled in next to Luke, we'd have had to resuscitate him.

Another person walks in and I throw up a little in my mouth. Shauna Creighton. I predict after graduation she'll have her own reality-TV show called *Bitch Intervention*.

There are stools stacked along the wall, and one empty chair next to Luke. She doesn't even move toward it; she just stands behind Mr. Rosen with her arms crossed, leaning against a shelf of pottery.

Mr. Rosen says, "Take a seat, Shauna. We need to get started."

"I'm fine," Shauna says.

"Please."

She expels a weary breath and walks over to pull out the chair next to Luke. She leans away from him like he's contagious.

Mr. Rosen kicks back in his seat, intertwines his fingers behind his head, and says, "This is going to be the most memorable prom Roosevelt High has ever known."

Mollie giggles.

Shauna says, "What does that mean?"

I answer her question: "We're having an alterna-prom."

"A what?"

"An alternative prom. Nontraditional. A prom that embraces inclusiveness and diversity."

Shauna slit-eyes Mr. Rosen. "Nobody told me that when I signed up this year."

Good, I think. *Maybe she'll quit.* I turn to Mr. Rosen. "What exactly do we have to do?"

Shauna answers for him. "Only pull off a miracle."

Mr. Rosen says, "I've never put a prom together, so I'm not going to be much help. Where do we begin?"

Shauna says, "We need to elect officers."

I sigh. "Do we really have to? There are only six of us."

"If we want organization and delegation of duties, then yeah," Shauna snipes. "We have to."

I know for a fact she's bucking for president. But this isn't her prom. "What's the next thing?" I ask.

"The theme," she says. "If we don't have a theme by this week, we're screwed."

"Oh, really? So I guess you've run the prom com before?"

"I was on the junior prom committee."

BFD, I think. *That makes you a prom pro.*

Mollie says, "Last year's prom was so super awesome. Everyone loved it."

"Since we're in a time crunch," Mr. Rosen says, "maybe the first thing we should decide is how often to meet."

Luke says, "I have play practice on Mondays, Tuesdays, and Thursdays."

On the days he has practice, I take the bus home or to

work. "I have to work after school, but I can probably change my schedule around our meetings," I say.

Connor says, "I have soccer every day, but it doesn't start until three fifteen."

Mollie and Haley go, "We have dance squad on Mondays and Wednesdays, and gymnastics on Tuesdays and Thursdays."

"Holy macaroni," Mr. Rosen says. "Would it be better to meet in the evening? Or before school?"

"Not before school!" Everyone starts whining about how early their first classes start.

Mr. Rosen holds up a hand. "Let me think about how to schedule this and get back to you."

"It better be soon," Shauna says. "Or we're up shit creek."

On the way out, I say to Luke, "Promise you won't give Shauna a paddle."

On my way to work I call Radhika, but her phone goes directly to voice mail. I tell myself it's because she's studying. She's not mad at me. She's never been mad at me. Is there really a first time for everything? I don't get why her parents are making her work so hard. She's already been accepted to Yale, yet she's carrying a full load of classes on the college track. Luke's going to art or theater school, and me? I'll be lucky to get into community college.

Every time I think about the three of us splitting up to go our separate ways, my stomach hurts. Luke, Radhika, and I are tight. They say blood is thicker than water, but it's not always true with friends as close as we are. I wish time would freeze so we could stay together forever.

Maybe that's why I want this prom to be a major blow-out, something we'll remember for the rest of our lives.

As I approach the door to the thrift shop, I leave Radhika a message that I'll call again when I get home from work. At the end, I say, "Love you," and hang up. One of these days I'm going to add, "I really do love you. And I mean that with all my heart."

Louisa, my boss, greets me. "Hi, Azure. I got a box of bona fide vintage clothes in today, and before I put them out, I thought you'd like to look through them."

"Seriously? Thanks."

Louisa adds, "Use your discount," then heads back into the donation room.

I don't agree with Louisa's policy that employees and volunteers at the thrift store can buy whatever they want for half price, and she knows it. Even if most of what we sell is discarded junk that would've ended up in a landfill or at Goodwill, the profits from the thrift store go to Kids with Cancer. How can anyone with a conscience steal from sick kids? I mean, what if it was *my* full-price purchase on a piece of junk jewelry that led scientists to discover the cure for leukemia?

As I'm arranging all the jewelry that came in sometime over the weekend, I spot these two ornate hairpins that I know Radhika would love. Sometimes she twists her hair in back, keeping it in place with scrunchies or bobby pins. Hair she absolutely *cannot* cut. Louisa priced the pins at

$125 each, or $230 for the pair. Ouch. As she passes behind me with an armload of clothes, I ask, "Are these real silver or something?" I point out the hairpins.

"I had my jeweler friend look at them, and he told me what collectors are paying for these old sterling silver pins from the turn of the century."

I imagine brushing Radhika's lustrous hair, curling it around my hand and pinning it up. I must be looking at the hairpins longingly because Louisa says, "Rethinking your half-price perk?"

"No way." I set them back on the velvet display card.

Louisa shakes her head, but smiles. "I'd be happy to put them on layaway."

Layaway. I glance again at the pins, visualizing Radhika's eyes gleaming when I give them to her. I make a decision. "Okay," I tell Louisa.

My cell jingles a text message and I sneak a peek at the caller ID. My heart leaps. The mountain of clothes in Louisa's arms begins to topple, so I rush over to catch them before they hit the floor. "Let me get these," I say. "I'm pretty good at pricing clothes."

"Don't price too high. And replace some of the older stuff on the front racks with new things so it looks like we have a bigger turnover."

I dump the load of clothes on the sorting table in back and read Radhika's text:

Sorry if I caught you at work. Don't want to get you in trouble.
Call later.

As I begin a text to Radhika, I remember when I first started working here, six months ago. I thought all the rooms smelled like musty old closets, so one day I brought in Glade air fresheners. Louisa beamed. "Thank you," she said. "I never even thought of that." Why wouldn't you think of that?

She really liked me after that. Before, I think, she had her doubts because of the way I dress and stuff. I mean, I have my own style, which combines glam, vintage, shabby, and chic. It's easy to make assumptions about people based on their style. My favorite color used to be black, but I've lightened up. Now it's dark blue.

I suggested to Louisa that the clothes are too crammed together in here and we shouldn't hang so many at once, and that we should organize accessories on the walls, and paint every room with bright colors to cheer up the place, and hang plants....

She said, "I'll get right on that."

Dad says I'm a total control freak. Like that's a bad thing.

So far my text back to Radhika reads:

No problem. I'm sorry if

I have too much to say, so I just call.
She asks, "Are you at work?"
"Yeah, but that's okay."
"I shouldn't be bothering you."

"You're never a bother," I tell her. "You know that."

At the same time, we both go, "I'm sorry about lunch," and laugh a little. Radhika adds, "I didn't mean to run out on you."

"I didn't mean to make a big deal out of prom com."

"It wasn't that," she says.

I hear it in her voice—a hesitation. "What's going on? Did you and your mom have another fight?"

"No. We're in truce mode. Walking on pins and needles."

"Eek. Bloody footprints on the Oriental rugs?"

Radhika laughs. "Did I tell you I absolutely loved that beaded necklace you wore today? Did you get that at the thrift shop?"

I don't want to discuss jewelry when there's an obvious crisis looming. But I don't want to upset her again, either. "Yeah. I keep telling you there's great stuff here. You need to come in."

There's a pause, then a change in Radhika's tone of voice. "Mom, do you mind? I'm talking to Azure."

I hear her mom say, "Tell her hello."

"Did you get that?"

"Say hi for me."

Radhika seethes under her breath, "I have no privacy at all. I feel like she watches my every move. My father, too. It's like I'm a prisoner in my own house."

"Have you talked to them about it? Maybe they don't realize—"

"They don't care. I'm sorry. I have to go." She hangs up.

"Azure, you through with those clothes?" Louisa eyes the lump of unsorted donations.

I shake out a rumpled shirt and think, *Shit.* I offended Radhika again. I need a self-affirmation—make that a confirmation—that reads: "For a control freak, you need to learn how to control what comes out of your mouth."

LUKE

Radhika calls me at 7:30 in the morning and says, "Will you pick me up for school?"

Like there's any question? "Sure."

"Not just today, but every day. I know it's an imposition."

"That word is not in my vocab. What about your college prep seminar—"

"I'm dropping it. If you don't want to drive me, that's okay. I'll find another way."

"I didn't say that. Did I say that? I'll be there in fifteen minutes."

She sounds snippy or mad, not like the chill Radhika I know.

I decide this is the occasion to bring out my big surprise. Radhika will be driven in style. It might even elevate me to prom stature in her eyes.

Radhika's gated community is on the way to Azure's

house, so she's my first stop. I press the buzzer and identify myself, and the gate draws open.

She's waiting for me on a porch step when I pull to the curb. Her gaze is fixed behind me, as if she's looking for my Kia. I get out and circle the Cadillac on foot. Her eyes widen. I open the passenger door in front and bow. "M'lady."

"Does Owen know you have this?" she says.

I click my tongue at her. "Would I steal his car?"

She just looks at me.

"Puh-leease. I value my life."

She tilts her head, those sultry eyes boring into me. I run around the car and hop in. As I start the ignition, Radhika peers into the back and says, "Roomy."

"I would've thought you'd ridden in hundreds of luxury vehicles, seeing as how your father is a sheik."

She laughs softly in that sweet, sexy way of hers.

"Not a sheik? A shah? A duke? The king of Siam?"

She shakes her head. I know he owns an international commodities firm, which means nothing to me except big money. Azure and I are sure there's royal blood running through Radhika's veins.

"How are you?" I ask. "I haven't seen you in a week. Which is forever and infinity."

"Okay." She stares out the side window, not sounding okay. Turning to face me, she forces a smile and goes, "But I miss being with you every day." My heart does a little flip. Does she mean me, personally?

"How are you?" she asks.

"Besides having to live with a sewer rat and working

32

my ass off to get this play done? I'm hanging, I guess. Then Azure signs me up to plan this alt prom." I sigh.

She sighs in exactly the same way. Now I know we're on the same wavelength.

"Have you decided where you want to go next year?" she asks.

"I've applied to UCLA, NYU, the American Conservatory Theater, the L.A. Film School, and the School of the Art Institute of Chicago. I doubt I'll get accepted anywhere."

"Luke. Don't be a pessimist. You know you're talented."

"Well, sure. *I* know it. But if I have to audition, I'll turn into a quivering mass of Velveeta." We pull into Azure's driveway and I check the dashboard clock: 8:05. We're going to be late if I don't haul ass. I honk. Smooth tone, like an English horn. I love this Cadillac Seville.

Azure tears out the door, then shuts and locks it. She pivots and stops dead, a priceless look on her face. Slowly, she advances toward the car. I get out and open the back door for her.

"Does he know you stole it?" she asks.

"Geesh. Not you, too."

Azure glances inside and sees Radhika. Her jaw drops to the ground and she opens the front door. She yanks Radhika out and hugs her. "I've been calling and texting you. I thought you were mad at me."

"No, I'm not mad. I just had a headache last night, then I figured I'd see you this morning."

Azure shuts Radhika's door and opens the back

passenger door. She climbs in and pulls Radhika in after her. "Drive, James," she says to me.

"What am I? Your chauffeur?"

"Duh," Azure says.

I stick out my tongue at her, which she misses because she's already babbling away at Radhika. I try to listen in, but it's girly talk and my mind drifts. I think about my play and how far I have to go to get it stageworthy.

There's a tap on my shoulder and I jerk back to the moment. Azure says, "How did you rate the Cadillac? Seriously."

"Owen said if I could get it running, it was mine."

"To keep?"

"That's what 'mine' means to me. He was ready to have it junked for parts, but I told him I'd trade my Kia for it. Naturally, he didn't want that hunk of junk. The Caddie only needed a rebuilt transmission. I got one from a guy on craigslist."

"Sweet," Azure says. "We should name it. Like, Moby Dickwheels."

Radhika laughs.

"Forget it," I say. "If Owen knows I'm even a little bit attached, he'll take it back."

Azure sniffs the air. "Why does it smell like bleach? Do you smell bleach, Radhika?"

In the rearview mirror, I see her nose wrinkle.

"It's not the car," I tell them. "It's me. Is it that strong?"

"It's lethal," Azure says. "Although there is a hint of Seduction mixed in."

She bumps Radhika's shoulder and they both smile. A tiny pang of jealousy ripples through me.

"Some kid had diarrhea all over the backseat of a taxi last night and Owen said he'd pay me twenty bucks this morning to get rid of the smell."

"Ew." That wipes the smiles off their faces.

A song comes on the radio and Azure leans forward. "Turn it up, Luke." It's Azure's new favorite band, Mercy Her. The song is "Now's the Time," which has dominated the airwaves and YouTube for weeks.

Azure and I sing along, but not Radhika. She says she's tone-deaf, which I don't believe for a minute. She's perfect in every way.

"Was your seminar canceled this morning?" Azure asks Radhika.

"No. I dropped it. Or at least I'm going to. Don't tell my parents."

I gasp. "You're rebelling against parental tyranny? You?"

Azure thunks me hard on the back of the head.

"Hey, that hurt."

"I'll be riding to and from school with you guys from now on," Radhika adds.

"Yay!" Azure cheers. "But won't your parents wonder why you're leaving so late?"

"No, because I told them the seminar time changed to two thirty."

"Genius," I say.

"I'll just study in the library until you're both ready to leave. Like I told Luke, I miss you. We never get to spend time together the way we used to. Just the three of us, you know?"

I know exactly what she means. I've been feeling nostalgic for the good old days myself. Not that they weren't without challenge. But thinking about graduating and having both of my security blankets ripped out from under me...

I feel a tear at the corner of my eye and swipe it away. I'm such a girl.

Mr. Rosen stops me on my way out of Life Skills and says, "We need to have a prom com meeting today."

"Today? But I have play practice after school."

"We'll keep it short. We just need to set up a schedule and get going."

Already I'm feeling pressured about dividing my time. Why did I let Azure talk me into the prom? "Yeah, okay. I might be a little late. I need to drop off the new and improved script. How often are we going to meet?"

"That's something else we need to talk about," Mr. Rosen says. He clamps a hand on my shoulder and smiles. My knees buckle.

Damn Azure. I never should've told her I had wet dreams about Mr. Rosen and me riding off into the sunset in a rebuilt Roadster.

After last period I race to the auditorium, where I almost collide with my stage manager, Ryan. "Hey," I say, pulling him aside. "Would you mind passing out this new script? I have to go to a short prom com meeting. Go ahead and do a read-through. You can play my part."

"M-me?" Ryan gulps.

I clap him on the back. "It's called acting."

"But…"

"There he is! Luke!" The cast swarms me before I can get away:

"We still don't have an opening song for Act Two."

"We're going to need sketches of the costumes if my mom's going to start sewing them."

"We need to start on the set design."

"People, people," I say, holding up my hands. "Chillax. Everything will come together. I'm working on songs for Act Two. I didn't like the direction it was going, anyway, so I rewrote most of it over the weekend."

"What?" Their communal echo reverberates in the auditorium.

"Come on. It's a challenge to fit everything into an hour and a half without an intermission. Where's Mario?" I ask.

I hear a keyboard riff and see he's already set up onstage. "Mario, I've got a few lyrics sketched out for Act Two songs. Do you want to work on the music?"

He responds with another riff.

"Ryan has the new script to hand out. I have to go to a meeting, but I'll be back."

I hear someone say, "This is going to be a disaster. I'm sorry I ever got involved."

That hurts my feelings. This play means a lot to me. It's a musical-slash-drama-slash-comedy, or musidramedy. I call it *Closets Are for Mothballs*. It's basically the story of my coming out as a bisexual. The whole school knows who and what I am by now, along with my family. But it was a long and painful process. I've known I was different since I was ten, and I was in the closet for a lot of years, until the walls closed in on me. It was either bust out or die trying. So my play is about liberation, freedom, and finding out who your true friends are.

Now I'm wondering if, after this "disaster" is over, I'm going to have any friends left. Except for Radhika and Azure, of course.

AZURE

"I still don't think we need officers," I say, trying my best to sound authoritative.

Shauna stares me down. Just as I'm about to wilt, she goes, "I guess we can do without, as long as we divide the tasks. But we really need to come up with a theme."

Luke rushes in and takes his chair beside me. "What'd I miss?"

"You were voted taskmaster," I say.

"Ooh," he goes. "Where's my whip?"

Mollie giggles.

Connor raises his hand. "Could we make some decisions quick? Because I have an early soccer meet in ten minutes."

Shauna goes, "Can we talk about the theme, please? Everything revolves around the theme."

"What about disco?" Luke says. He does his best impression of John Travolta, and everyone laughs. Except Shauna, who purses her lips at him. "Or a masquerade ball," Luke says. "I like wearing costumes and masks."

"They did that a couple of years ago and I heard hardly anyone dressed up," Shauna replies. "Costumes are for Halloween, not prom. What about Under the Sea?"

I groan.

Shauna snaps, "We did it last year and everyone seemed to like it."

Haley says, "I saw the decorations and they were super awesome."

Mollie echoes, "They were."

I ask, "How many people came?"

Shauna cuts a glance at Mollie and Haley. "I don't know."

Haley says, "Not that many. There were, like, hundreds of party favors left over. Maybe we should switch up the theme."

Shauna's eyes drop.

I say, "We're here to reinvent prom. Right, Mr. Rosen? To get more people to come."

"Well, we still want it to represent the spirit of prom," he replies. "Just in a more inclusive way."

"Like how?" Shauna asks.

My mind is buzzing with ideas. Just as I open my mouth, Luke says, "What about Arabian Nights? Or Burlesque?"

"Why do we need a theme at all?" I ask.

"Because it's a *prom*," Shauna answers.

"But it's *not*," I counter.

"Let's decide this one issue and move on," Rosen says. "Everyone who wants a theme?"

Shauna raises her hand immediately. So do Mollie and Haley. Connor raises his, so Luke puts his up slowly. My blistering gaze at Luke makes him pull his arm down fast.

Mr. Rosen says, "Decided. Who has theme ideas? We know Luke does. Um, for Azure's sake, something original?"

"If we have to go with a stupid theme," I say, "we need to do something that speaks to diversity. Like, Over the Rainbow."

"No way," Shauna says. "I don't want my prom to be gay."

I feel my anger boiling over. "Maybe I don't want my prom to be straight."

Mr. Rosen leans forward in his chair. "This is good. I like healthy debate. Let's keep the discussion going."

This is healthy? At any moment I'm going to lunge across the table and claw out Shauna's eyes.

"I have to leave in five minutes," Connor reminds us.

Mr. Rosen says, "I want everyone to think about the theme and come up with one that'll entice every, um, persuasion here at Roosevelt to consider attending prom."

Shauna says, "Even the geeks and nerds and stoners?"

"Don't forget the prommies." I mock-smile at her.

Mr. Rosen says, "Everyone."

Shauna shakes her head. "I can't believe we're starting so late. We'll never get everything accomplished. Do you even have Prom Central up yet?"

"What's that?" I ask.

She rolls her eyes at me. If she disses me one more time… "The online bulletin board for prom information."

"We have an online bulletin board?" Luke asks.

Shauna doesn't answer.

Mr. Rosen smacks his forehead. "I almost forgot. The Sheraton where we usually have the prom will be closed for renovations this year. We need to find a new place, and it has to be within our budget, which is tight."

"Are you insane?" Shauna cries. "We'll never find a new location in time."

"Now, Shauna, think positively. Any volunteers to start the search?" Mr. Rosen asks.

No one raises a hand, then Shauna and I both raise ours and lower them simultaneously.

Connor, who's shouldering his backpack, says, "I could make some calls."

"Me, too," Luke chimes in.

"Me three," I say.

"Groovy." Mr. Rosen pushes to his feet. "You'll want to go check out the locations, too. See what they're like."

"What day is prom, exactly?" I ask.

Mr. Rosen laughs. "That would be helpful information." He shuffles through his papers and pulls out a folder. "April sixteenth."

Shauna says, "If we have to move it, is that a problem?"

"Any later and you'll be running into finals and senior activities. We might be able to move it to a Friday night. Say, April fifteenth?"

"No way," Luke says. "That's the night of my play."

"Come to think of it, I'm not sure I have the authority to move the date, since it was set last year." Mr. Rosen sticks his folder in his backpack and says, "Can we meet on Mondays, Wednesdays, and Fridays? At least until we have all the tasks assigned. If anyone has a problem with that, come talk to me."

Luke gives me a despairing look. He'll have to cram his play practices into two days, or reschedule altogether. *Sorry*, I mouth.

His cell rings and his eyes dart around the room. "Excuse me," he says. He answers the phone and Connor says, "Now you have my number. Give me a call."

Connor leaves and Luke stares at me, slack-jawed. I say, "He meant when we're ready to call hotels."

I need to remind Luke that crushing on straight people only leads to rejection. Or maybe I should remind myself of that.

My affirmation is a joke: "Be your true self in every way."

I'm a phony. An impostor, a hypocrite. I want Shauna's prom: the gown, the shoes, the hair and makeup. I want to pick up Radhika in a limo and pin a pink or purple orchid on her dress. I want a picture of us together, holding each other or gazing into each other's eyes so that one day I can show my daughters or sons or grandchildren the most beautiful girl in the world, and tell them about how we danced all night, how prom was magical and mystical. I even want a stupid disco ball to shower us with a rainbow of sparkles as we twirl around the dance floor.

Luke calls and asks if I want to go to a movie or something tomorrow. Tomorrow's Saturday, and I have to work. "Is Radhika going?" I ask. If she's going, I'm calling in sick.

"No. I can't get hold of her. Which means…"

"She's studying," we say together.

She's the only person I know who studies on the weekend. "I guess that's the price you pay to get into an Ivy League college."

"Yeah," Luke says. "It's so cool, though. Our own Radhika a Yalie."

My Radhika, I think. "Has Connor called yet about checking out hotels?" I ask Luke.

"You'll be the first to know," he says. "Take that back. I'll be the first to know. You'll know by the heavy breathing on your cell like a woman about to give birth because I'll be in the labor of love."

Oh, brother. "Luke. Give it up."

"Hey, you never know. He *is* in the Diversity Club."

"Yeah, as a straight ally."

"Or a mothball in the closet."

"He smells better than a mothball."

"You've sniffed him?"

"Oh, yeah. He's always shoving his armpit in my face."

We talk for a while about Luke's play, until he says he really should hang up and work on it, especially now that his time is limited by the prom com, which is supposed to make me feel guilty.

"Oh, come on. Prom com gives you that special, special time with Connor Spears. Not to mention Mr. Rosen. So much testosterone in one room, I can hear your voice lowering as we speak."

He snorts. "Off to pump iron." We disconnect.

I wander out to the kitchen and Dad's at the breakfast bar, drinking coffee. I pour myself a mug of his sludge, then stir in four teaspoons of sugar and half a cup of milk. I sit and rest my elbows on the counter, gazing into the middle distance.

Dad says, "Penny for your thoughts."

I blink back to consciousness. "It'll cost you more than that," I tell him.

He quirks a smile and sips from his own mug. "A plug nickel?"

"Not even close. Did you go to your high school prom?"

He arches his eyebrows. "Are you studying ancient history?"

I sneer at him. "Just answer the question."

"Sure, I went to prom. Junior and senior years. Why? Don't tell me *you're* going to your high school prom."

"Why wouldn't I?" I snap.

"I just meant... Prom doesn't seem like your thing."

He's right. I crank it down. "Everyone has this image about prom being a ritualistic coming-of-age event for straights with dates. A person who's just a little off the social grid shouldn't even bother to feel like they're welcome. But I'm going to change that."

"Oh?" he says, sounding worried, like I'm going to commit a felony or something.

"I'm on the prom planning committee this year, and we're going to have an alternative prom."

"Hoo boy. Look out, Roosevelt High." Dad slides off his stool and yanks one of my little ponytails as he passes behind me. "I'd like to get your opinion on something," he says.

"Okay. Quit your job and sell magazines door-to-door."

He doesn't hear me because he's retrieving something from his desk. He returns and spreads out three printed pages. "Which one would you choose for me?"

It takes me a moment to read the header: MEET YOUR PERFECT MATE!!!

I gasp. "Tell me you're not online dating."

"I haven't yet. I put in my profile and got matched with these three women. I hope they're women. What do you think?"

"I think you're crazy." I gather the pages and slide them across to him. "Losers do this, Dad. Not guys like you."

He gives me a long, hard look. "I'm lonely. Can you remember the last time I went out on a date?"

I think back. "That lady with no eyebrows. She had to draw them in, or she had them inked."

Dad frowns. "Who?"

"You know. She laughed at everything you said, like you were funny or something."

He shakes his head at me. "I think you're talking about my cousin, Roxanne."

My eyes grow wide. She seemed really into him, and not in a family way.

"It's been more than a year," Dad says. "A couple of guys on the force used this online site and met really nice women. So come on. Help me out here."

He's serious. I had no idea my dad was lonely. Mom left us when she ran off to Florida with her boss, but that was eight years ago. She's married now with two more kids, which works for me, since it means she's not on my case about coming down for "family time."

Poor Dad. I understand what it means not to have a special someone in your life. It's miserable.

I spread the pages across the counter and inform him, "You're not a loser."

He goes, "I never said I was."

I begin with the first page. Lynda. No last names, only IDs. Her picture is far away and kind of blurry. On purpose? Hard to make out her facial features. I say the first thing that comes to mind: "Hasn't she ever watched *The Biggest Loser*?"

"Azure!"

I hunch my shoulders. "Sorry." She's not really that heavy. "If you marry someone who can cook, I'll walk you down the aisle."

"I'm not marrying anyone," Dad says. "I just want companionship."

The first profile question is: What are you looking for in a partner? Lynda answered: Honesty, trustworthiness, humor, stability, a man who loves children…

"Uh-oh," I say to Dad. "What if it slips out about your record of child neglect? Of course, I'd always testify on your behalf. If the price was right."

He fake-threatens me with a fist. I read from Lynda's profile, "She's a third-grade teacher. Single mom with two kids, ages ten and twelve."

Ugh. Do I really want stepsibs?

I admonish myself: *This isn't about you.*

"She seems okay." *Kind of boring,* I think. I take a look at the next profile.

Mercedes. A lawyer. "She's pretty," I say. Shoulder-length wavy hair, dishwater blond, a nice smile. It looks like a professional shot; she's propping her chin on the back of her hand. "I like her funky glasses." Round, aqua frames.

There's not much warmth in her eyes.

"You hate lawyers," I remind him.

"It doesn't specify her law specialty. She might be a patent attorney."

"True." If she's a defense lawyer, their first date will last approximately ten seconds. Dad thinks too many criminals go free over obscure loopholes in the law.

"She's been divorced twice," I say.

"One more than me," Dad goes. "Practice makes perfect?"

Or there's something seriously wrong with her. "She's

looking for a person who's sober, employed, faithful, and doesn't have an Oedipus complex."

Geez. Poor judgment in previous relationships much?

I slide the page across to Dad. "You're a match made in heaven."

"You think?" he says.

"No. I'm appalled."

"Cloud," I read the final profile. "I like her name." A massage therapist, belly dancer, poet, and singer. "Okay, I'm in love. She describes herself as a free spirit. You could use some fun in your life."

Dad takes the profile from me. "She was my last choice."

"Why?" I take it back from him. "She's perfect."

"You're enough free-spiritedness for anyone." He gets up and loads his cup into the dishwasher, then buckles his gun holster.

"So?" he says. "Lynda or Mercedes?"

"I think you should try all three," I tell him. "At least take them out to dinner and see if you click."

He makes clicking noises in his mouth as he heads for the door.

"One thing," I add. "I'll want a full report on how it all goes down."

"Roger that, Sherlock." He pulls a mock trigger finger as he shuts the door.

LUKE

Saturday morning I get up to find that Owen has left a trail of dirty clothes from the front door all the way to his room. Unless he's into drag, he didn't sleep alone. I sleep like a rock. If there was moaning and groaning going on, I missed it. I kick aside a bra and a woman's high heel. Then I wonder if it's my size and slip my foot into it. Only my big toe fits. "I'm up," I call, hoping to startle Owen and whoever's desperate enough to sleep with him. Muffled voices seep out of his room.

Since we have company, I head back to my room to get dressed. I check my cell to see if Connor called while I was sleeping. No such luck.

In the kitchen I see the same thing I see every morning: a sink crammed with dishes, cartons of Chinese take-out, or a pizza box, or burger wrappers and soda cans. Without me, this place would be a pigsty. No offense, pigs.

I don't even have to look in the fridge to know it's

empty, except for a twelve-pack of Coke. Owen's addicted. I'm starving, so I check my wallet to see if I have enough cash to go to McD's or Subway for breakfast. Without warning, Owen sweeps out of nowhere. He snatches my wallet out of my hand.

"Give it back."

He holds it above his head. His gut sags over his boxers and his arms are flabby. He's a disgrace to the male anatomy.

A girl wanders out of Owen's bedroom, raking her hand through her brassy red hair. "Jean-Paul?" She yawns. "Where'd you go?" She's wearing one of Owen's football jerseys from Western State. He went there one semester, then dropped out. "Who's this?" She peers around him to gawk at me.

"Tell her, Jean-Paul," I say.

He tosses my wallet in the air toward me and I snag it. "My brother," he mutters to the girl. He elbows me aside and kicks through the trash to the fridge.

"Hi." She smiles. "I'm Saralee."

I can't help myself. "Nobody doesn't like Saralee."

She flips her hair over her shoulder. "Why does every guy have to say that? It's so lame."

She's right. Her name probably isn't even Saralee. "I'm going to go get a breakfast sandwich or something," I say. "Do you want anything?"

Owen pops the tab on a Coke can. "Bring back three breakfast burritos from Twisters for me. Saralee, you want food?"

"I'm full." She grins at Owen. He turns the grin on me.

I want to hork.

"Give me some money," I say to Owen. He finds his jeans on the floor, digs in the pocket, and slaps a ten-spot in my open hand. "I know how much they cost, and I want the change," he says.

Did I mention he's a cheapskate?

It takes me forever to find the car keys in my backpack. Nobody-Doesn't-Like-Saralee says to Owen, "Your brother's cute. Why didn't you tell me you had a brother?"

"Yeah, Jean-Paul. Why didn't you tell her?" At last I find the keys on the coffee table.

"We try to keep the dirty laundry in the closet." Owen offers her a Coke and she declines.

"What does that mean?" she asks Owen.

"He's bi-beastial."

He must think he's amusing because he shoots me a crooked grin. I head for the door and Saralee says, "You mean bisexual? I *love* bisexual people."

My hand freezes on the doorknob.

"What's your name?" she says, strolling up behind me.

I pivot slowly and meet Owen's eyes. "Pierre-Paul," I say.

She runs her hand down my arm and I shiver. Peering coyly from me to Owen, she goes, "Do you guys want a three-way?"

Owen's face changes from pale pink to bile yellow. Mine's got to be raging scarlet.

"No, thanks," I manage to croak before exiting. A shudder shakes me all over. I feel a little unsteady on my feet. I've always fantasized about a three-way, but not with my brother.

Blech. The thought of it sends my appetite south.

As I'm driving through Twisters, I have this flashback of Owen and me playing catch in a yard somewhere. We moved around a lot, being Army brats. Owen must've been about seventeen or eighteen because I was just a kid. He was coaching me: "Cover the ball with your opposite hand when you catch it in the mitt." It was his mitt, and it kept falling off my hand. Owen didn't laugh at me; he was patient. He did say, "You throw like a girl." But every day after school we'd pitch and catch until I was good enough to join a rec league. Then we'd move and have to start all over again. We grew up. Owen graduated and I lost interest in baseball.

What happened to that brotherly love? I guess I know the answer: It died the day I came out.

When I get back to the house, Owen and Saralee are at it again. I leave his burritos on the table, hoping they'll be stone-cold by the time he gets done. Still no call from Connor. I pack up my netbook to head to the library. On a whim I call Radhika to see if she's free.

"Hi, Luke," she says. "I was just about to call you and Azure."

The sound of her voice makes me forget whatever I was remembering.

"You want to go to a movie or something?" she asks.

"Definitely!"

"Great. Come and rescue me now."

"I'm already in the car," I tell her, hustling to the Seville.

It's starting to snow lightly as I pull up to the gate and get buzzed in. Radhika comes out the door. Mrs. Dal's behind her. "Hello, Luke," she says as I climb out to usher Radhika into the car. Under her breath, Radhika goes, "Quick. Drive."

"Um, hi, Mrs. Dal." I hate to be rude. I shut Radhika's door and stand there, jingling my keys.

"What are you going to see?" Mrs. Dal asks.

"Uh" — my eyes cut to Radhika, then back to Mrs. Dal — "we haven't decided. A bunch of movies start around one. We should be back by four or four thirty at the latest."

"Well, have fun." She bends down and waves at Radhika. Radhika is facing forward and doesn't wave back.

As we pull away, Radhika says, "You're saving my life, Luke. My dad's out of town and my mother wanted me to spend the day with her at the art museum." She wrinkles her nose.

"Horrors," I go, even though I could spend a year at the art museum. "What do you want to see?" I ask.

"Nothing, actually. Let's just go to the mall. I'll call Azure and see if she can come, too."

"She has to work today," I say.

"Oh. Well, I guess it's you and me, then." She turns on that radiant smile of hers and I feel the sizzle under my skin.

It's a blast from the past hanging out at the mall with Radhika. We try on sunglasses and jewelry. She sits and watches while I get my colors done at Macy's. We decide to play a game of black-light putt-putt and Radhika beats my ass by about a million points.

"You know I let you win," I tell her. "I hate to see girls cry."

She goes, "Just for that I'm letting you pay for lunch."

It's long past lunchtime, but by now I'm starving. And since I'm the one who paid for the putt-putt, I'm officially broke.

"I would, but…" I pull out my wallet and show her it's empty. "I might have a quarter in my pocket. I could get you a gumball. Or we could shoplift a ski mask and hold up the ATM machine."

She looks at me and bursts into laughter.

"Okay, I'll pay," she says. "But you'll owe me."

"And I always pay my debts."

She links her arm in mine and tugs me close. "I know you do."

I veer toward the food court, but Radhika says, "Let's get out of here. I've been dying for something really greasy, like Sonic."

The snow has deposited a layer of white crystals on all the trees. It looks like a scene from Disneyland. Being alone with Radhika makes it even more bedazzling.

The closest Sonic is down by Sloan's Lake, about fifteen minutes away. When we pull in, there are only a few empty slots.

"Weird," Radhika says. "It's not even lunch- or dinnertime."

"It's always time for Tater Tots," I say.

We call in our orders and I turn up the heat because I see Radhika shiver. She says, "You're lucky your parents aren't here controlling every minute of your life."

"Yeah, well…Owen brought home a"—I glance sideways at Radhika—"rhymes with *Poe*."

Her eyebrows arch. "No way."

"Her name was Saralee."

"Not seriously."

"I almost asked if she was gooey."

Radhika covers her face. "You're so bad," she says in a smothered laugh.

Our orders come and I hand over Radhika's hot dog and Tots, then take a sip of my limeade Chiller.

"Owen's such a douche," I tell her. "Here's the best part: Saralee wanted to do a three-way."

She chokes on a cheesy Tot and I have to slap her back to help her get it down.

"Did you?"

I screw up my face. "Girl. I am *not* that desperate. Yet."

A second stream of cars rolls through the Sonic with guys and girls hooting and squealing. "There must've been a game or something," Radhika says. One car passes behind us and pulls into the adjoining slot. My stomach flutters when I recognize the driver.

"Luke," Radhika whispers.

"What?"

She thumbs at the window.

"Yeah, so?" My heart's crashing like a bass drum. It's Connor.

Radhika doesn't go on; she just gives me a coy smile. She's been talking to Azure. I am *not* in love with Connor Spears.

I see Connor calling in everyone's orders as I suck my Chiller dry and nibble my fries. His car door opens. When he passes in front of us, he turns to peer in through the front window. He squints, then stops and comes around to Radhika's side. She searches for the button to open the window. I press the one on my side that operates hers and mine. "Hey, Radhika." He leans in through her open window. "Hi, Luke. Oh, shit. I was supposed to call you, wasn't I?"

All I can manage is a weak shrug.

"Sorry. I had a soccer tourney today. How 'bout I call you tonight?"

"Um, sure. I'll be home." Damn. Why did I say that? I don't want him to think I sit around alone on Saturday nights. Which I do.

"Whassup, Radhika?" Connor says to her. "I haven't talked to you since you stopped coming to Diversity Club."

"I've been busy," Radhika says. "How's Tarah?"

Connor hesitates. "We broke up."

She gasps. "Oh my gosh. I'm sorry. I didn't know."

"Yeah, she's going out with a girl now." His eyes glaze over.

It's a phenomenon, girls breaking up with their boyfriends to date girlfriends, and vice versa. Hey, works for me.

"We won the tourney today." Connor's voice perks up again.

"Awesome," Radhika says.

"Props." I reach across Radhika to fist-bump Connor. Can I help it if a tingle races up my arm?

He stands there, leaning on the window frame for a long minute, studying the dashboard of the Caddie. "How does this pimpmobile handle?" he asks me.

"Depends on who's behind the wheel. If you want to take her out sometime, let me know."

Connor smiles. "I'll do that."

"Hey, guess what?" Radhika says. "Luke got invited to a three-way."

Blood rushes up my neck. Connor acts like he doesn't hear, or care. "Would it be okay if I called you sometime?" he says to Radhika.

She blinks. "Sure. I guess."

"Spears, go take your leak," someone hollers from his car. "Hurry up."

"Shove it," he barks over his shoulder. He snitches a cold Tot from Radhika's order and says to me, "What's a good time to call tonight?"

"Any time," I say. Shit on a stick. Why not just tell him 24/7?

"Say hi to your folks," he says to Radhika. He swaggers off toward the front of the Sonic.

I watch him halfway, then see Radhika watching him

all the way in. "Do you know we've gone to school together since first grade?" she says. "Isn't that weird? It's like we grew up together, and I barely know him anymore."

"Did you have to tell him about the three-way?"

She turns her gaze on me. "I didn't know it was a secret. I thought it was funny."

I cram my empty cup into the Sonic bag so hard the bag rips. Then I hold it out for Radhika to dump in her trash.

"Are you mad at me?" she asks.

I take a deep breath and force a smile. "No. Of course not." How could I be mad at her? I'm not even sure why I'm angry. Except all the way back to Radhika's this mocking voice swirls through my brain: *Would it be okay if I called you sometime?*

Mrs. Dal comes out on the porch again as I pull up.

"God, was she watching for me this whole time?" Radhika yanks on her door handle as I get out and come around. "Thanks, Luke," she says. "That was fun." She gives me a quick hug, then squeezes past her mom and into the condo.

Mrs. Dal says, "Would you like to come in, Luke? Have a cup of chai?"

I see Radhika behind her mom, motioning *no, no, no*.

"I have to get going...."

"I made three batches of tandoori and froze them," Mrs. Dal adds. "Radhika doesn't like it and now there's so much, I don't know what I'll do with it all. Would you take some home for you and your brother?"

Real food? "OMG yes," I say. "Thank you."

I follow her in and Radhika sprints up the stairs. As soon as her mother's out of range, she stands at the railing and sticks her finger down her throat.

I want to tell her, *You don't know the junk food I'm forced to live on.*

Mrs. Dal comes out with a tub of frozen tandoori and hands it to me.

"Thank you, thank you, thank you." I clutch it to my chest.

On my way out, I see Radhika still standing at the railing, fake-strangling herself. Unfortunately, her mother sees her, too. The temperature in the condo suddenly drops to subzero.

Radhika backs into her bedroom and shuts her door, leaving me alone with Mrs. Dal. She turns her ice-cold stare on me.

Awkward.

AZURE

Luke calls at seven PM, just as I'm curling up to watch a rerun of *Grey's Anatomy*. "Connor's on the line," he says. "He wants to know how to call hotels."

"Basically, you punch in the number and say hello."

Luke clicks his tongue. "Who should we call and ask for? And what do we ask? Like, if they have a ballroom? Because I'm guessing Motel 6 is off our list?"

I say, "Conference me in and let's all talk about it."

"Hang on." There's dead air for a second, then a beep. "Azure, you there?"

"Yeah."

"Connor?"

"I'm here."

"So how do we do this?" he says.

I say, "We should split up the hotels in our area and call to see if they have a ballroom available for a prom on April sixteenth." Are guys dumb, or what?

Luke says, "I think we should go visit places. I'm available tomorrow."

"We don't have any places to visit unless we know they have space available," I go.

Even over the phone I can feel Luke's glare, aka desire to be with Connor, but get real. There are millions of hotels. We have to narrow it down first.

Connor says, "A ballroom for how many people? Because I think they have bigger rooms and smaller rooms. My sister had her wedding reception at the Marriott, and it didn't look like a room that'd be big enough for a prom."

Okay, that's a valid question. Luke says, "We could call and ask Shauna. She might know."

"She doesn't know," I say immediately. "At least, she had no idea how many people went last year, so how would she know about this year? All we can do is estimate. The senior class is what? Six hundred? If everyone brings a date that's twelve hundred people."

"Not if people come by themselves," Luke says. "Which we hope they will, right? Or come with a group of friends. Which could make it even more."

"And seniors might ask other seniors, which could make it less," Connor adds.

Maybe they're not so dumb. "You're good with numbers, Luke. Come up with an estimate."

"It'll be a wild guess," Luke says.

"So be wild."

"Woo-hoo. Eleven hundred and forty-three people."

"That seems like a lot," Connor says. "Last year it didn't look like there were more than two or three hundred."

"But we're going to change that," I go. "We're going to make people want to come. Everyone in the senior class, I hope."

There's a long silence.

Luke finally speaks up. "Let's say we start at a thousand. Do hotels charge by the person?"

Who's he asking? Because I don't know.

Connor says, "I don't think so. Unless you have a meal or something."

"Do they have a meal at prom?" I ask.

"A cake," Connor says. "That's what we had last year. And kibbles and punch."

"Hopefully that won't take a big bite out of our budget. Ha," Luke says. "Get it?"

Neither of us laughs. "Do we even know what the budget is?" I ask.

"No," Luke and Connor say together.

"Maybe Shauna knows," Luke pipes up.

I grit my teeth. Shauna knows diddly squat. "We can deal with the budget later. Just find out if they have a place available, and how much it'll cost for a thousand people."

Luke says, "How do we decide which hotels to call?"

Do I have to do all the thinking? "Connor, you take A through G. You have H through O, Luke. I'll take P through Z."

Connor says, "I assume we can eliminate places like the Big Bunny and the Red Garter Motel?"

Luke giggles.

"Bring your lists to the next meeting and we'll go from there," I tell them. Just in case Luke wants some special, special time with Connor on the phone, I say, "Signing off," and disconnect.

In addition to watching *Grey's Anatomy*, I grab my laptop and log on to Facebook. On the off chance Radhika's online, I log in to chat. Yes!

Azure: cheater, cheater start the meter. shouldn't u be studying the holy grail of yale?
Radhika: i'm taking a break from writing a paper on Kant ☹
Azure: someone told me once never to say kant
Radhika: lol. we need to fix Luke up with some hot guy so he'll stop mooning over Connor
Azure: good luck w that. he's a goner
Radhika: sorry u couldn't go to the mall with me and Luke. it was like old times

Wait a minute. Luke told me Radhika couldn't go. Or was it that he couldn't get hold of her? Still, once he did, he should've called me back.

Radhika: how's prom com?
Azure: chaos. i don't know what we're doing. everyone's going in different directions and some people are a pain in the ass (I won't say who). OK, u forced it out of me. Shauna Creighton. our philosophies don't exactly mesh

Radhika: i trust you'll pull it all together
Azure: or unravel it completely. what if it's a complete and utter failure?
Radhika: stop it. What's your affirmation for today?

I tell her to hang on a sec. The one for today says: "You are a gift unto yourself." Which is idiotic. I rip off tomorrow's and bring it back to the living room. I should've read it first.

Azure: i am a highly creative, intelligent, attractive, and energetic person

In what altered state? I wonder.

Radhika: see? told u so

Luke's IM lights up and Radhika says:

Luke's here. want to do a 3-way? ☺

Was that a double entendre? I doubt she even knows what that is. Not that she isn't smart enough. Just…naïve. And pure.

Azure: sure

We sync our chats. Luke's the only one of the three of us to have created a unique Facebook ID.

Singlr_sensashn: azure, arent u supposed to be making phone calls?
Azure: aren't u? i'll start tomorrow
Singlr_sensashn: Connor was telling me about last year's prom. no matter what we did this year it couldn't be worse than last year. no live band. no pyrotechs. boring boring boring. even the food tasted like it came from sams club

That makes me feel a little more hopeful.

Radhika: u guys will do a fabulous job
Azure: i wish you were on the committee with us
Radhika: i'd never have time. plus, all my xtra curricular activities must be filtered through the rents. u know that
Singlr_sensashn: how did u get to be in diversity club?

I've wondered that myself.

Radhika: they honor diversity. why do u think they let me hang with u 2?
Azure: ☺
Singulr_sensashn: bet i could bribe your mom to let u join if i promised to keep her freezer emptied
Radhika: can we change the subject? how's the play coming?
Singlr_sensashn: on a scale of 1 to 10? it's terminal. i'd like to trash the whole thing and start over. i'm a nervous wreck
Radhika: u r so insecure. i can't wait to see it
Azure: me neither

Singlr_sensashn: i don't know. i've lost perspective. sometimes i think it's funny and other times i think it's the work of a desperate housewife
Radhika: lol. my mom's coming up the stairs. see u guys monday morning

She logs off and Luke says he should go, too. He's still not crazy about the second act of his play, specifically the ending.

I write:

just hold up an APPLAUSE sign. and THE END
Singlr_sensashn: thx.

He logs off.

I sit and think about our conversation for a while. Think about Radhika. It's strange and mysterious how she and I have been friends seemingly forever, but it's only recently that she's turned into this irresistible object of desire. Maybe it's the fact that I'll be losing her soon and I never made my move.

I've had three girlfriends in my life. The first was when I was fourteen. Her name was Brianne, and she lived in South Carolina. We met in the Oasis chat room, where she used to post these amazing poems and short stories. I started commenting on her work, and eventually we began to text and IM. We talked online every night until Dad got curious about who I was chatting with and gave me the whole lecture about online predators.

Yeah, yeah.

I told Brianne we needed to Skype to ease my dad's mind, and, okay, maybe mine, too. That was the scariest moment of my life. What if she loathed me at first sight? Back then I was more into goth and wore lots of black makeup and dark lipstick.

Turned out she wasn't a forty-year-old creep, but this gorgeous blond who was funny and nice. She had the sexiest accent. We were together for eight months, then the distance became more than geographic. Like, we'd set a time to IM and she'd blow it off, or conveniently forget. I was crying so much, Dad asked me to break off the relationship. Brianne saved me the trouble by dumping me. No more online relationships, I vowed.

I met my second girlfriend, Ami, at eco camp. She was two years older than me, seventeen, and totally radical. Her head was shaved and she had all these piercings, which expressed her attitude. I loved that about her. She was passionate about saving the planet, not only for ourselves, but for future generations.

She was a passionate person in every way. Yeah, that was a summer camp I'll never forget. Ami lived in Evergreen and we saw each other almost every weekend. What eventually tore us apart was jealousy.

Ami would show up at my house unexpectedly to see if my friends were there — Radhika in particular. I kept telling Ami that Radhika and I were just friends.

She never bought it.

She called me at all hours to make sure I was alone. It

got really annoying, and not only to me; Dad finally put his foot down. He never did like Ami all that much, and honestly, it was a relief to break it off. She was intense.

I heard she went to Wellesley. At the beginning of this year I got an e-mail from her informing me that she had a new girlfriend and wouldn't be able to wait for me. Like, huh? Was I supposed to be counting the minutes?

My third girlfriend, Desirae, I met in Diversity Club. She was a freshman and I was a junior. She was really sweet and shy, just coming to grips with being a lesbian. She said if she ever told her parents they'd kill her, and I told her that her coming-out journey was hers alone to take. She could choose who and when to tell, and she should never feel pressured.

I think that really brought her out of her shell, because she began to open up to people at school.

Looking back now, I wonder if Desirae wasn't my rebound girlfriend after Ami. I was lonely, and I like the feeling of being in love. Desirae and I went everywhere together — to movies and parties, and just riding our bikes or hiking. We'd find a shady spot under a tree and make out for hours.

I loved Desi. Then one day I didn't. We were lying on her lawn in a sleeping bag, watching for shooting stars, and I knew she wasn't The One. I couldn't picture us spending our lives together — not that we were married or engaged, although Desirae talked about us in future tense. I started avoiding her at school, not returning her calls. I know — cruel.

When I broke up with her, she took it hard. She sort of disintegrated. I told her, "It isn't you. It's me."

No matter how many times I told her, she didn't believe me. She was so insecure anyway; of course she'd blame herself. She'd come to school with puffy eyes and I'd feel like a total jerk.

I figured I'd be paying penance for the way I hurt Desirae.

That's it, isn't it, God? My punishment for Desirae is to be in love now with someone I can never have.

LUKE

I'm not the last to arrive in Studio 2B, so I get my choice of seats. Azure or Connor? Azure or Connor—

"Hey," Connor says. I slide in next to him and convert from solid to liquid.

Mr. Rosen opens the meeting with, "I'm afraid Mollie and Haley decided to drop out. They still want to participate, but maybe on the decorations committee, after all the planning is done."

Azure's hand shoots into the air. "Can we ask someone else, then?"

"We can't all agree now," Shauna says under her breath.

Azure seethes. "Well, if we have to do as much as you say, we're going to need more people." She says to Mr. Rosen, "It's Radhika Dal. I don't know if you know her, but she'd be a real asset."

"Yeah, because she'd be on your side," Shauna goes.

I see smoke coming out of Azure's ears.

"I vote for Radhika," I say.

Connor goes, "Radhika'd be awesome. I'm for asking her."

Without even meaning to, I mimic to myself, *Radhika'd be awesome.*

Mr. Rosen looks like he can't decide. Azure makes up his mind for him. "She's in the library. I'll go get her." She takes off.

"Did you find a new location for the prom?" Shauna's eyes dart between Connor and me.

"I got a few hits," I say. I unclasp my man bag to take out my netbook.

Connor reaches into his backpack and pulls out a folded sheet of paper.

"There weren't too many hotels with a ballroom available on April sixteenth," I say. "Or even a big enough meeting room."

Shauna crosses her arms, like, *Told you so.*

Azure returns, practically dragging Radhika behind her. "You're at school anyway. You said you wanted to spend more time with us, and here we are."

"Azure…" Radhika scans the room, checking everyone out.

Mr. Rosen introduces himself. He asks Radhika if she knows everyone. Radhika nods and says, more to Azure than to Mr. Rosen, "I really don't think I can be on this committee."

"Please," Azure implores. "We need you."

I think, *I need you. In ways you can't even imagine.*

Shauna clears her throat. "We were talking about hotels?"

Mr. Rosen says, "It might be a good idea to elect a secretary. To record our decisions and keep minutes."

"I can do it," Azure says. She pulls Radhika down beside her.

"You can't even read your own writing," I say. "Here, I'll key the notes on my netbook." I open a Prom file.

"So what did you come up with?" Shauna asks.

I return to my Hotel file. Every hotel I called, I noted yes or no as far as availability. I also keyed in cost. "I ended up with five that said they had a room big enough for a thousand people."

Connor says, "When I mentioned it was for a prom, no one had a room, like we were juvie d's planning to torch the place afterward."

Azure goes, "I only found two hotels. One's clear out by the airport, and the other's at the Tech Center."

Mr. Rosen asks, "Are all of these within our budget?"

"You never told us what the budget is," I say.

"Didn't I?" Mr. Rosen fake-stabs his forehead. "Space case." He opens his folder and flips through the first couple of pages. "We have two thousand dollars budgeted for prom out of the student activities fees. Plus around eight hundred from corporate sponsors."

All at once, Connor, Azure, and I say, "What?"

"My lowest-priced hotel is four thousand dollars," I say. "And that's with their biggest discount."

"Mine's thirty-five hundred," Azure goes. "How do

73

they expect us to stay within the budget when it's impossible?"

"You guys." Shauna shakes her head. "Don't you know anything?"

We all stare at her.

"We have to do fund-raisers. That's how we can afford to put on the prom at all. In addition to the site, we have to pay for food and decorations and favors and the photographer and the DJ...."

"We want a live band, don't we?" I say.

Azure says, "We *have* to have a live band."

Shauna says, "Then we have to find a way to pay for it."

"It's a little late to do much fund-raising." Mr. Rosen sighs.

Shauna goes, "Duh."

Mr. Rosen says, "Unfortunately, Grease Monkey and Ace Hardware had to drop out as corporate sponsors. The economy, you know."

I don't know why it strikes me funny that Grease Monkey would be a corporate sponsor, but I start laughing. Then I can't stop, and Connor has to smack me on the back. When I get myself under control, everyone is gawking at me. "Sorry," I say. "I'm on my period." I don't even want to ask who else sponsors us. But now I have to know. "Who else sponsors us?"

Mr. Rosen consults his list. "Black Forest Bakery, Midwest Bank, and Artful Framer."

I'd used Artful Framer once for a watercolor I did for my parents for Christmas. They charged an arm and three legs. Mr. Rosen adds, "It'd be nice if we could find a couple of replacement sponsors. Would anyone like to take on that project?"

Shauna says, "That's not usually something we have to worry about. Mrs. Flacco always found the corporate sponsors."

Mr. Rosen hesitates. "Okay. That'll be my responsibility. Make a note, Luke."

Radhika speaks up. "My dad might have some contacts. I could ask him."

Mr. Rosen looks like he wants to kiss her. *Me first*, I think.

Azure says, "Too bad we don't have a nice gym or cafeteria. We could save big bucks." Roosevelt High should be condemned. Neither the gym nor the cafeteria is big enough for a prom. A new high school is being built, but it won't open until next year, after we've all graduated.

"Everyone I talked to said I should get my reservation in now," I tell the committee. "The party and conference rooms fill up fast. And we should go check out the hotels to make sure they're not dives."

"I can't go any night this week because I have soccer," Connor says. "What about Saturday?"

"I can do Saturday," Shauna says.

Azure goes, "I thought Connor, Luke, and I were looking at sites."

"But we should all go. It needs to be a group decision."

"I can't go." Radhika lowers her eyes. "Sorry."

"That's okay," Azure says.

We go back and forth about when we all have free time, or could make time. Finally, we settle on Sunday. Shauna sulks because it's the one day she can't make it.

I say to Shauna, "We'll take pictures, okay? Like you said, we need to divide and conquer if we're going to get everything done in time."

Shauna must realize she's lost the battle. She moves on, saying, "We need a way to communicate with each other. Last year we had a Google docs file. Do you want me to set one up?"

"That'd be super," Mr. Rosen says. "Thank you, Shauna."

"And we should clear out Prom Central and get it ready for this year. But the first thing we need is a theme."

Azure groans.

"We do!" Shauna insists.

Connor scoots back his chair. "Sorry, guys. I have to leave."

Is it three fifteen already?

Mr. Rosen says, "Think about themes for our Wednesday meeting."

Azure says, "Can we also talk about how we're going to make this prom different? More alternative?"

"Sure," Mr. Rosen says. "It's your prom."

"It isn't yet," Azure mutters.

On the way home, Radhika says, "Please, please don't let my parents know I'm on this prom committee."

"Promise," Azure and I say in unison. That must mean she's going to join!

I add, "Thank your mom for the tandoori. It was tan-delicious. And gone before Owen could sniff out the curry."

"I never asked you this, and tell me if you don't want to talk about it, but how is it living with Owen?" Radhika asks.

Azure snorts.

"He's your basic butthole of a brother. I'll survive."

"Not to mention bigot," Azure goes.

"Yeah, there's that. It's only for a few more months, though. If I don't get accepted to an art school, I can always go to Germany and live with my parents. Except I'd probably travel around Europe instead."

"Take me with you," Azure pleads. "I can fit in your backpack."

"With all your piercings, you'll set off every train and airport scanner."

Azure sticks out her tongue at me. Her silver stud glistens.

Radhika jumps out at home and races inside without even stopping to wave good-bye. Azure climbs into the front seat and turns to me. "Do you think we forced her to do something she didn't want to?"

"I don't know," I admit. "She'd tell us. Wouldn't she?"

Azure worries her tongue stud until I drop her off.

Owen's in the driveway with a bucket of soapy water and the hose, washing his black stretch limo. His prize possession. He calls it Black Panther. It must've gotten a microscopic mud splotch on it, because it came back from detailing two days ago, and he's already washing it again.

Steam rises from the hood and Owen's breath is visible in the chilly air. A sane person would just run his cars through a car wash, no?

He hitches his chin at me, like he acknowledges my existence. It's a first. I sling my man bag over my shoulder and walk up to him. "Did you go to your prom?" I ask.

He stops for a second. "My prom?"

"In high school. Did you go?"

"No." He dunks his sponge in the water.

"All the hos had johns that night?"

He doesn't even bother to squeeze out the sponge before he pitches it at me. It smacks me square in the face. He tries to stifle a laugh, but can't. I want to drop everything and attack him, take him down and pulverize his acne-scarred face and bust his nose and just scream, "I hate you!" But I know he'd kick my ass. Anyway, I have my dignity and gender queer pride to protect.

I turn and saunter casually into the house. *Four months*, I count to myself. *Four months to freedom.*

AZURE

My affirmations don't match the days anymore because I keep ripping them off until I find one I like. I stop at: "You are kind and caring in a way that comforts others."

I try to be kind and caring with Dad, with my friends. With Radhika.

I'm thinking about this affirmation as these two women, who look like mother and daughter, come into the thrift shop carrying armloads of red dresses. The older woman says, "We'd like to donate these."

The younger one scans the shop, looking horrified.

I rush around the front desk to help the woman unload the dresses onto a receiving table. "Wow," I say. "These are beautiful."

They're full-length gowns, satin and strapless. Instantly, I catch on. Bridesmaid dresses. I know because we have four other sets in the formalwear room in back. "Let me get you a receipt," I tell the woman, reaching across the desk for the receipt pad. "How many are there?" I ask.

"Six," the mother says. The daughter—I assume she's the daughter—hugs herself loosely, staring at the floor.

As I'm writing out the description of the donation, I say to the daughter, "Thank you so much. All the proceeds go to Kids with Cancer. It's a really worthy cause."

"At least *something* good will come out of this fiasco," the mother carps.

The daughter's lips purse.

I'm dying to know what happened, why the wedding was called off, whether the bride reneged or the groom did. As I hand the receipt to the mother, she says, "He might've had the courtesy of breaking off the engagement *before* all the arrangements were made."

Which answers my question.

I say to the daughter, "What a jerk. I'm really sorry."

She snaps at me, "You don't know anything about it." She whirls and heads for the door.

My shoulders hunch. Yeah, I'm so kind and caring.

The mother sticks the receipt in her bag and says, "Take my advice: Elope."

The door whooshes shut and those gorgeous dresses draw me to them. I hold one up, thinking, *No way will I ever elope.* I want a huge wedding with all the trimmings. Flowers, cake, champagne, music. I want to dance with my bride long into the night, and toss my bouquet over my shoulder to the next bride-to-be. My wedding dress will be pure white with a mile-long train, and I'll have a flower girl and a ring bearer.

"Did those just come in?" Louisa jolts me out of my reverie.

"Yeah," I tell her. "Bridesmaid dresses."

"I guessed that. They're gaudy. Who'd choose red for their bridesmaids?"

I would, I think. "I'll take them to the formalwear room," I tell Louisa.

She folds the dresses over my arms. "Don't put them up front on the rack. They'll scare customers away."

Or invite them in. Everyone has different tastes.

As I'm hanging the dresses, I fantasize about my wedding. Every time I get to the end, where the pastor says, "You may kiss the bride," the person who lifts my veil is Radhika. Getting married to Radhika, having a wedding, becoming legally wife and wife...

"Hey."

I turn at the sound of the voice.

"I heard you worked here."

"Desirae. Hi." She looks different, like she grew taller, or older.

"Oh my God. Those dresses are awesome." She circles around me to where I'm hanging the last one.

"I know, huh? They're bridesmaid dresses from a canceled wedding."

She licks her lips. My stomach does a little flip; I remember those lips, soft and sweet. I shake off the feeling.

"I didn't think you'd ever speak to me again," I say.

She looks at me and frowns. "Why?"

Do I really have to tell her?

"It wasn't me. Right?" She smiles a little.

I shake my head. "Right. Stupid thing to say. I'm sorry."

"Don't be. If it's not meant to be, it's not meant to be. Anyway, I found someone else." She turns toward the dresses, away from me.

You'd think I'd feel relieved about that, but a knot of jealousy clenches my stomach. I have no right to be jealous. Anyway, knowing she doesn't hate me lifts my spirits.

"I'm glad," I say. "Do I know her?"

"Could I try one of these on?" Desi asks.

"Um, sure. The dressing room's over there." I point to the closet with the curtain.

We riffle through the sizes looking for a twelve. "They've probably been altered," I say.

She takes a ten and a twelve to the dressing room.

"How've you been?" she asks through the curtain. "I see you around with Luke and Radhika. I've been too busy with French club and Science Olympiad to get to Diversity Club much. Where are you going to college next year?"

I'm embarrassed to tell her I haven't thought much about it. "I might be traveling in Europe with Luke."

"Seriously?" She draws back the curtain. "How cool. I wish I was graduating." She twists to check out the back of the dress in the mirror. "What do you think?"

I step forward and retie the silk belt at the waist so it's full and even. "It's gorgeous."

"It is, isn't it? Do you have any shoes that might go with it?"

"Let me look." I run to the shoe area and dig through the pumps. "What size?" I call back to her.

"A seven or seven and a half."

I should know that. I find a pair of silver heels, clear plastic pumps that look pretty cheesy, and some gold stilettos a stripper must've donated.

Desi takes them and tries each pair on in front of me. We agree that none of them really works.

"How much is the dress?" she asks.

Louisa and I didn't discuss price, and I haven't settled on one. Louisa doesn't even like the dresses. "How much would you be willing to pay?"

Desi's eyes grow large. "I don't know. Like, a hundred dollars?"

"Think lower." I cringe at my impulsiveness. *Think Kids with Cancer*, I tell myself.

"Fifty?" she says.

"Sold."

"Oh my God." Desi engulfs me in an embrace and I can barely breathe. It's not only because she's crushing me. It's been so long....

She releases her hold and says, "I'm going to wear this to prom. It'll be perfect."

"Perfect," I repeat, the sensation of her nearness lingering.

"I don't have the money today, so could you hold it for me?"

"Absolutely," I say.

As she exits, she blows me a kiss and I catch it. Her new GF must be a senior if Desirae's going to prom.

After my shift, I log in my hours, then ask Louisa, "Would it be okay if I tried on a few things? I saw some boots I really like."

"Be my guest," she says.

I return to the formalwear room. A lot of the dresses in here are probably leftover prom dresses, or cocktail dresses cleaned out of an old aunt's closet. I love everything with lace. If I had money to burn, I'd buy all the lacy dresses, the black and blue clothing, boots, gloves, and hats in this place. Then I'd accessorize with jewelry. Most of the gowns are in good shape, and an idea begins to solidify in my brain. Girls—or guys—who wanted to go to prom on the cheap could shop here. I bet I could get Louisa to give them a discount, since dresses like these don't usually move very well. I make a mental note for the next prom com meeting.

When I get home Dad's not there. Instantly, I freak. Then I see he's left me a message on the fridge. It's a picture of that one lady, Mercedes. Dad wrote in the top margin: *My first victim.*

I lie on the sofa to watch TV and wait for him to get home. I wait and wait. *He must be having a good time,* I think. If he plans to stay over at her house—ew, the thought of my dad having…you know—I hope he'll call to let me know. Not about the…you know. Radhika phones around eleven, after her mom's in bed, so we talk about nothing and everything. I ask her point-blank if she really wants to be on the prom com and she says yes, which is a relief. By the time we hang up, I'm feeling so light-headed and sleepy in a romantic, dreamy kind of way that I drift off to blissville.

The next thing I know Dad's covering me with a blanket and tucking it in around me. "How was your date?" I ask him in a yawn.

He smiles.

"You're home early," I say. "What happened? Did you show her your gun?"

He tickles my ribs until I'm writhing around, squealing with giggle pain.

"Go to bed," he says. "Or I'll show you my guns." He starts to roll up his sleeve.

I don't care to see any part of his anatomy, so I scramble to my room.

LUKE

"Luke, will you read the notes from the last meeting?" Mr. Rosen says.

"We're out two corporate sponsors. You and Radhika were on the case."

"My dad's out of town," Radhika says. "He should be home sometime this week."

"I've been swamped the last two days," Mr. Rosen says. "I may not be able to start until the weekend."

"It's already the last week in January!" Shauna cries. "We only have two and a half months."

Mr. Rosen smiles at her. "Thank you for updating the calendar."

Azure makes a sound in the back of her throat.

"I'm just saying…"

"And we ended the meeting by discussing the theme," I cut in.

Azure says, "Before we discuss the theme, can I bring

up a few ideas I had about making this a more alternative prom?"

Shauna sighs audibly.

Azure ignores her. "We have to get more people to come, so I think we definitely want a drag show."

"What?" Shauna goes.

"And a karaoke contest."

"At a prom?"

"And a gamers' competition."

"I suppose you're going to say we don't need to elect a prom king and queen."

Azure shrugs. "Is it really necessary?"

"Of course it is!" Shauna says. "What's a prom without royalty?"

I raise my hand. "Could I be the queen?"

Shauna shoots me with eye bullets.

"Luke makes a point," Azure says.

"I do?"

"We don't need a prom king and queen, unless there are no gender limits."

Shauna opens her mouth, then snaps it shut. Under her breath, she mutters, "Whatever."

I put in my two cents: "We could have spotlight dances, like they do at the skating rink."

"Definitely," Azure says. "What do you think, Radhika?"

Up to now Radhika's been doodling in a notebook, like she's lost in thought. She glances up. "Whatever you decide is fine with me." She resumes her doodle.

"Of course, we'd want strippers in the spotlights," I continue.

Connor jumps in, saying, "I like that idea. I can guarantee strippers will get every male in this school to attend prom."

"And some females." Azure grins.

"Male strippers, too," I say. "We don't want to limit anything by gender. We want Chippendales, or the Thunder from Down Under. Then all the girls, not to mention queer boys, will show up."

Mr. Rosen goes, "Guys, please. No strippers. We're getting way off track."

"But we still want an alternative prom, right?" Azure goes.

"Can we talk about the theme?" Shauna says.

This time Azure sighs heavily.

"You know I like Under the Sea," Shauna says. "But I wouldn't be against something different."

Azure says, "I hate Under the Sea. It's so...prommish. What about something having to do with rainbows, as a symbol of inclusiveness?"

"A rainbow only means gay," Shauna says. "And you know it."

I sort of have to agree with Shauna. At least, that's how people would perceive it.

Mr. Rosen says, "Maybe we should just put the theme up for a vote."

"That's not fair." Shauna pouts. "It'll always be them against me." She scoots back in her chair, grabs her purse, and walks out.

Girls are so melodramatic. Which might be why I like them.

Mario, my musician, left me a message on Facebook that he reworked the opening number to add more percussion. He attached a YouTube link. I click on it and watch him at his keyboard. He's such a cool dude, with his Mohawk and seemingly endless collection of tees with band names. He sings:

Odor-Eaters
BO beaters
Closets are for mothballs.
Suffocate
Can't go straight
Closets are for mothballs.

I beam. The lyrics are mine. Mario can't sing worth shit, but I like his techno take. He's really into my musidramedy. I can't wait to hear the Mothballs' rendition with Mario's upbeat changes.

Owen comes in from outside and tosses his chauffeur's cap onto the coffee table. "How long are you going to be on that thing?" he asks.

"It's called a laptop. And what's it to you?"

"Dobbs and the guys are coming over to play Texas hold 'em. Just thought I'd let you know," he says.

"Why? So I can get lost? I live here, you know."

Owen shakes his head. "I'm just saying you might want to work elsewhere."

"Elsewhere. Whoa. Big word."

He stands there, gazing down at me.

"What?"

"You take everything I say wrong."

"You want me to make myself scarce. I get it." I shut my computer and head for my room. At the threshold, I stop. "What do you see in Dobbs?" I ask Owen. "He's a total loser."

Owen pops the tab on a Coke. "We go back to elementary school. He's always been my wingman."

I click my tongue. "Maybe it's time to fly solo. Birds of a feather..."

Owen narrows his eyes. "What does that mean?"

"Nothing." It just flew out of my mouth.

I shut my bedroom door behind me.

Sometimes I think I have Owen pegged, and other times...What we have is a failure to communicate. Or in his case, medicate.

I lie on my bed and fire up my laptop again. Linking to the Oasis chat room, I see that it's fairly active. There's a group of bisexual guys on Oasis who chat every night. I haven't contributed much lately. I've been busy with school and the musidramedy. One guy wants to know if we feel it's cheating to date a girl and a guy at the same time.

I've wondered that myself. I could see myself falling in love with two people at once; let's say, for instance, Radhika and Connor. But I don't think either of them would be too keen on sharing.

As if reading my mind, one guy responds,

if they don't care, i think it's ok 4 u 2 date both of them. u should tell them tho.

I agree — about the honesty.
Another guy writes:

I don't believe in it. I want to be in an exclusive relationship. Period.

I agree with that, too. Identifying as bisexual can be confusing and messy. I write,

just b yourself, dude. and b honest. that's what counts.

Owen asked me once about my sex life. His comment was, "If you plan to bring a guy here, let me know so I can clear out."

"What about a girl?" I asked.

He didn't answer.

No worries, bro, I wanted to tell him. *I'm still a virgin.*

Last year I had a long-distance relationship with this guy named Seamus. He lived in Sydney. As in Australia. Not a lot of touchy-feely with an LDR. He totally broke my heart when he told me he was going back to his ex, who also lived in Sydney. I got the feeling he only used me to make his ex jealous. That hurt like hell. I'm so ready to be in love for real. Which I am. Now all I need to do is let Radhika in on the secret.

AZURE

We walk into the Holiday Inn and Connor pinches his nose. "Anyone bring their Speedos?"

The stench of chlorine is overpowering, since the swimming pool is right outside the lobby. "Maybe we could put up Glade air fresheners," I suggest.

Luke and Connor look at me.

"It was a joke."

Luke says, "Our theme could be Finding Nemo."

Connor adds, "Finding Nemo Under the Sea."

We all crack up. I know it's not nice to make fun of Shauna, but she makes it so easy.

"I don't think we even have to look at their ballroom. Do you guys?" I say.

We turn and head out the way we came in. As we veer toward Luke's Caddie, I tell them, "That's the last hotel on the list."

"What are we going to do?" Luke says as we all get in the car.

No one has any ideas.

We drive out of the parking lot and Connor points up the street. "There's a Starbucks. Let's get something to eat or drink. My treat."

Luke pulls into the strip mall and we pile out. Even though the breeze is brisk, the sun is warm, so we sit on the patio with our drinks and sandwiches and muffins. "What about rec centers?" Connor says.

"They probably reek of chlorine, too," I say. "Not to mention locker rooms."

Luke inhales deeply. "I love the musky smell of gym shorts."

Connor says, "You would. The theme could be Athlete's Footloose."

Luke giggles and I groan.

"Oh, come on." Connor elbows me. "It wasn't that bad."

"Yeah," I say. "It was."

We all eat and drink for a while, then Connor's watch beeps. "Crap. I need to get to work."

"Where do you work?" Luke asks.

Connor makes a face. "Sonic."

"No way," Luke says.

"Way. Just got the job. Don't hold it against me. I had to learn how to skate." He crumples his sandwich wrapper and stuffs it into his cup, then takes all our trash to the can.

As we're driving to Sonic to drop off Connor, he says, "Have either of you talked to Radhika since Thursday?"

"Yeah," we both say.

"Did she mention anything about me?"

Luke cuts a look my way.

"No," I say. "Why?"

"I asked her to prom and she said she'd get back to me. But she hasn't."

I feel my throat tighten. Luke sounds like he's gasping for air. Does she like Connor? She'd confide something so personal to me, wouldn't she? We drive up to the Sonic and Connor gets out. Before he shuts the door, he says, "If Radhika asks you guys what she should do, tell her to say yes." He grins.

Luke backs out before Connor can even step away from the car.

Luke and I turn to each other. In unison, we go, "He asked her to prom!"

I pull my cell from my bag and call her. "Voice mail," I say to Luke. I write a text for her to call me ASAP, but I don't send it. I decide I want to talk to her in person.

I look at Luke and see that his jaw's set. "What do you know about this?"

"About what?" he goes.

"You know what. Connor and Radhika."

"What makes you think I know anything?"

He doesn't meet my eyes. He's lying, or he's holding something back, which is the same as lying. What's going on, and why are both Luke and Radhika keeping things

94

from me? I've never been a paranoid person, but now I know what it feels like.

Her cell goes to VM every time I call. "Grr." I punch it off for the hundredth time. I wait for her to call, but she never does. All night long I'm awake, tossing, turning, stewing up a maelstrom in my mind. I have no right to be mad at Connor, or frustrated with Luke or Radhika for not communicating, when I'm the one keeping the biggest secret of all. Why didn't I ask her to prom first? Why don't I just tell her how I feel? How does she feel about Connor? Does she like him?

I don't want to go there, but I can't help thinking that if she does like Connor, it's a good thing I've kept my mouth shut.

LUKE

I call Radhika as soon as I pull into the drive at home. VM. VM again. Owen's got his head under the hood of Black Panther. I'm surprised he even knows how to unlatch the hood, so I wander over.

"Do me a favor and turn over the ignition," he says. He's slipping the dipstick back in the slot and he's got his hand on the distributor cap.

"Um, you might want to —"

"Just do it."

The guy has a death wish. Sliding into the front seat, I twist the key and brace for sparks. There's a *thunk* when Owen's head slams against the open hood. He yells, "Shit!" He jumps around going, "Shit, shit, shit."

The human hand is a mighty electrical conductor. He flaps his hand, folding and unfolding it.

I get out of the limo. "You okay?"

"Do I look okay?"

I don't answer that. And I don't hide my smirk.

Owen says, "It stalled on Pena Boulevard and I missed a fare into Denver from the airport."

"I told you the carburetor in this limo needed work, did I not?" The last time he allowed me to park Black Panther in the garage, I could feel it running rough. I was surprised at the time that he even let me drive it ten feet.

"Yeah, I should've listened." He unfurls his fingers. "So fix it." He grabs his Coke off the ground and stalks into the house.

I smile. He hates that his queer bro is a gearhead. Because then, of course, that makes me the manly man around here.

I call Radhika three or four more times, and each time her line either is busy or goes straight to VM. Then I call Azure and her cell's busy. Maybe she got through to Radhika. I'm dying to know what Radhika said to Connor. Dying, I tell you. On a whim, I check my e-mail and see that Mom sent me a message. She said she deposited a hundred dollars in my account. I already assumed that because she does it every other Friday. I guess she just wanted me to know she didn't forget. I feel like a jackass getting an allowance at my age, but if Owen would let me drive or pay me for anything I do around here, I could contribute to expenses. Since he's never asked for rent, I suspect Mom's paying him directly.

Except he'd never take money from Mom and Dad. He's spent too many years trying to prove his worth to them.

Mom wrote, "We'll be Skyping you two on Wednesday at 4:00 PM your time. Please tell Owen to be home if he's not working."

If I tell Owen, he'll be working.

I check my Facebook and Radhika's not online. Because she's talking to Azure, probably. It's not fair. If they're talking, why don't they conference me in, the way we used to? I want to know what she's going to tell Connor. If she hasn't decided, I can make up a list of hideous offenses he's committed. Something. Anything. I'm desperate here.

While I'm waiting to get through, I comment on all my friends' comments on FB. We have a separate page for *Closets Are for Mothballs*, and a few members of the cast have written on the wall. "Cool script change," Gabe wrote. Three people liked his comment. I have one message I don't even have to read, since I know the gist. T.J., who plays my second BF in the play, wants a bigger role. More lines. A song. He's such a play hog. I've already expanded our scenes together, even though I have most of the lines. But that's only fitting; it's my story. I reply to his message, "I'll think about it." Which I won't.

I send a message to Ryan, thanking him for taking charge last week. I pause at his profile. He's changed his picture. He's got this Justin Bieber-ish hairdo, and his pic's in black-and-white. Very arty. I check out his albums. He has one labeled "Who Am I?" and it's full of artwork. Most of the pieces are abstract, disjointed, like he's searching, exploring himself. Full of color, though, and mesmerizing.

I understand. I've been there.

My cell rings and I lunge for it. It's Azure. "What'd Radhika say?"

"I thought you were talking to her."

"I wasn't. Every time I called it went to VM." We're both quiet for a minute.

Azure asks, "What do you know about her and Connor? I *know* you know something."

"We saw him at Sonic a couple of weekends ago. Not working. Hanging with his friends. It was that Saturday I asked you to come to the movies with us...."

"Which I would have if you'd told me Radhika was going."

Oops. My bad.

"Anyway, they talked. Sounded like they hadn't seen each other in a while. She said they'd been friends since they were both in swaddling clothes. He said, 'I'll call you.'"

"Huh," Azure says.

"Yeah. Huh."

Azure hesitates. "Is that all?"

"Would I lie to you?"

She doesn't reply. "There's other stuff she's not telling us," she says. "I can feel it."

"Why? Doesn't she trust us? What'd we do?"

"I don't know. I thought we told each other pretty much everything. Of course, some things are personal and private."

"Like what?"

"Like, I don't tell you everything I'm thinking and feeling. But it's not because I don't trust you. I just think some things are…"

"Personal and private." I'm dying to tell her how I feel about Radhika, but if there's stuff she's not telling me…

Azure says, "Did I mention my dad is computer-dating?"

"OMG. No. Where? E-Harm-Me?"

"No, this other site. I'm not sure what it's called, but he went out with a woman named Mercedes, a lawyer."

"Ooh. Dish, girl."

"I couldn't get anything out of him, except that she talked a lot. And drank a lot. And I only got that much by hand gestures. You know, blah blah. Knock back a few?"

I picture it in my mind and giggle.

"Did he Taser her and cuff her to the bedposts?" I ask.

Azure puffs out a breath of disgust. "You're talking about my dad. I'm sure he was a perfect gentleman. He has two more matches," she adds. "Hopefully, one of them will work out."

"Do you want your dad to get remarried?" I ask her.

"I don't care. I just want him to be happy."

"I hear you. We should all be happy."

"Amen to that," she says.

AZURE

I'm the last one to the prom com meeting because I fell asleep in Poli Sci and had to stay late to copy the notes from the whiteboard. All day I've been comatose because of my lack of sleep.

Radhika's head is lowered as I rush in and take my seat next to her.

I think we're discussing the location again, or still, because Connor goes, "My dad suggested country clubs, so I called a few and they're either booked or cost as much as the Taj Mahal."

I key into my phone: Are you going to prom with Connor? I show the message to Radhika.

Radhika reads it, keys a short reply, and slides the cell back to me.

No, she wrote.

My heart leaps to the ceiling.

She takes the cell back and writes: but i haven't told him yet, so please don't say anything

Like I would. I zip a quick text off to Luke because it's only fair that he's filled in, then stuff my cell in my bag and concentrate on the discussion, as much as possible. The message seems to perk Luke up.

Mr. Rosen shakes his head. "It's my fault. I should've confirmed the Sheraton earlier. Then we would've known about the renovations."

Shauna says, "Mrs. Flacco must've known. Why didn't she say something?"

A look crosses Mr. Rosen's face. Is it...anger?

Shauna must see it, too. "What's going on? I heard Mrs. Flacco got fired from the committee. Is that true? Is she trying to sabotage it now?"

"She got fired?" Luke and I say together.

Can you be fired from a committee? Under the desk I see Luke pump his fist.

Mr. Rosen says, "I'm sure it's nothing like that. All I know is, I was asked by Mr. Gerardi if I wouldn't mind taking on the prom this year. And I'm happy to do it."

We all look at him, like, *Sure you are.* Mr. Gerardi doesn't exactly "ask."

Mr. Rosen says, "So, we're back to not having a location."

"What about sponsors?" Shauna asks.

Mr. Rosen hangs his head. "I couldn't find any. But I haven't given up." He turns to Radhika. "Did you talk to your dad?"

She shakes her head. "He had to extend his trip. I promise to talk to him as soon as he gets back."

A glum silence settles over the group. I finally say, "We can keep looking for locations, right? And there's plenty of time to find corporate sponsors."

Luke says, "Why don't we talk about music? We absolutely, positively have to have a live band."

"I'd rather have a DJ than some crappy garage band," Shauna says.

"Hey," Connor cuts in. "I'm the front man for my crappy garage band."

Shauna's face flares.

"Really?" I say. "You have a band? Are you any good?"

"In my garage, yeah."

Luke smiles. "What are you called?"

"The Crappy Garage Band."

Luke's giggling borders on hysteria.

Mr. Rosen stands and says, "I'm sorry, guys. I have to go to a faculty meeting. If you want to get out of here, go."

He leaves and Luke says what I'm thinking: "Wow. I've never seen Mr. Rosen mad."

"He has every right to be," Shauna says. "He gets this catastrophe dropped in his lap, and if it fails, he'll be the one to blame."

"Not really," I say. "We will. And we should be. There's no reason we can't pull this off if we put our heads together and get creative." Knowing that Radhika isn't going to prom with Connor has freed up my mind for productive thoughts. "My church has a big empty room where we hold community events."

"You go to church?" Shauna widens her eyes at me.

"I know you think queers are all heathens who are going to hell—"

"I never said that," Shauna snaps. "I've never even thought that."

I continue, "Jefferson Episcopal Church welcomes everyone. We even have a transsexual pastor. You should come sometime, Shauna, if you're up to diving into the depths of diversity."

Shauna says under her breath, "I hate church. My parents make me go, and they're total homophobes." She tells us, "I have nothing against gays. And I've never once said I thought gays and lesbians were going to hell."

Luke and I exchange glances. "What about bisexuals?" he asks.

Shauna looks straight at him. "Not even transgenders."

Wow. I'm surprised she knows they exist.

Luke says, "If we find a church, we could go with an O Holy Night theme."

Connor and I laugh, and even Shauna smiles. I wish I had Luke's gift of lightening the mood.

"You know what?" Connor says. "My dad's company had a reception at the Museum of Nature and Science. In that glassed-in atrium where we ate lunch when we took field trips in elementary school. Remember the atrium, Radhika?"

She lifts her head and blinks at him. "Yes," she says. "It's gorgeous."

"That'd be so cool," Shauna breathes. "To have our prom in the museum."

Connor goes, "Our theme could be Night of the Living Dead."

Luke says, "Or Diorama Drama."

We all laugh again.

Connor says he'll call the museum, and I volunteer to check with my church. Luke says, "I'll go to that church over on Alameda that looks like a big mushroom. I've always wanted to see what it's like inside."

Connor says, "I'll go with you."

I walk out with Radhika and Luke, while Shauna trails behind. Connor says, "See you guys next time. Call me, Luke." He takes off for the exit.

Luke hollers, "Count on it."

Radhika says to me, "Is there anything I can do to help with locations?"

Shauna says, "Me, too. Just tell me what to do."

When did I become the leader? "Radhika, you're still on corporate-sponsor detail. That's enough."

Shauna says, "If you find anything, leave a note in our Google docs. Everyone give me your gmail addresses, or create one, and I'll set you up. The file is called RHSPROM."

I'm suddenly thankful for her organizational skills, since I have zero.

"Does anyone know Connor's gmail?" Shauna asks.

Radhika says, "I'll call and ask him."

I almost say, *I'd rather Luke called.*

It doesn't matter. She's not going to prom with Connor, so what difference does it make?

My affirmation of the day is: "I will believe in my own potential." That seems prophetic. Yesterday I felt powerless to effect change, and today I'm leading the prom com. Of course, I may lead them into quicksand.

I remember this one time I must've been paying attention in science class. Our teacher explained synergy as "the multiplied power of people working together toward a common goal." I think that's what we have now on prom com.

I can't figure out Shauna. I'm trying to tolerate her, the way we're supposed to, but it's hard. I hate that word, *tolerate.* It seems like the lowest form of acceptance. I know I can't change Shauna, so the only power I have is to tolerate — make that *accept* — her for who she is.

Honestly, all I know about her personality is what I've seen at prom com. I haven't taken much time to get to know her, really. I just know her type.

Note to self: I will once and for all stop classifying people by "types." I despise that tendency in others, and I hate it in myself.

I decide to walk the mile to Jefferson Episcopal Church, where maybe I'll find strength in a higher power, and also a location for prom. I love how the spire rises above the old lodgepole pines and how the sun catches a stained glass window so it looks like Christmas every day. From the moment I first stepped into this church, I felt a sense of belonging.

Pastor Thomas is floating down the winding stairs in his long white robe as I enter through the Hall of Fellowship. He used to be Pastor Ruth, until he transitioned. He's always been a really spiritual person, sort of what I imagine angels to be.

"Azure, hello," he says.

"Hi, Thomas." There are no formalities here, because, like Thomas says, "Everyone is equal in the eyes of the Lord."

"What can I do for you?" he asks.

"I need to ask a question. Or a favor."

"Come with me. I have a baptism in fifteen minutes, and I'm running late."

I have to hurry to keep up with him. "I'm on the prom committee at school, and we're looking into places to hold the dance because our usual hotel isn't available, and I was thinking we have that big community hall here."

Thomas arranges a white silk cloth on a table and sets a silver basin atop it. "We might be able to arrange that."

"Cool." I'm already imagining how we can decorate to make the room look totally romantic.

"When's the dance?" Thomas asks.

"April sixteenth."

He pauses with the water pitcher over the basin. "I'm afraid the month of April is out. We have our food drive, remember?"

My spirits sink. I want to say, *Can't we collect and store food in PODS or trucks instead of the community hall?* Then I realize I'm putting our prom before a *food drive.* Selfish, selfish, selfish. How self-centered can I be? New affirmation: Stop putting yourself first when others are in need.

"I'm really sorry, Azure." Thomas meets my eyes.

"No. That's okay." I can't hold his gaze. "I just forgot." I take in the baptism scene — the basin and candles and flowers. It's beautiful.

"What else? You look like you have something you want to talk about."

How does he do that? Read minds, or hearts? "I don't want to interrupt your baptism."

"Do you hear any screaming babies?"

I smile.

"Do we need to go to the Vestry?" he asks. The Vestry is where he talks to people in private.

"No. I didn't murder anyone."

He laughs, then indicates a step up to the podium. He sits beside me and clasps his hands in his lap.

"There's this girl I like," I say.

Thomas's eyes widen.

"She's straight. But open-minded. She's also my best friend." He's quiet for a long minute, so I go on. "I don't have very good judgment, do I?"

"I wasn't thinking that at all. You're wondering if you should tell her how you feel."

Our conversation is halted abruptly by the aforementioned screaming baby. We both stand. Thomas places a hand on my shoulder and says softly, "Follow your heart, Azure. I know you'll do the right thing."

The right thing being…?

I guess I'll have to wait for a sign from above. The only problem is, will I know it when I see it?

LUKE

Right on time, Mom and Dad call for our Skype visit. The conversation is always the same: "How's everything going?" Dad asks.

"It's going."

"Are you keeping your grades up?" Mom says.

"Define *up*."

"Is your brother there?" Dad asks.

Owen stands on the other side of the computer, out of view, snarfing a burrito. He burps.

"Owen?" Dad says.

Busted, I want to say. Owen shakes his head at me, like, no, no, no.

"Yeah, he's right here. Hang on."

I turn the computer around so the camera's on him. He flips me the bird thigh high, out of camera range.

"How's business?" Dad asks.

"Never better," Owen deadpans. "Here's Luke." He twists the computer back to face me.

"Is he on something?" Dad says to me. "Because he can't be driving if he's high and putting lives at risk."

Owen's never done drugs that I know of.

I catch the fire in Owen's eyes before he storms out of the living room and slams the front door.

He and Dad have a hate/love relationship, in that order. Dad wanted Owen to enlist after high school, but Owen had his own plans. Like working at crapola jobs for years to support himself. I have to give Owen credit for starting his own business and being The Man. Dad doesn't, of course. What is it with parents and their expectations?

I think it pisses Owen off even more that Mom and Dad still love me, even though I'm queer. It took a while, but they're fine with it now. In a way I have Owen to thank for that—he's such a disappointment to them.

"What are you doing in your free time?" Mom asks me.

"Watching porn and doing Jell-O shots," I say.

"Oh, Luke. Is that what Owen does?"

"Oh, Mom," I say. "He works. That's all he has time for." I don't mention Saralee. Owen's a guy. He's got needs.

The phone rings in their off-barracks apartment and Dad says, "I better get that. Take care. And let us know if you change your mind about coming to live here. You can always get your GED, or make arrangements to finish school here, then stay or go back to the States for college and live in the dorm." He disappears from the screen.

I won't change my mind. My play, my friends — they're too important.

"I'm on the prom committee," I tell Mom.

"You are?"

"Why do you sound shocked? Queers know how to party."

She says, "You mean study."

"Did I say party?"

She smiles.

"Did you and Dad go to prom together?" I ask.

"No. We didn't meet until later. After boot camp. But I remember my prom all right. It was pouring rain, and we'd rented this old barn that leaked."

"You had your prom in a barn?" I say. "That's thinking outside the ballroom."

"It was great. Lots of atmosphere."

"Like having to clean the cow pie off your shoes?"

She says, "Do you have a date?"

"Our connection's breaking up," I say. "Oops, I just lost the visual. Good talking to you, Mom." I call louder, "You, too, Dad." I hang up.

I wonder if that barn is still standing, and leaking. If there are mice or rats, dead bodies to be unearthed. Maybe if we hold our prom in a house of horrors, no one will notice I'm there alone.

I call Radhika, but her cell goes to VM. Again! I'd better find the nerve to ask her soon, before someone *else* beats me to it.

Just as I'm thinking that, my cell rings and it's Radhika. "My mother would like to invite you to dinner tonight. If you're not busy. Say you're busy."

"I cannot tell a lie. I'm bored and starving." It's fate. I'll ask her tonight.

Radhika sighs. I hear her ask her mom, "What time?"

Mrs. Dal says, "Sixish?"

"Six," Radhika tells me. She lowers her voice to a whisper. "Please, please be careful what you say about you know what."

"Cross my heart and hope to die a gruesome and bloody death if I even bring it up."

"Let me give you the gate code so I don't always have to buzz you in." She rattles off a sequence of numbers and symbols. I note them down. I feel so special to have 24/7 access to her.

As soon as Radhika hangs up, Azure calls me. "Will you pick me up?"

"For what?"

"Dinner at Radhika's. Duh."

She's invited? I imitate Radhika's sigh, doubly loud. "Are you ever going to get your driver's license?"

"Maybe when I can afford an electric car. We have enough pollution killing the planet."

"You don't mind riding in my Caddie. At best it gets eight miles to the gallon. And that's if I run all the red lights."

She doesn't have an answer to that. "Could you just pick me up?"

It's a little after four, so I have an hour and a half to

primp. I saw this men's grooming segment on a talk show once where it said the best way to put on cologne without drenching yourself was to spray a mist in a crosswise motion, then walk through it. Just enough cologne should land on your clothes and skin to give you a fresh, manly scent.

As I'm doing this I hear a donkey bray at my bedroom door. It's Dobbs. "Owen, come watch your zitwit of a brother," he calls out to the living room.

Owen appears. I slip into my shoes and head out, but Dobbs blocks my exit. "Where you off to, fag rag?"

"Leave him alone," Owen says. He returns to the living room, but Dobbs stands there bobbing back and forth to keep me from advancing.

"Dobbs!" Owen says.

Under his breath, Dobbs goes, "You make me sick."

I almost say "Ditto." But I don't want to show up at Radhika's with a fat lip or a severed spleen.

Azure's dressed up, as far as I can tell under her bulky ski parka. She's wearing lacy leggings and shiny boots. Top-of-the-line thrift fare.

"Did Radhika tell you to be careful—"

"About mentioning prom com. Yeah. Zipped lips." Together, we pretend to pull zippers across our lips.

As we approach the gate to Radhika's condo, I feel a flutter in my stomach in anticipation of being with Radhika, even though we won't be alone together in a romantic setting. Mrs. Dal greets us at the door. "Luke." She hugs me. "Azure." The same. "How nice to see you both."

"Thank you for inviting us," Azure says before I can.

"Radhika," Mrs. Dal calls up the stairs, "Luke and Azure are here."

She emerges and I go all goose-pimply. "Hey," she says, smiling. It looks forced.

"Dinner will be ready in a few minutes," Mrs. Dal says. "Make yourselves comfortable."

We move to the living room. The Dals' condo is a miniature HGTV Dream Home. Very stylish. Pricey furnishings. I love all the Indian art and collectibles.

The aroma wafting from the kitchen makes my mouth water.

"Why didn't you guys have anything to do tonight?" Radhika asks, flopping onto the sofa between Azure and me.

"Stop it," Azure says. "We used to come over to eat all the time."

Radhika slumps. "I know. I'm sorry. It's not you."

Azure reaches over and puts her hand on top of Radhika's, which is resting on the cushion. "What is it? What's going on?"

Radhika's eyes pool with tears and Azure scoots closer. I do the same.

A tear rolls down her cheek just as Mrs. Dal comes in and says, "Dinner is served."

Quickly, Radhika wipes away her tears.

"We'll talk later, okay?" Azure whispers.

Radhika nods.

We sit down to eat, Radhika taking a chair across from the two of us. Mrs. Dal says, "I don't know why I've been craving Indian food lately. Radhika is not a fan." To confirm, Radhika sticks out the end of her tongue. Mrs. Dal points to a dish. "This is chicken and lamb korma. And basmati rice." She indicates a bowl of green, spinachlike goop. "Saag," she says. "And fried vegetables. Lentil soup with naan."

I sing, "Heaven. I'm in heaven."

Mrs. Dal smiles. She pours us each a cup of chai.

I take a sip and it's so sweet and creamy, my eyes roll back in my head. I'm already thinking about making a plane reservation to India.

"What do you hear from your parents?" Mrs. Dal asks me as she slides into her chair.

"We Skype occasionally." I pass the korma to Azure and she spoons some onto her plate.

"And what have you both been up to?"

"I'm working on *Closets Are for Mothballs*," I reply. She looks confused, so I explain, "It's a musical drama comedy. And Azure and I are both on the prom planning committee."

Azure chokes. Literally.

I look at her and she scalds me with a glare. What? That didn't give anything away.

"Did you go to your prom?" I ask Mrs. Dal.

"Oh, yes. My prom was unforgettable. My date was so handsome in his tuxedo. He even wore a turquoise cummerbund to match my sari. I wore a turquoise and magenta silk sari with bangles and haar."

Azure says, "Did you go with Mr. Dal?"

"No. He still lived in India then. But our marriage had been prearranged."

Azure's jaw unhinges. "You're kidding. People still do that?"

"In our culture, yes."

"*Your* culture," Radhika says under her breath.

Her mother casts her a veiled look. "You should be proud of your heritage, Radhika. In this country especially, where difference is celebrated."

"It's not that easy to be different, Mother," Radhika says.

Azure and I exchange a knowing glance.

"I understand that," Mrs. Dal replies. "Your father and I were both persecuted in this country at various times. That doesn't mean we aren't proud of being Indian."

Azure asks, "Do you get a choice about who you have to marry? I mean, what if you hate the person? Can you say no?"

"Of course. But families know their children well, and get to know the other family, so the bride and groom are usually very compatible. Vadish and I were acquainted since childhood. We were friends long before our marriage."

"You mean people get married without even being in love?" Azure's voice rises an octave.

"Ninety percent of arranged marriages are successful,"

Mrs. Dal tells her. "As compared to only, what? Fifty percent here?"

I'm only half listening, since I'm scarfing food down like I haven't eaten in months. Which I haven't. Finally, I take a breath and go, "OMG. This food is to roll over and beg for."

Mrs. Dal laughs. "Thank you. What do you have to do on the prom committee?"

"Everything, practically," Azure says. "We found out the hotel we had reserved is undergoing renovations, and we can't find any other place in our price range. Then two of the corporate sponsors withdrew."

Mrs. Dal turns to Radhika. "Maybe we can talk to your father about whether his company would be willing to sponsor your prom."

For the first time, Radhika looks up and meets her mother's eyes. "Do you think they would?"

"It can't hurt to ask."

Azure and I elbow each other.

"What we want to do—what we're charged with doing," Azure says, "is coming up with something completely different. Sort of an anti-prom. An event that's not so exclusive, you know? One that *does* celebrate difference. Right now the only people who ever go are the preps and jocks. Not to label people or anything."

"Which you just did," I say.

Azure curls a lip at me.

She adds, "We're pretty tolerant at our school about race and sexual orientation, stuff like that. Not everyone is rich enough to go to prom, and a lot of people don't go because they don't have girlfriends or boyfriends, or even arranged prom partners." Mrs. Dal grins at that. "Not everyone can afford a tuxedo," Azures goes on, "let alone a dress they'll probably wear once. Although, if they can, that's cool. I'm not saying it's bad to be rich." Her cheeks flush. "I bet two-thirds of the juniors and seniors aren't into prom because it's—"

"Pretentious," Radhika finishes Azure's sentence.

Mrs. Dal stares at Radhika. Static fills the air. At last, Mrs. Dal says to us, "I understand completely how you'd want more people to feel included, like it's their prom."

"Exactly," Azure goes.

"It's such an important night in a young person's life. Do you all have dates?"

The conversation halts again.

"Never mind. It's none of my business," Mrs. Dal adds. "It was nice talking to Connor the other day, though. Maybe he'll take you, Radhika."

For the first time in my life, I see Radhika blush.

She seethes, "Can we just drop it?"

We all eat in silence until Mrs. Dal says, "What are you going to do about a location?"

"I don't know." Azure takes a sip of chai. "I guess until we find more money, more corporate sponsors..." She grimaces at me.

Open mouth, stuff in boot.

"Where did you hold your prom?" I ask Mrs. Dal.

"Oh, that was the best part." She smiles. "It was outdoors, in the Highlands Pavilion."

Azure and I say, "Where's that?"

"In northwest Denver. I wonder if it's still there."

"How much was it?" Azure asks.

"I have no idea. I guess the prom planning committee took care of that. Now that I think about it, what would we have done without a prom planning committee? We had a wonderful theme: Under the Sea."

Azure, Radhika, and I all cough.

Azure stifles a short laugh under her napkin.

"Did I say something funny?" Mrs. Dal asks.

"No," I go. "That's a super-awesome theme."

Under the table, Azure kicks me.

After dinner we head toward Radhika's room, but at the bottom of the stairs, she stops. "I feel a migraine coming on. Would you mind if I just went to bed?"

Azure and I tell her no, not at all. "Thanks for coming." She hugs us both. "And thanks for...you know."

"Not a problem." Her smile radiates through me.

On the way home, Azure tells me to look up the location of the Highlands Pavilion. "It's probably rubble by now, or replaced by apartments or strip malls."

"It's probably underwater," I say. "As in..."

"Under the Sea," we say together and whoop with laughter.

AZURE

Dad's dressed in his best black suit with a white linen shirt and a gray-striped tie. "Wow," I say. "Who died?"

"Me. Help me with this tie, will you?" He's standing in front of the full-length mirror, pulling out the slipknot.

I move over in front of him and begin it again. Over, under. His cologne tickles my nose and I suppress a sneeze.

"Too much?" he asks.

"Nope. Just right." It's the cologne I got him for Christmas. Yves Saint Laurent's L'Homme. I spent fifty dollars, but it was worth it. I slide the knot into place and Dad buttons his suit coat. He looks hot. He even got a haircut. "Let me guess," I say. "Cloud."

"Lynda. She has tickets to *Tosca*."

I let out a short laugh, then slap a hand over my mouth. "Have you ever been to an opera?"

Dad shoves his wallet into his back pocket, along with a tin of Altoids. "How bad can it be?"

"Remember how I got a D in Music Appreciation? It was because when we covered opera, I slept through every class."

Dad tugs my earlobe. "Well, I am much more cultured than you."

The only CD dad plays in his car is Bruce Springsteen.

At the door he says, "Don't wait up."

I say, "When you drift off, don't drool in Lynda's lap."

I need to make a pit stop before the prom com meeting, and as I'm leaning over the drinking fountain afterward, I feel a tap on my shoulder. I turn and Desirae's there.

"I got the dress," she says, smiling. "I can't thank you enough, Azure. There's no way in the world I could've afforded a dress like that."

"I'm glad you found each other," I say.

Our eyes meet and hold. A thrill of electricity runs through me and I have to look away. I can't be feeling this.

"I'll see you around." She touches my arm and the jolt about sends me through the roof. As I watch her go, I let out a stuttering breath. We're over. She has someone new. I'm in love with Radhika.

Perspective, Azure, I tell myself.

When I walk into Studio 2B, Luke spins me back around and says, "Field trip."

"Where are we...?"

"Pavilion," he whispers in my ear.

"You found it?"

He hands me a page of directions from MapQuest.

"Where to?" Mr. Rosen asks.

"You'll see," Luke answers. He says confidentially to me, "It looks pretty cool online."

Sweet, I think.

We all cram into the Cadillac and buckle up, including Mr. Rosen.

"Where's Radhika?" I ask.

"She went home with another migraine," Luke says.

I check my cell and see that she texted me after lunch. How did I miss that? Luke has this look of concern in his eyes that I feel. I want to call her, but she's probably in bed. Shauna says, "I need to let my mother know if I'm leaving the school grounds."

I say, "After school? You're kidding."

Shauna's voice hardens. "Just tell me where we're going."

"Tell your mommy we're going to Wally World to buy Tampax," Luke says.

Shauna shrinks visibly in her seat next to Connor. Luke should be smacked for that remark; even I'd cringe with guys around.

"Read the directions, Azure," Luke instructs.

I scroll down the sheet. "Turn left at the light and get on Sixth Avenue." Mercy Her comes on the radio and I turn it up.

Shauna says, "I hate this song."

I turn it up louder, then think, *Tolerance*, and turn it down again. We almost miss the exit because my head is back on Desi, wondering what that was about. You always want what you can't have? At the last minute, I say, "Luke,

123

get off here." He has to swerve across two lanes of traffic to catch the off-ramp.

"Geez," he says. "Give me a wedgie."

Mr. Rosen's beside me, hyperventilating like he's going to have a heart attack.

"Okay, now we have to get on Tennyson Street," I tell Luke.

He turns at a light.

"Slow down. It must be somewhere inside this loft community."

"There." He indicates a huge concrete structure at the end of a drive. We park in the lot and all pile out.

"Where are we?" Shauna asks.

I answer, "The location for prom. Maybe."

The pavilion might've been something in its day, but it's all boarded up now. Luke says, "It didn't look like this online."

"I know this place," Connor says. "My mom said there used to be a carousel in here when this whole area was an amusement park. Then they moved the carousel to the zoo and transformed the pavilion into a concert space. I've been here a few times in summer to hear bands. And my parents have come to dances."

The pavilion is like something out of Victorian England. Ornate patterns are molded into the concrete columns, which support a domed roof. The roof is undamaged, but a lot of the concrete pillars have been tagged. It's gone ghetto, as Luke would say. But if you use your imagination...

If we cleaned it up...

There's no entry that I can see — only a knothole in the plywood planking, where I peek inside.

Oh, wow. It's spacious. Cavernous, actually. The plywood siding would have to be removed, but there's a wooden floor, like a dance floor. If we can get permission to use the pavilion...if it's in our budget... "This would be awesome for our prom," I think aloud. "Who do we talk to about renting it?"

Mr. Rosen says, "The city, I suppose. Although it might be privately owned. If you want, I'll check into it."

"That'd be great," I tell him.

"Since I failed miserably at finding any more sponsors, it's the least I can do," he says.

As we're leaving, I glance out the back window and can see it: the pavilion all lit up like a palace, and people dancing long into the night.

I call Radhika on my way to work and she says she's feeling better. "We went to the pavilion today, where your mom had her prom."

"It's still standing?" Radhika goes. "I figured it'd be in ruins by now."

I wish I would've thought to take pictures to send her, but we don't even know if we can get it. I hear the train coming and say, "I'm glad your headache's gone." Her migraines are debilitating. "If you feel like it, call me later." She promises she will and my spirits soar.

The first thing Louisa says to me when I walk in the

door is, "Your friend came in to pick up her dress." I cringe, wondering if Louisa's going to fire me for practically giving it away. But she says, "You have a real knack, Azure. I couldn't have bribed anyone to take that ugly dress off our hands."

I exhale relief. She adds, "I was thinking about clearing out that whole room and making a space for used appliances."

"No!" I cry. "You can't."

She cocks her head at me.

"I mean, you can. It's your store. But I was thinking people could come here to buy prom dresses. A lot of the vintage clothes are back in style, and we do have gobs of old prom dresses in there at really reasonable prices."

Louisa looks like she's considering it. "When's your prom?"

"April sixteenth."

"I suppose I could hold off until then."

Impulsively, I give her a hug. I don't think you're supposed to hug your boss, but I don't care. "Would it be okay if, after my shift, I took some pictures of the dresses and suits? I can post them online for people to see."

"Sure. And tell you what: Anyone who comes in to buy something for prom gets a twenty-percent discount. Tell them that."

"I will. Thanks." I'm torn because I want all the money to go to Kids with Cancer.

Just as my shift is about to end, the door opens and

Desi walks in. "Hi." She smiles. "I was hoping you were working tonight."

She has another girl with her and I wonder if it's her new girlfriend. "This is Christine," Desi says. "She saw my dress and asked where I got it, so I told her, and she wanted to come check out the thrift store herself."

"Be my guest," I say.

As I'm sweeping up the front, Desi returns from the back room and says, "Do you have any jewelry that might go with my dress?"

"You can look." I show her the jewelry cases. As she's examining the collection of earrings, I say, "Everything you buy for prom is twenty percent off."

Desi swivels her head. "Seriously?"

I nod.

She returns to browsing. I study her from the back—her hair, which she's streaked with purple, and her cute, round butt in her tight jeans. I shouldn't be admiring her butt.

She says, "Would you show me these red and gold ones, and the hoops?"

I rest my broom against the shelf and skirt around the counter. I unhook the gold and garnet studs from the velveteen board. She holds them up to her ears and studies them in the mirror.

"You like?" she asks.

"Yeah. They're perfect."

She checks out the price and goes, "Eek!"

"I know. Some of the jewelry's pretty expensive. Especially if it's antique."

Her GF reappears from the back with the dress I've had my eye on for a month. "I'll take this," she says. "Can you put it on layaway, or hold it until I can come back with the money?"

I want to say no because it's my dress. "Sure," I say, and take it from her.

"Everything's twenty percent off for prom," Desi tells her.

"Wicked cool," she answers.

Who says that anymore?

Desi asks her, "Which of these earrings do you like?"

Christine asks her to hold them up. "Actually, neither. I like these long beaded gold ones. Can we see them?" she asks me.

I unhook them from the display card.

"Yeah, those are the ones."

Desi pooches out her lips. I want to say, *Buy the garnets. They're so much prettier.* But Desi goes, "Okay. Would you keep these out for me, Azure?"

I take the earrings and grab the dress. As I'm walking them to the back room, I'm wondering what Desirae sees in Christine. She seems overbearing, a little like Ami. It's none of my business, though, and I certainly have no place telling Desirae who she should and shouldn't see. The bell over the door tinkles and Desi sticks her head through the curtain. "Azure," she says, "forget the long beads. You're right. I want the garnets."

LUKE

I leave a message in our Google docs that the mushroom church is a bust. It's amazing inside, like a spaceship. There are prayer meetings and services on Saturday nights, though. I see that Connor's left a message that if the pavilion doesn't work out, he may have a lead on a cheap hotel. Just seeing his name stirs my latte, no whip. *Lust*, I tell myself. *Nothing more.*

The phone rings and rings as I'm buttoning up my jeans for school. Owen must be out on a run, so I pick up. "A-1 Car Service."

"Is this a person or a machine?" the guy asks.

"Flesh and blood," I say.

"The limo service that was recommended to us is out of business, and we need a ride from the airport to the Hotel Teatro in Denver."

I scramble to find a pen and paper. "We can handle all your needs, sir," I tell him. "How many passengers?"

"Five," he says. He hollers to someone, "What hangar?" He relays to me, "Hangar three. How soon can you get here?"

I guesstimate the time to Denver International. "Forty minutes?"

"That long?"

"I could make it in thirty."

He sighs audibly. "Can you keep it on the DL that we're in town? Otherwise, we'll be swarmed with screaming teenyboppers."

"Privacy is our mantra." I just made that up. I wonder who "they" are. If they care, they're obviously high-profile.

I rush to Owen's bedroom and knock. No answer. I could call his cell....Then again, I could prove to him what a valuable member of his team I'd be if he'd only give me a chance.

It snowed overnight, about an inch, and it's still coming down. The town cars are all out on calls somewhere, and anyway, five people is too many to cram into a town car. The only vehicle available is Owen's Black Panther. Oh, God. Maybe I should call him, leave an urgent message. I check my watch and see that six minutes have already elapsed while I've been wussing out.

As I slooooowly back out of the garage, I think, *Crap*. I have two tests today, and a final oral project that's sixty percent of our grade in Civil Liberties. It's Flacco, too, who hates me. I call Radhika and explain the situation. I tell her about my exam, and she says if I'm not there in time, she'll stop in and make an excuse for me so Flacco won't flunk my ass. She says she'll drive to school and pick up Azure.

I love that girl so much.

Oh, shit. The gas gauge is fluttering on empty, but I can't stop now. I pray I have enough fuel to get me to and from the airport.

The side streets are slick, but I-70's been plowed, so I make up time there. Pena Boulevard is plowed and sanded, too. The snow is heavier here, though, and I feel the back of the limo swerve on icy patches. I almost fishtail into a ditch and my heart thrums in my chest. *Get a grip, Luke*, I think. Deep breaths. I've never been to the private-jet hangars, so it takes me a while to find them. By the time I squeal into hangar three, I'm fifteen minutes late.

A guy in a skullcap saunters up to me. "You from A-1?"

"Yes, sir," I tell him as I get out. I scurry to the rear door to open it. He scans me up and down and says, "You don't look like a chauffeur."

"My uniform's at the cleaners." I should've grabbed one of Owen's company caps.

"You don't even look old enough to drive."

"If you'd like to see my chauffeur's license…"

He waves me off. "Our ride's here, ladies," he calls to a group of girls sitting on instrument cases, shooting the breeze.

Oh my God! It's Mercy Her!

"Hey," Leilani says. She's the lead singer.

She hands me her guitar case and slides into the back of the limo. All the band equipment piles up at my feet. The guy, Skullcap, must be their manager. He says, "Well? Are you going to just stand there, or put those in the trunk? There's luggage, too."

I load everything as fast as humanly possible.

OMG. I'm driving Mercy Her. Azure will die. My hands sweat as I crank over the ignition and check the side-view mirrors. I head for the exit and Leilani says, "Do you have any bottled water?"

Shit. I forgot to equip the limo after Owen brought it back from detailing.

"Sorry, I don't. I could stop...."

"No, that's okay." She rolls her eyes at the other band members. Owens's right. I'm a spaz.

The band members joke around, or key into their iPhones and BlackBerrys. I try not to eavesdrop or slide off the road. But it's Mercy Her, for God's sake.

Owen's told me about all the times he's driven celebs from the airport: basketball players and politicians and once even a Saudi Arabian prince. I thought he was full of shit.

My cell jingles and I pull it out. It's Radhika.

"Mrs. Flacco is not happy about your Civil Liberties project. I told her you were on your deathbed, but I don't know if she's going to let you reschedule."

"Thanks anyway," I tell her. Then I lower my voice: "Guess who I have in the limo at this very moment?"

"You're driving a limo?"

"Yes, and quite capably."

"You shouldn't be on your cell, Luke."

"Mercy Her," I say.

"What?"

"I'm driving Mercy Her."

"I'm hanging up so you don't get stopped by the police or get in an accident." She disconnects.

No one will believe I'm driving Mercy Her. Unless...I lift my phone over my shoulder and snap a picture. The manager, or whoever he is, grabs my cell. "Didn't I say no paparazzi?" He figures out how to delete my pic, then throws my cell over the seat. "Kid, you just blew your fare."

The whole thing?

Leilani catches my eye in the mirror and fake-kisses me. Now I'm thinking she's kind of a bitch.

We roll up to the Teatro and I get out to open the back door. Everyone scoots out. As I'm unloading the luggage with the help of the hotel porter, Leilani comes up to me. "You're cute," she says. "Here." She hands me a wad of cash.

I silently take back the bitch thing.

She says, "What's your name?"

I tell her and she calls to the band. "Come over here. One or two pictures with Luke, okay?" She says in my ear, "We're only here to play a private party, so don't post it on your Facebook or tweet it."

"I wouldn't even know how," I lie.

She cricks a smile. The manager's disappeared inside, so she asks the doorman to take a few snaps with my cell.

The limo is running on fumes now, and I have to pee a river. As I turn onto Colfax Avenue, an ambulance comes screaming out of the hospital. It's heading right for me. I slam on the brakes, skid, and hear squealing brakes behind me. An SUV has to jackknife out into traffic to avoid hitting me.

The ambulance speeds off and I sit for a minute, my heart palpitating.

Air clogs my lungs and I release it in a burst. There's wet between my legs. Damn. I've pissed myself a little.

The SUV behind me hasn't moved. I get out to see if anyone got hurt. The window is up and I rap on it. I indicate that I was in the limo and the window rolls down.

It's a lady with two kids in the back. "Are you okay?" I ask.

She nods, sort of dazed. "I think so. Did I hit you? Because if I get into another accident, my husband's going to kill me."

A millimeter more and we'd have been sharing a grave. I tell her that her children will not have to grow up without a mother, and my brother will not crush my balls.

A cop stops to make sure everything's okay. Traffic is backed up now, and the cop gets it moving again. I climb back in the limo and pull in at the first gas station I see.

My cell rings and I almost answer, then see that it's Owen. He never calls me at school, which is where I should be right now. He must be home, wondering where the limo is.

There are times to answer your cell and times to throw it in the glove box.

I need to pee *and* I'm starving. I quickly pump five bucks of gas in the tank and head for the cashier and restroom. As I'm paying for the gas, I see a pickup truck pull into the bay across from mine.

Three guys get out. They cross the island and check out the limo. I have to pee so bad, but I don't trust these guys. I pay the clerk and hurry outside. "Excuse me," I say from behind one of them.

He steps aside, but bumps my shoulder hard. "Excuse *me*," he goes.

"Give us a ride, dude," another one says.

They're not getting a ride in Owen's Black Panther. When I go to open the door one of them grabs me from behind, spins me around, and gut-punches me.

PAIN. As I crumple to the ground, my bladder empties.

Someone kicks me in the face with a boot and I cry out.

"Hey, get away from him," I hear. A scraping sound fills my ears before the guys actually scatter. Their pickup squeals out of the station.

"Are you okay?" It's the clerk from inside.

I roll over, pushing to my knees. My stomach hurts and there's blood all down my front. One eye feels like it's swelling shut. "The limo."

The clerk helps me to my feet. "Is there someone I can call to come get you?"

"I'm fine." I'm dizzy, but my first thought is that I have to get the car home.

Wobbling, I turn around. The part of my stomach that isn't throbbing begins to roil and I freak. *Please, God*, I pray. *Tell me I'm hallucinating.*

Right there on the cement I hurl.

There's a deep gouge where the thugs keyed the whole entire length of the limo.

AZURE

Mr. Rosen says, "Does anyone know where Luke is?"

Radhika replies, "He called me this morning and said he was going to be late."

"I haven't seen him all day. Let me call him." I dial Luke's number and it goes to voice mail immediately. He never turns off his phone. "Huh. Maybe he had a dramedy emergency. Why don't we go ahead and start? I can keep minutes today."

Mr. Rosen says, "Well, the pavilion is run by a foundation and has been declared a historic landmark. Not that that's relevant. But I talked to the person in charge of renting it out, and she told me it doesn't open until May."

I deflate. My visions of dancing under the stars go dark.

"I found a Ramada Inn with a ballroom," Connor says. "They'll rent it to us for fifteen hundred dollars."

"Do they have free parking?" Shauna asks.

"I...think so," Connor says. "They do for guests."

"But you don't know about visitors. What about security?"

"Why would we need security?" I ask.

"Because there are sickos in the world," Shauna says. "I want to feel safe."

"It's also a school policy," Mr. Rosen says. "We do need security at any school event."

"How much does that cost?" I ask.

No one seems to know.

"How much is the damage deposit?" Shauna says.

"I don't know." Connor grits his teeth.

Shauna drops her eyes.

"Why didn't you tell us to ask these questions when we volunteered to check out sites?" I say.

She goes, "You never asked."

I so want not to tolerate her. "We still have time to find more corporate sponsors and do a couple of fund-raisers," I tell her. "I say we go ahead and make the reservation. What do you think, Radhika?"

"About what?" She glances up from her paper, where she's tracing over an infinity sign.

Shauna adds, "You may need to reserve the room, Mr. Rosen. They'll probably require a credit card or something."

His eyebrows shoot up. "Just promise I won't end up paying. You might've heard about how dismal teachers' salaries are?"

"Wah-wah." I mock-play my miniature violin.

"I'll get answers to the other questions when I call to

make the reservation," Connor says. He hands over the Ramada information to Mr. Rosen, who sticks it in his prom folder.

On that note, the meeting ends. As we're walking out to Radhika's car, I ask, "Have you told Connor yet?"

"No. And I know I have to. I just can't think of a kind way to do it." She expels a long breath. "I don't know why he asked me when he has a hundred, if not a thousand, girls to choose from."

"Because you're beautiful and fabulous, and who wouldn't want to go with you?" I say.

She bumps shoulders with me, which sends tingles up and down my arm.

As we get into the car, she adds, "Why did he ask me, anyway? We're just friends. That's all we'll ever be."

I try not to decompose in her presence. My chances with her just plummeted.

Luke calls to tell me he won't be in school tomorrow and asks if I can catch another ride with Radhika. He sounds strange — upset or something — so I ask what's wrong. He goes, "Next subject."

Geez. Why is he chilling me out?

He says, "Connor might've found a place for prom."

I tell him, "The Ramada. If you'd been at the meeting, you would've known that."

"Yeah, thanks," he says and hangs up.

I'm taking my discouragement out on him and he

doesn't deserve it. Still, Luke doesn't usually react so dramatically. I mean, he does, but not in a negative way.

I call Radhika. "Have you talked to Luke?" I ask.

"Not since he called to tell me he was going to be late to school because he was picking up Mercy Her at the airport."

"Oh, right. I'm so sure."

Radhika doesn't reply. "That might've been a secret."

"Come on."

"That's what he said."

Good one, Luke.

"Let me call him," Radhika says.

"Conference me in."

My phone doesn't ring. A few minutes later she calls back. "He's not answering."

"I'm going to leave a message and wait for him to call me back," I say.

"I will, too. Don't mention the part about Mercy Her, okay?"

Damn. I so wanted to call him on it. Lying to me is one thing, but lying to Radhika is like blasphemy.

I try to study, but can't concentrate. The last couple of weeks have been an emotional tsunami. I get on Facebook and see that Radhika's there. I IM her:

i never heard from Luke. did u?

Then I wait for an answer.

She IMs back:

Radhika: no. i thought he might be online. usually if he sees me here, he IMs me
Azure: did you talk to Connor yet, about you know what?
Radhika: no. i want to do it in person when i can catch him alone. i'm not looking forward to it
Azure: he's a big boy. he'll survive
Radhika: it's not him I'm worried about. much. it feels like the prom is coming together. i mean, all we need is a little more money. and if ur wondering whether i've asked my father about being a corporate sponsor yet, the answer is no
Azure: i wasn't even thinking about that

Which is true. I'm stuck on how and when I can ask Radhika to prom, and what she'll say, and if I should do it or live with the regret of never even trying and wondering what might've happened if I had expressed my true feelings....

Radhika: he only got back today and I want him to be in the right mood. whatever that is

Who's she talking about? Oh, right. Her dad.

Azure: no hurry. don't feel pressured
Radhika: b cuz time is on our side, right?

Is she being sarcastic? That's not like her.

Radhika: what r we really doing differnt 2 get people 2 come?
Azure: the drag show. karaoke. gaming competition
Radhika: we haven't decided on those things 4 sure, have we?

I thought we had. Maybe I'm the one who decided.

Radhika: u know what we should do? A survey monkey. Get
everyone's opinions so they feel involved in the prom

Brilliant. She's brilliant. She should be the leader, not
me. I know about survey monkeys because we had to team
up in Sociology the first semester of this year to poll people on the issues that affected their school lives, like dating and drugs and bullying. The survey monkey was cool
because it compiled all the answers and spit out a report.

Azure: ur a genius. which is why you're going to Yale, of course

Radhika doesn't write back for such a long time, it
feels like she's waiting for me to write more. Just as I start
to ask if she's excited, she writes back:

Radhika: we should all come up with questions and post the survey online at Prom Central
Azure: u don't think Shauna will go bananas ☺ when we tell her
we want to invade her precious Prom Central?

That was a joke, of course.

Radhika: if u want i'll post a message in our Google docs asking prom com what they all think about the idea
Azure: sure. that'd be gr8

I can predict who'll be in favor and who won't.
My cells rings and it's Luke.

Azure: Luke's calling! Hang on

I answer, "Where have you been?"
"Hello to you, too. I need to talk to you about something."
"Radhika's on IM. Why don't you log on…"
"Later." He disconnects.

Azure: that was weird. he wanted to talk about something, then he hung up
Radhika: can I ask u a question, Azure?

My heart hammers in my chest.

Azure: u no u can

Ask me. I'll say yes, yes, yes.

Radhika: do you really think Luke is bi?

Why does she care about that?

Azure: only on tues, thurs, and sat

Radhika: LOL. What about Haley? he did love her

Azure: i'm not sure he knows what love is. I think it was a lost case of lust

Radhika: it sure seemed like love. anyway, I better go. i still have at least two hours of homework. ☹

She logs off. I sit there rereading our conversation, picturing her in the glow of her computer screen. *Do it*, I tell myself. *What's the worst that could happen? She'd say no and you'd feel like a jerk. Then everything would change and she'd drift away from you; maybe never speak to you again.* I'd die. I would actually, seriously cry every day for the rest of my life.

LUKE

Owen didn't kill me. Obviously, since I'm still alive. He was pacing on the porch with his cell to his ear when I drove up. Shutting it, he stalked over. I got out and he froze solid.

He didn't speak at first — working through all the ways to murder me, I assumed. "Who did this?" he asked.

I stared at the jagged gouge across Black Panther. It represented the total loss of trust Owen would ever have in me. "I don't know," I said flatly. "They didn't sign their work."

"Not the stupid car." Owen hitched his chin. "Your face."

That's when I began to cry. Everything just poured out of me. All the pain and humiliation and fear. "I'm sorry. I'm sorry. I should've called you. I should've peed before I left. I shouldn't have taken your Black Panther. Please don't hate me. I shouldn't have taken your Black Panther."

"Forget the car!" Owen yelled. "I can *fix* the car. I *can't* fix you."

I swiped at my bloody, snotty nose. "I know you think I'm broken, but I'm not. I'm just me."

"I didn't mean that," he muttered. "Although this is what I'm afraid of when you flaunt it."

I didn't think they beat me up because I was gay. I mean, I wasn't even wearing anything with a rainbow on it.

At that moment the pain in my gut caught up with my brain and I doubled over.

"What?" Owen placed a hand on my back. "Luke...?"

"I'm fine," I wheezed.

"No, you're not. I'm taking you to the ER. Change your bloody shirt."

Which I couldn't do. I couldn't raise my arms over my head without screaming. Owen said, "Just get in the taxi."

All I could do was cry, it hurt so bad.

I know he wanted to call me a sissy, but instead he said, "I'll kill the bastards. Where did this happen?"

"I don't remember. I was in a state of shock." I didn't want to tell Owen because he has this scary temper. I'm not afraid of him for nothing.

It turned out I had bruised ribs and a broken nose. But the doctor was dreamy. As we were leaving the ER, I told Owen, "Guess who the fare was? Mercy Her."

"What's that?" he asked.

"A band."

"Never heard of them."

I'd forgotten about the cash Leilani had given me. I pulled it out of my pants pocket. Owen took it and counted. "Fifty-three dollars," he said. "I hope it was worth it." He shoved it back at me.

I take a day off to recover from the trauma. The next morning when I pick up Radhika, I have to recount the whole story to her and her mom. Then, when I pick up Azure, I have to relive it again. Radhika's all concerned about my health, which is why I love her. Azure doesn't believe I drove Mercy Her. I show her my cell pics. I honor my vow of silence, though, by making them swear not to tell anyone.

Even though my nose is bandaged and I have two black eyes, Flacco is totally unsympathetic. She won't give me an extension on my oral report, even by a day.

"You shouldn't have waited until the last day for your presentation," she tells me. "Since you're late, I'm going to have to mark you down at least one grade."

I consider calling the ACLU, then think, *Screw it.*

At play rehearsal the entire cast and crew run up to me and want to know what happened. Some of the girls start crying, and I mean wailing. "I'm okay," I tell them. "It looks worse than it is." Which isn't true, but it's weird how sympathy can suddenly make you feel a hundred percent better.

T.J. says, "I can stand in today if you can't sing."

"Nah. I'm fine." He's so transparent.

I get through rehearsal, but just barely.

Ryan comes up to me after and says, "I'm really sorry this happened to you. It's why I'm so scared to come out."

"I didn't get beat up because I'm queer. They just wanted a ride in my brother's limo."

Ryan looks doubtful.

"Look, you can't let the haters get you down," I tell him. "There'll always be people in the world who hate on you for one reason or another. Being openly queer is just being who you are."

He gazes into my eyes, and I see how deep down his fear goes. I wish I could reassure him. But my ribs start to ache and I question my own declaration of freedom and independence. No, I don't. Closets are for mothballs, dammit.

Shauna says, "Do we really want to let people vote on the theme? Because if we do, we need to give them specific choices. Otherwise, we'll get asinine write-ins, like...like..."

"Under the Sea?" Azure says.

Shauna slit-eyes her.

As they offer suggestions, I begin a list on my netbook:

Somewhere Over the Rainbow (Azure)
Somewhere Over the Monochromatic Rainbow (Me)
Under the Ocean (Shauna)

Azure groans.

Under the Stars (Azure)

Shooting Stars (Shauna)
Bollywood (Azure)

Radhika says, "Please, no."
Azure looks embarrassed.

Swinging on a Star (Me)

"I like that," Azure says.
"Pirates of the Caribbean," I say.
Connor goes, "Aargh," like a pirate.
"We need to get serious about this, people," Mr. Rosen
cuts in. "That survey should be posted this week so we can
have results by the end of next week."
"Over the Moon, Under the Stars," I think aloud.
"That's perfect." Connor smacks the table.
It's not really. He's just too nice to mention how
unoriginal I am. Confirming my suspicion, he adds, "We
should leave a blank for people to fill in a theme. They
really might have better ideas than ours."
Shauna says, "We are going to ask people on the survey
about the royal court, right? Do they only want a king and
queen? Or do they want a couple of princesses and princes?"
"And frogs and beasts," I say.
"People." Mr. Rosen rubs his eyes.
That reminds me of something I've been thinking
about. Make that obsessing over. "We know not everyone
will have a date. How do we encourage singles or friends to
come as groups?"

"They come in groups anyway," Shauna says.

Azure corrects her: "They come in cliques."

"Would singles sign up on Prom Central?" I ask, meaning me. "Everyone would be able to see that they don't have dates."

The committee seems to ponder the question. Shauna answers, "We could match singles, like on eHarmony.com."

Azure coughs.

"It was just a suggestion," Shauna snaps.

"I don't mean it was a bad idea. My dad uses an online dating service."

"Really?" Shauna's eyes widen. "So did my mom. They advertised, 'Meet Your Perfect Mate!!!' She got matched with my current stepdad, who I despise. Now my aunt's using it."

Azure's eyes bug out. "Is her name Mercedes or Lynda or Cloud?"

Shauna makes a face. "No."

"Thank gawd. Anyway, a lot of people are dying to ask someone to the prom, but are too shy or afraid," Azure says.

"What can we do about that?" Shauna asks.

Radhika answers, "I bet I could write a quickie program where people can connect with others who want to go to prom. Singles could get with groups of other people who share their interests, and shy people could hook up online. I don't mean hook up, literally."

"Actually, that could be cool," I say.

"Or a complete disaster," Shauna mutters.

"Geez." Azure throws up her hands.

"Well, what if you get matched with someone you absolutely hate? Then you'd have to spend the whole evening with them."

"It wouldn't be like a blind date. You'd know who you were going to go with," I explain to Shauna and Azure.

"Maybe our theme should be Masquerade Ball, like Luke suggested," Connor says. "Then everyone could come incognito."

Shauna blows out a shallow breath. "I don't want to wear a costume to my prom."

"Fine." Connor lifts his pack and stands. "I have to get to practice."

Radhika gathers her things and says something in Azure's ear. She rushes out after Connor.

Azure grimaces at me. I think that means Radhika is going to do the deed.

Shauna says, "What's happening?"

Azure and I say, together, "Nothing."

"If everyone could put the questions you want to ask in Google docs by tomorrow," Azure picks up the discussion, "Radhika or I could get the survey in Prom Central by Friday. Then we'll make an announcement for people to answer the survey over the weekend, so we'll have reports by Monday."

"We should give people a little more time," Shauna says.

I feel Azure tense up. "How's Wednesday, then?"

Shauna nods. She says to Azure, "Tell them their answers

will be anonymous, even though they have to log on to Prom Central with their student IDs."

Mr. Rosen goes, "Groovy, peeps. Why don't we skip our Monday meeting and wait for the survey results?"

Shauna says, "I think we should discuss fund-raising. We still don't have nearly enough money."

"That brings me to something else I wanted to talk about," Azure says. "I think a lot of people don't go to prom because it costs so much. Which is one of the questions we should ask on the survey: If you wouldn't go to prom, why not? I bet a lot of people will say it's too expensive. The tickets alone are seventy-five dollars. I mean, get real. Who can afford that? Then they have to buy prom dresses and rent tuxes. We need to let people know this prom isn't going to be like that. If they want to come in casual clothes, they can."

"People can't wear jeans to prom!" Shauna cries. "They have to dress up, at least."

Azure inhales, exhales, then says calmly, "I know where people can get formals for cheap. At the thrift store where I work."

"I'm not buying my dress at a thrift—"

"I don't care where you buy your dress." Azure cuts off Shauna. "All the benefits go to Kids with Cancer, so maybe that'll give people extra incentive to shop there. *Some* people."

Shauna shoots to her feet. I see tears in her eyes as she scoops up her backpack and races out. "Nice going," I say to Azure.

"I didn't mean to imply...She just gets to me. One minute she's—"

"Maybe post some pictures on Prom Central of dresses and suits that people can buy," Mr. Rosen says. "Along with the prices."

Azure says, "I was going to."

"Are we done?" Mr. Rosen asks, standing. He looks like he wishes he'd never heard the word *prom*.

AZURE

As we're waiting for Radhika at the Caddie, I tell Luke, "I'm sorry. I'm not judging her, but everything we want to do is wrong in Shauna's eyes."

Luke says, "She does have experience at this. I think we're making her feel really left out."

He said "we," but it's clear he meant me.

I ask Luke, "What did you want to talk to me about when you called the other day?" Just then Radhika comes around the corner of the building and hurries toward us. Her head is down and her hair is covering her face.

Luke says to me, "Later." He asks Radhika, "How'd it go?"

She opens the back door and climbs in. We get in after her. Radhika says, "I never, ever want to hurt someone's feelings like that again."

"He'll get over it," I say. "Everyone's feelings get hurt once in a while."

"What did you tell him?" Luke asks.

I go, "Duh. She told him she wasn't into him."

We drive out of the lot and, to distract Radhika, I say to Luke, "Can we see the pictures of Mercy Her again?" I reach over the seat back.

Luke digs out his cell and hands it to me. Without warning, Radhika bursts into tears. Luke meets my eyes and I see on his face the alarm that I feel.

"Connor will be okay," I say.

Radhika wails, "I don't want to go to Yale."

Luke swivels his head around. Radhika bends over, crying so hard her pain is palpable.

What brought this on? I smooth a hand down her back. "Let's go somewhere to talk. Okay, Radhika?"

She sort of nods. "Will you call my mom and tell her I'll be late? Tell her…" She raises her head and sniffles. "I don't know. Make something up."

I still have Luke's cell in hand, so I scroll through his contacts. He has Radhika first on the list, preceded by three stars. But that's her cell number. Her home number is under *Dal*. I call and her mother answers.

"Hi, Mrs. Dal. This is Azure," I say. "Would it be okay if Radhika came with me and Luke to check out the pavilion for our prom?"

Mrs. Dal says sure, that'd be fine, and asks if I know where it is. "Yeah, we printed out directions," I tell her.

She asks the question I was hoping she wouldn't: "Where's Radhika now? Why didn't she call me?"

"Um, she's in the restroom. Lunch was salmonella stew, and it sort of went right through her."

Mrs. Dal hesitates. "If she's not well, she should come home."

"No. She's okay. She just, you know. She really wants to see the pavilion where you had your prom."

Another pause. "All right. But don't be too late."

I hang up.

"You had to tell her Radhika has the runs?" Luke asks.

"Well?" I say. "I don't think fast on my feet."

"Or your ass," Luke says.

"Shut up."

Radhika sobs into her hands. I tell Luke, "Let's go to my house."

As Luke drives, I put my arms around Radhika and she leans into me. "It's okay." I caress her head. "Why didn't you tell me?"

She's crying so hard, she can't speak. I knew something was wrong. I knew it.

Dad's on duty, so we have the place to ourselves. As I remove my muffler and hang it on the coat tree, I say, "I'll make us some hot tea." I take Luke's and Radhika's coats as well.

They disappear into the living room while I put on a teapot of water and stick a pan of pizza rolls in the microwave. As I join them in the living room I hear Radhika say, "Connor was so great. He told me good luck at Yale, and that's when…" She hiccups a sob. "I just couldn't keep it in anymore."

Luke says, "You never had to. Not with us. Have you told your parents?"

I don't hear Radhika's answer. Probably because she can't stop crying. It breaks my heart to hear and feel her pain. We sit on either side of her and try to calm her down. The microwave dings, so I get up for the pizza rolls. I bring them in on a plate, which I set on the coffee table.

Luke pops a pizza roll in his mouth and flaps with both hands, going, "H-h-hot."

I take Radhika's hand. "*Have* you told your parents?"

She shakes her head no.

"If you don't go to Yale, where would you go?" Luke asks.

Radhika swipes her nose. "Nowhere. I don't want to go to college."

Luke and I gape at each other.

"At all?" he says.

"I'm tired of school. I'm sick of studying all the time, and I'm even sicker of my parents always telling me what to do. I'm eighteen. I can make my own choices and decisions."

"Of course you can," I say. "So what do you want to do?"

Before she can answer, the teapot whistles and I jump up to make a pot of apricot tea—Radhika's favorite. When I return, Luke's offering Radhika a pizza roll and she's declining. I pass her a mug.

"You could take a gap year," I say.

"Yeah," Luke agrees. "Travel or something."

"Or just stay here." *Where I'll be.*

"I've been thinking about joining the Peace Corps," she says. "Making myself useful to the world."

"That's an awesome idea," Luke goes. "I know this guy who joined the Red Cross and went to help rebuild in Haiti."

Radhika sips her tea, gazing off into the shadows. She sets down her mug and says, "My parents will never allow it."

"But it's your life," I say. "It's your choice."

She turns to me. "Tell *them* that."

We talk awhile, until Radhika's composed and Luke has her laughing as he's tossing pizza rolls in the air and making her catch them in her mouth. Once the pizza rolls are gone, Radhika says, "I better get home."

On the way back from her condo, Luke says what I'm thinking: "Holy shit. Did you have any idea?"

"No. I thought she was stoked. Although she hasn't really talked much about it." I just figured she didn't want to constantly remind us how much smarter she was than us, which she totally wouldn't do. It makes me feel inadequate for being so out of touch with her. "I hope her parents don't kill her. She's going to have to tell them sometime."

"Or suck it up and go to Yale," Luke says. "Which I can see her doing just to please them."

He's right. It's so Radhika.

"It's so not fair," I say.

I see Dad pass my bedroom door, heading for his room to change out of his blues.

"Hey," I call to him from my bed as I pull out an earbud. "Back up."

He returns. I prop myself on an elbow. "I'm working Saturday morning, so we'll have to postpone our handball game." We play handball every Saturday unless one of us has to work.

"No problemo," he says in a yawn.

"We can go Sunday," I tell him. "After church."

I've been trying to get him to come to church with me, but he's not into the concept of a higher power, and I'd never push him.

"I forgot to ask," I add. "How was the opera?"

"You won't believe this," Dad says, "but I actually enjoyed it."

I clutch my chest like I'm having a heart attack.

"I liked her. We laughed a lot."

"During *Tosca*? I didn't think it was a comedy."

He makes a face, then disappears down the hall. I follow behind and say, "Hypothetical. Let's say I was accepted into a prestigious Ivy League college."

Dad pivots and makes the same heart attack gesture I did.

I smack him on the arm.

"Then let's say I decided not to go," I continue.

"Why would you do that?"

"Because I wanted to join the Peace Corps instead. Change the world. You know?"

"I'd say you were crazy." He enters his room.

I linger in the doorway. "Why? I'd be doing important work."

"Sure you would," he says. "But passing up an opportunity like that would be pretty stupid. And I assume you're not stupid if you got into an Ivy League school. You must've worked your butt off."

He's right about that.

"You could join the Peace Corps after college," he says, unbuttoning his shirt.

I trek to the kitchen to make mac and cheese for dinner. As I plop a tablespoon of fake butter into the fake cheese, I consider what he said. Is it worth being miserable for four years of college so you can do what you really want when you get out?

Dad's changed into his sloppy jeans and a grungy sweatshirt. He sprawls on the sofa and turns on the TV. I hand him his dinner and he says, "Thanks, Paula Deen."

I say, "So if I told you I didn't want to go to Yale, you'd make me go anyway?"

"Yale?" He swallows a spoonful of goopy macaroni and eyes me. "Azure, I can't make you do anything," he says. "It'd be your decision, babe. But some opportunities only come around once in a lifetime, and Yale is one of them."

It always confuses me when he sounds right.

"So," I say, changing the subject, "when are you taking out Cloud?"

I motion for him to lift his legs, and I slide in underneath. He clicks around and settles on the Colorado Avalanche game. "I'm not sure I will. I really like Lynda."

"Dad, you can't tell by one date." Which, I realize as soon as I say it, is absolutely untrue. You know right away if there's chemistry.

"For your information, Lynda and I are going out again on Saturday."

"Nice," I say. "Where's she taking you?"

He's practically inhaled his dinner and sets his bowl down on the coffee table. I know he's still starving, so I give him the rest of mine. He says, "This time I get to choose."

"Ooh. Where are you going?"

The Avs are losing six to one, so he switches to the Denver Nuggets game. "To the shooting range."

"What? No, Dad. Are you nuts?"

He leans forward and sets my emptied bowl inside his. "She wants to learn to shoot."

I get up and toss a pillow at him. "Yeah, so she can kill you in your sleep. Does anyone do a background check on these lonely women?"

The pillow hits me in the face and it's an all-out war.

LUKE

Azure and I try to keep the conversation light on the way to school, but I can tell Radhika's lost in her own little world. When we pull into the parking lot, the first thing she says is, "I didn't have to ask my dad about corporate sponsorship for our prom. My mom brought it up at breakfast, and he said it was out of the question to expect his company to give us money. Then he made it sound like prom was the most superficial thing in the world, and he and Mom got into a huge argument. Which means if I ever bring up Yale, it might be cause for divorce."

"Can you get divorced if you're in an arranged marriage?" Azure asks.

Radhika snips, "Of course." She sucks in a breath. "Sorry. I don't mean to take any of this out on you. I know you both love and support me, no matter what."

"We do," we assure her.

In the rearview mirror, I see Azure take Radhika's

hand. I wish it were me back there. Why do I always have to play chauffeur?

"I put the survey up on Prom Central," Radhika says, "so we should make an announcement this morning that seniors can begin to vote."

Azure goes, "I think you should do it, Luke. Say something funny so people will want to log on and express their opinions."

"No pressure," I tell her.

The announcements are at the beginning of second period. I sprint from Flacco's room to the office with no time to gargle or practice different voices. At least I wrote down what I wanted to say during Flacco's lecture on... whatever it was.

In the microphone, I say in my radio-DJ voice, "Coming to you live from K-I-S-S MY ASS. It's time to pimp your prom. That's right, folks. This year you — yes, you — get to participate in what you want your prom to be. Your prom committee has created a survey to gather all your opinions so we can make this the best prom EVAH. Just log on to Prom Central with your student ID, password PIMP, and link to the survey. It should only take ten minutes or so, and your answers are anonymous. Since we're, like, way behind, move your ass, class, and get your answers in by Monday." From his chair next to me, Mr. Gerardi scowls. I hand the microphone back to him. Was it *pimp* or *ass* I shouldn't have said? Anyway, I got it done.

At play practice, the Mothballs ask if I've thought about costumes for them. I have and haven't. Most of my creative talents have gone into writing the dramedy and song lyrics. Britny, who plays my mother and my short-lived girlfriend, Haley, and who is also in the chorus, says, "I might be able to get my mom to sew us big round balls that we could stuff with batting."

I form an image in my mind. "Make it so your heads and arms and legs stick out. 'Cuz you'll have to dance and sing."

Ryan clears his throat. "Have you thought about set design?"

"Actually, I have. I saw some of your art in your Face-book album. I was wondering if you'd paint simple black-and-white backgrounds. We only need the three scenes: one at home, one in the closet, and one in school."

"You looked at my art?" Ryan says.

"Yeah. It was amazing."

He lowers his eyes. "Not as good as yours."

Well, no. But I don't work in black and white.

"I think the closet should shrink around me. In the second act, it gets so claustrophobic, I have to break out. What do you guys think?"

Everyone goes, "Cool."

Mario says, "I'll write a few dramatic bars for your breakout."

"Perfect," I tell him. "Okay, so let's do a quick run-through. Mothballs, you're on."

When I descend the stage steps to direct, I see Radhika in the back row. She's not alone. Gabe's there, with his head bent close to hers. I walk back and tell Gabe, "We're ready to start."

"Oh, all right." He tells Radhika, "Laters," and she smiles at him.

A smile that would make Haley Zeligman, now Gabe's girlfriend, put a hit out on Radhika—everyone knows Haley has a short leash on Gabe. It makes me glad she didn't have time to rein me in. "Do you mind if I study here?" Radhika says to me. "I promise not to watch."

"You can watch all you want. I'd really like your feedback."

She turns that smile on me and I melt into a pool of dark chocolate.

"We could sell roses for Valentine's Day," I suggest, since VD is so soon and I know just the person I'd give a rose to.

"Where are we going to get money to buy roses?" Shauna asks. "What about a cupcake sale? I bet if we asked the PTSA, we could get a bunch of moms to bake the cupcakes for free. My mom's president of the PTSA."

I don't even have to look at Azure to catch her reaction.

"We're going to need more than a cupcake sale," Azure says. "What about a silent auction, or a tag sale? Everyone has junk to sell."

"That'll take too long to organize," Shauna says.

Before Azure blows, Connor jumps in. "What about a Battle of the Bands? We could charge the bands who want to play, like, twenty-five bucks, and also charge admission. If one of the bands wasn't major suckage, maybe they'd agree to play at the prom."

Major suckage. I love that.

"Has anyone even talked to a photographer?" Shauna asks. "Do we know how much they charge?"

Everyone's quiet.

Azure says, "We can ask the photography club if one of them wants to do it."

"I don't want some amateur photographer taking blurry pictures of my senior prom," Shauna says.

"Fine." Azure huffs. "But if a professional is going to charge us something like a thousand dollars, we're going to have to sell a shitload of cupcakes."

"Unless we get more corporate sponsors." Shauna looks directly at Mr. Rosen. His head's bobbing forward, like he's drifting off. "Mr. Rosen," Shauna raises her voice. He jolts awake. "Have you found any more sponsors?"

"No," he says. "Sorry. I just don't have time. Not with evaluations coming up. You guys may be on your own."

Shauna turns her attention to Radhika.

Radhika says softly, "My dad can't help us."

Shauna sighs. "What about favors? Have we talked about that?"

"What exactly are favors?" I ask. "Like, friends with benefits?"

Connor stifles a laugh.

Shauna deadpans me. "Party favors. Keychains and

pens and candles and picture frames. Mints, buttons, tote bags—"

Azure says, "I didn't know we had to finance Target."

"It's tradition," Shauna says. "People like having something to take home with them that they can keep forever to remind them of prom."

"How much do the favors cost?" Azure asks.

"I don't know. Ten dollars or so per person, I guess, if the decorations committee buys in bulk."

Azure goes, "So they're responsible?"

"Yeah, but it still comes out of our budget."

"Anything else?" Azure asks Shauna.

Shauna considers. "No, I think that's it."

"Thank gawd," Azure mutters.

This is adding up to be more of a royal wedding than a prom.

AZURE

My self-affirmation for the day is: "Love can be found in surprising places." Since I've flipped so far ahead, I check today's date and see that it's Valentine's Day. My favorite day of the year—when I have a girlfriend to lavish with love. Since I don't…but I'm working on it…I find some construction paper and cut out a heart for Radhika. In my drawer are lots of lace gloves that I've sheared the fingers off of, so I choose a pink one and cut out a small heart, which I glue to the paper. I also trim my affirmation in the shape of a heart and stick it inside. I sign it *Anonymous*, even though she'll know it's from me.

As soon as Luke, Radhika, and I split up to head for class, I run back and slip the heart through Radhika's locker vent.

After first period, when I open my locker, something drops to the floor. It's a computer-generated card, with a rose-petal border and a poem that fills the page. The title is "Longing for the One You Love," and it's by ShirLotta Tidwell. It says things about longing to touch my face and kiss my beautiful lips. Longing to sing and dance. Longing to be with me and join hearts…

The signature is a hand-drawn heart filled in with red ink. *Wow*, I think. *Romantic.* This isn't a card one friend would give to another. And it's all about longing. Dare I hope? My insides glow. She must've slipped it in my locker between first and second periods.

She slides in across from me at lunch and I smile at her. She smiles back. I'm going to ask her. I am. I know now she'll say yes.

"I got four valentines," she says. "I know one of them is from you. Thank you."

Four! My self-confidence dissolves. I have to ask her before someone else does. I open my mouth, but the words won't form. Instead, she asks me how she should tell her parents about Yale and I launch into my regular incoherent babble. Lunch ends without me asking her to prom.

Gaw. I have to do it today, on Valentine's Day.

The next time I see her is after school in Studio 2B. Before I can even whisper a word, Shauna says, "Do you have the survey results?"

The survey. I almost forgot. I reach into my backpack and pull out the stack of stapled reports.

"Wow," Luke says. "Who organized these?"

"I did."

"I'm impressed."

I mock-sneer at him. "Let's start with page one," I say.

"Oh, I wanted to start at the end." Luke fake-sulks.

I kick him in the shin.

"Ow!" he cries. "You just bruised the walking wounded."

He's right. "I'm sorry." It pains me to even look at his two black eyes.

Shauna reads from the survey, "Sixty-eight percent of respondents chose Under the Sea for the theme." She gloats. I bite my tongue. "Second place was Starry, Starry Night. Combined, the three Rainbow themes didn't even add up to thirty percent."

"Only ninety-two people responded," Radhika says. "Maybe if we'd given them more time…"

"No one really cares," Shauna says. "All we did was waste a week."

I glare at her, and I'm not the only one.

"I'm just stating a fact. Look at the survey."

We turn the page and Connor and Luke must read the write-in themes first, because they break into laughter. The list includes:

Psycho Killer in the Crowd
Nude Beach Party
Tranny Transformers
Food Fight
Vamps and Tramps
Send in the Clowns

Shauna says, "I warned you about letting people write in their own ideas."

I sigh. "Let's turn to page three."

We flip in unison. Music. Fifty-one percent want a live band, while forty-nine percent want a DJ. Pretty even. That's all we asked, but there are, like, fifteen write-ins for bands people want us to get.

Lady Gaga. I'm so sure.

The Black-Eyed Peas.

Mumford & Sons.

"Hey," I say, "someone wants Mercy Her. Since you have a close, personal connection, Luke, why don't you see if you can get hold of Leilani? I bet she's waiting for your call."

He curls a lip at me.

I read from the survey, "Rockabilly Willy?" I snort. "Are they for real?"

"Hey," Connor goes, "don't diss my dad's band."

Shauna giggles. It's a weird sound coming from her.

Radhika says, "It's hard to know if these are real bands or made-up ones. If they're local and legitimate, we might be able to hire them."

"I recognize a couple of the names," Connor says. "Maybe if we organize a Battle of the Bands, we can audition them and see how good they are."

We turn to the next page. Prom traditions: Do you want a prom king and queen? A royal court? If yes, what kind of royal court?

More than ninety-three percent answered yes. The royal court was prince, princess, duke, duchess, blah blah blah.

"They're not thinking outside the box," I say.

Luke says, "Or even outside the closet."

Shauna shrugs. "That's what people want."

We have no response to that.

The next page forces people to open their minds a crack. I'm the one who came up with the question: If we have a nontraditional prom, what activities would entice you to come?

We gave them choices like a drag show, karaoke, and a gaming competition.

"Hey," Luke says, "who removed Chippendales and the Thunder from Down Under?"

"I did," I say.

"Party pooper."

Around thirty percent liked our ideas. More were added:

Pony rides
Tatting and piercing
Car show
Face-painting
Disco dancers
Street-dance contest
Poetry slam
Paintball war
Free weed
Pin the tail on the prom com donkeys who are
    planning this prom

"They're making fun of us," Shauna says.

"You think?" Connor goes.

Shauna's cheeks flush.

He adds, "People are just so closed-minded."

"Exactly," I say. "I guess we could do face-painting. A car show might get more guys there."

"I really, *really* want a drag show," Luke says.

"Or we could have a drag *race*," I suggest.

Shauna asks, "What's a drag race?"

Luke explains, "People in drag race. But it's hard to run in heels."

It takes her a minute, but she actually smiles.

"Let's look at the last page," I say. There are lots of positive responses for the people-matching program, and for signing up to join groups on Prom Central. The only write-in is blind dates.

"I *hate* blind dates," Shauna says.

"Me, too," everyone chimes in.

We mull over the numbers and suggestions. I say, "The only way to please everyone is to go with everything. How much are pony rides?"

"Get real," Shauna says. "That was a joke."

"How do you know?" I reply. "You're the one who said to give them what they want."

Shauna's jaw clenches. "Mr. Rosen?"

He glances up from the survey. Up until now he's been quiet.

"You know a lot of this is bogus," she says.

"Maybe. Maybe not," he answers.

"Come on!" Shauna cries.

"Did we say this was a democracy, that we'd act on the majority vote?"

We all look at him. Is he suggesting that we…cheat?

He leans his elbows on the table. "Okay. We know the majority of people will always go with the status quo. It's what they know and what their expectations are. Remember, your prom is about maintaining the status quo while expanding the traditional prom to pull in the outsiders."

"Right," I say.

"Pony rides?" Shauna goes.

"We might leave that one off the list." Mr. Rosen smiles.

"We did get some interesting ideas," I admit. "And band suggestions. And people said they want to come in groups. The survey shows there are those who'd come if they had a date, so I think Radhika should work on the matching program."

"It's already done," she says. "All I have to do is put it up on Prom Central."

Connor says, "If it's okay, I'll post the Battle of the Bands and see who signs up."

"Fine with me," I say.

Shauna sighs loudly. "We *still* need a theme."

"*Not* Under the Sea," I plead. "Please?"

"I love Over the Rainbow," Radhika says.

I so want to kiss her.

"Me, too," Connor says.

I'm pretty sure Luke's thinking he'd like to kiss Connor.

"Do I get a vote?" Shauna asks.

No one answers.

"Go ahead," Rosen says to her.

"You can't actually go or be *over* the rainbow. I prefer Under the Rainbow. Then we can have rainbow-colored arches for couples to walk under. And they'll look pretty in the prom pictures."

I'm shocked speechless. Which is rare for me. "Cool," I say.

Shauna grins, looking pleased with herself. She should be; I think compromising isn't easy for her.

After the meeting's adjourned, Luke catches my arm and whispers in my ear in this singsong voice, "I got a valentine."

"Oh, yeah? From who?"

"A secret admirer," he says. "It was signed with a heart."

My bubble isn't completely burst, because of course Radhika would show her love to both Luke and me. Still, I can't imagine she gave Luke a romantic poem like mine. I'm dying to ask, then decide I'd rather keep what's left of my bubble intact.

The meeting's over and I don't get one single second alone with Radhika. I feel like I'm going to explode. At home, Shauna's already written in Google docs that she talked to her mom and thinks they can pull together a cupcake sale by next Tuesday. She says we need to make an announcement and put up posters tomorrow. I write that I can help with posters, since I don't have to work tonight.

Radhika calls and asks if she can come over and help with posters for the cupcake sale.

Yes! It'll be the perfect opportunity to ask her.

Since I'm in Google docs, I write in all the suggested activities for our alt prom. I add, "Unless anyone has a problem, Shauna can go ahead and post them in Prom Central."

When Radhika arrives, she's thought ahead. She has poster paper and markers. As we get set up in the living room, I feel all jittery. I need to work up to the Big Moment. I ask if she's told her parents about Yale yet and she says no. "I might just run away from home. If you can join the circus, I assume you can join the Peace Corps."

I laugh. She's so cute. "You wouldn't do that." I know her better.

"What would you do?" she asks.

I clear off the coffee table and reply, "I'd tell my dad the truth."

"He wouldn't be angry or disappointed in you?"

I don't want to let on that Dad and I had already discussed it. "I don't think so. I think he'd tell me I was passing up an opportunity that might never come my way again."

"Is that how you feel?" Radhika's eyes drill into my soul.

I can't hold her gaze. "I think it's your decision."

We start our posters, and I'm sweating bullets because the only words on my tongue are, *Will you go to prom with me?*

Radhika says, "You want to watch a movie or something? Maybe listen to music?"

Music. Romantic music.

I sprint to my room and grab a handful of CDs. Dad's got *Tosca*, of all things, in the CD player. Did he buy this at the opera house? I put on Mercy Her, which I think is romantic, and return to my poster.

Radhika's cupcakes resemble actual cupcakes. The first one I draw looks like a boob on steroids. As I watch her work, her lettering perfectly even and perpendicular, my stomach twists. I'm going to ask her. Right. Now.

"I was wondering…" I start.

Radhika's cell rings and she turns away to snag her purse off the sofa. Sighing, she flips it open and says, "Yes, Mother." She makes a face at me. "Oh. I forgot. Okay. I'm on my way." She stands and shoulders her purse. "My aunt's birthday is tonight and we're all going out to dinner." Crossing the room toward the coatrack, she adds, "I can't imagine how I could've forgotten about that." She crosses her eyes and I force a short laugh.

At the door, as I'm waving good-bye, I let out a long breath. Tomorrow. Tomorrow for sure.

LUKE

Mr. Rosen wrote in Google docs that since the cupcake sale is Tuesday, we should help with that instead of meeting on Monday. Connor wrote that so far no one has signed up for Battle of the Bands. The idea might be a total bust. I don't think it is, but time is running out, and fast.

On the off chance we have to find a local band, I dig out Owen's *Westword* from a pile of trash to be taken out. *Westword* is this yuppie subversive paper that lists all the bands playing around town. The first one I see is named Bad Sex. Sounds perfect to me.

They're playing a couple of weekends at a club called Herman's Hideaway. I call the club and a guy answers.

"Who's this?" I ask.

"Who's this?" he says.

Great. A comedian. "I'm looking for a band to come play at our prom. I was wondering if Bad Sex was available."

"Bad sex is always available, dude."

I can feel the smirk on his face.

I repeat, "I'm looking for—"

"I heard you. Listen, Bad Sex is bad, but they're not *that* bad."

"We'd pay them."

"Sorry," he says. "I know those guys, and they're off the prom and wedding circuits." He hangs up on me.

I mutter a curse. I flip through the entertainment pages and see there are dozens of bands. I call three different clubs and have to leave messages because they're not open. In the classifieds, I see an ad for a band called Sanity's Edge. I call and this guy answers, "Yo."

"Hi," I say. "I'm trying to get hold of Sanity's Edge."

"Aren't we all?"

Another smart-ass.

"Why?" the guy asks.

"For a possible gig," I tell him.

"What is it?"

I swallow hard. "A prom."

The guy laughs. He hollers to someone in the background, "You want to play a prom?"

I don't hear their response. The guy comes back on. "How much?"

This buzz of excitement burns in my belly. "Um, two hundred?"

He disconnects.

"Three hundred?" I say to dead air.

Owen comes in with a bulging bag from Carl's Jr. and

the aroma makes me salivate. He sits at the table, opens the bag, and pulls out a thick, juicy burger. He chomps into it while removing the bag of fries. "We got any catsup?" he asks me.

I get up, breathing in the burger's delectable aroma. I go to the fridge for the bottle of Heinz. Who knows how old the bottle is? The catsup is still red, and not fuzzy. I stand across from Owen, drooling like a werewolf.

"Well," he says, "sit. Dig in." He shoves the bag at me.

He bought me a Carl's Jr.? OMG. The first bite is heaven. So are the second and third and fourth. We finish our burgers at exactly the same time, wiping our mouths with napkins. Mom would be proud to know Owen's remembered his manners.

Owen spots the *Westword* and sees that it's open to the ads. "Whatcha doin'? Checking out personals?"

"I'm looking for a band for our prom."

Owen makes a sound in the back of his throat, like, *Good luck.*

"Yeah. You'd think I was asking them to play for a six-year-old's birthday party." I dip a fry in catsup. "We may have to settle for a DJ." Which would only be acceptable if all the bands were major suckage. I like that expression. I'm adding it to my use-as-often-as-possible dictionary.

"I know a few bands at the clubs," Owen says. "You want me to ask if they'd play a prom?"

"And get laughed at in your face?"

"You're paying them, right?"

"Yeah," I say.

"How much?"

"That's the problem. We don't have a lot of money," I tell him.

"If you can offer five Cs, it's a legit gig. If they don't want it, screw 'em."

Even if I was lowballing, I wish I'd approached it with that attitude. Maybe it's part of my having come out as queer, but I take every rejection personally. Owen's phone rings and he gets up. "What's the prom date?" he asks over his shoulder.

"April sixteenth."

He answers his phone, "A-1 Car Service." He jots down whatever the caller is saying on the back of the Carl's Jr. bag. "Yes, ma'am. I'll have a taxi for you in ten minutes."

He rips off the address and looks at me. "You want to take this?"

My eyes bulge. "Really?" I jump up and snatch the address.

"Keep the fare, too," he says.

All of his drivers have to split fares with Owen 70/30. Now I'm suspicious. What am I going to have to do to earn it? Clip his toenails?

"Why?" I ask.

He smacks the back of my head. "Because you're my bro. And that's the way bros roll."

In whose landslide? I wonder.

I hear the noise from the gym before I get there. Inside, hordes of people are gathered around tables and tables of cupcakes. I see Azure and sidle up to her. "There must be a million cupcakes. We're going to make a fortune."

Azure says, "We might if they weren't priced so high." She points at a poster.

I read it. "Five dollars each? Are they filled with liquid gold?"

Shauna appears out of the crowd. "My mom thinks we've priced them too high, but I told her it was a fund-raiser."

Azure mumbles under her breath, "We're not raising money for Kids with Cancer. It's just a prom."

Shauna looks worried. "If we don't sell anything…" She gazes at the door, where people are leaving. "I'd hate for the PTSA to have gone to all this trouble for nothing."

Azure says, "We have to lower the price. What about two for five dollars?"

"That still sounds high," I say.

"But it's a fund-raiser," Azure and Shauna say together. They look at each other, as if voicing the same idea freaks them out.

Shauna goes, "Let me ask my mom." She takes off.

Connor appears, chomping on a half-eaten cupcake. "Delish," he says. "Have you seen Radhika? I made her this." He shows us a cupcake with a swirl of icing and red candy hearts on top. "You can decorate your own at the last table." He indicates the table with his chin.

Just then Radhika comes through the gym door with a tray of cupcakes that I assume her mother made. "There she is," Connor says. "Catch you later."

Grr, I think. *He could've made me a cupcake.* "He's kind of dense, isn't he? She told him she wasn't interested."

Azure says, "Oh, let him buy her a cupcake. What do you care?"

If she only knew. Maybe this is the time to tell her....

Shauna returns. "Mom said we should try two for five." She hurries over to slash the price sign on the door.

I see more cupcakes getting sold after that. When the crowd thins, I make my way around the tables. I eat as I go, mostly anything and everything chocolate. I buy a plain chocolate cupcake to decorate for Radhika. I build a mountain of rainbow icing with glitter and sprinkles and stick a pirouette cookie in the middle. Radhika's out in the crowded hall, talking to Azure.

As I whip out my cupcake from behind my back and hand it to Radhika, she laughs. Not because it's amazing and incredible, but because she has a paper plate full of cupcakes. "I'll be in a sugar coma for a week," she says.

I whisper in Azure's ear, "Who else gave her a cupcake? Besides Connor?"

"I don't know," Azure replies. "By the time I got to her, she already had three."

Crap, I think. I have to work up the nerve to ask her to prom. Not here, though, where she's surrounded by people.

Tomorrow, I vow. Hopefully, I'm not too late.

AZURE

Radhika doesn't ride to school with us the next morning. "A migraine," Luke explains.

"She must've eaten those chocolate cupcakes." She's especially sensitive to chocolate. "Did you give her a chocolate cupcake?"

Luke blanches. He knows full well....

When I walk into the art studio later, she's there! "Sorry I missed lunch," she says to me. "I ate at home, then came in for the rest of the day."

I clench her hand under the table. "Are you feeling better?"

Radhika nods and smiles.

Shauna interrupts. "We only made two hundred and eighty dollars on the cupcake sale. And there were, like, three hundred cupcakes left over. I feel really bad that the PTSA went to so much trouble for us."

"We can sell them all week," I suggest.

"That's a good idea," Luke says. "But we should discount them daily as they become petrified rocks."

I make a face at him.

Shauna goes, "I can't ask my mom to make any more cupcakes. She baked most of those herself."

"My mom baked some," Radhika says.

Yeah, I think. *Don't take all the credit.*

Shauna adds, "Even if we sell cupcakes all week, we're not going to make that much money."

Connor says, "This is a lousy time to bring this up, but only one band signed up for Battle of the Bands, and I've heard them."

Luke goes, "Major suckage?"

"Worse. Plus, it's not much of a battle with one band. Which means we should start looking for a band."

Luke says, "I talked to my brother, and he might be able to find us a local band. He drives to lots of the clubs, so he knows the managers and band members. But…" Luke exhales a dramatic breath. "He says the minimum we should offer is five hundred."

"What?" Shauna explodes.

"What are they, like, grunge bands?" Connor asks. "Or screamo bizarro?"

"Probably," Luke says. "Who knows what my brother's taste is. It'll be an alt band, for sure."

"We'll need another fund-raiser or two," I say.

"What do you suggest?" Shauna asks.

How about what I suggested before and you blew me off? "A silent auction. Everyone has stuff that they don't want or need. You know what they say: One person's junk is another person's treasure."

I'm expecting them all to diss it. Except Radhika. I turn to her, but it's Shauna who says, "I'll be happy to work on it with you."

I want to keel over dead.

"Awesome," I say. "We should give people a week or so to bring their stuff in, then we can go through it and organize it. Do you think we should hold the auction at night or during the day?"

"We might get parents to come if we hold it at night," Shauna says.

"That's what I was thinking." I can't believe Shauna and I are on the same wavelength.

I ask Mr. Rosen, "Can Luke make an announcement about it in the morning?"

He goes, "Yes. But please, Luke, keep it short and tasteful."

Luke slaps his chest. "I'm crushed. My taste is impeccable."

I say, "Also, we need a room where we can lock up the things people donate. We don't want anyone's junk getting stolen."

Shauna lets out a short laugh. Genuine. I guess that did sound kind of funny.

"I'll ask Miss Wells if we can use the costume closet in the theater department," Luke says. "I'm sure it'll be okay."

Mr. Rosen gets out the school activities calendar and we set a date for the auction. There's so much going on, we can't do it until the second week in March, right before spring break.

"That's cutting it close," Shauna says.

"We should think positively," I say. "Why don't you go ahead and check out bands?" I say to Luke.

"Can I go with you?" Connor asks.

Luke looks like he just peed his pants. "Why not?" he says coolly.

Mr. Rosen goes, "The ticket committee wants to start printing and selling tickets. All the committees would like to get an idea about how many people to plan for, so can we put up a short survey to ask?"

"I can do that tonight," I say. "Add it in your announcement, Luke."

Mr. Rosen adds, "Make sure the survey says they're not locked in if they respond yes. And that they'll still be able to buy tickets at the door if they say no."

Again, Radhika and I don't get any time alone. When Luke drops me off, a wave of relief washes over me. Why? There's something holding me back from asking Radhika, besides the fear of rejection. I know this sounds weird, even to me, because it's everything I want, but what if she says yes? Our relationship will definitely change, and if it goes the way of all my past relationships, I'll lose Radhika forever.

LUKE

Owen and the bouncer do this high-five handshake, like they're old army pals. The guy says something to Owen behind his back and Owen replies, "Yeah, they're underage, but they're not drinking. We're only here to listen to Hex Angelis."

The bouncer scans us up and down. "Man, I dunno, Owen. This one especially looks like a kid." He means me.

I see Owen slip the guy a folded bill. The bouncer bends down to tie his shoe, accidentally on purpose opening the door for us with his rear end.

If Owen's going to have to bribe every bouncer to let us into clubs, this is going to cost him a fortune. He must be reading my mind, because he says to me, "This is coming out of your allowance."

Actually, he yells that because it's so loud in here the walls are shaking. I see stairs leading up, but Owen heads for the dark open room where the band is playing. Make that strumming guitars with the bass turned up so loud the reverb is doing demolition on my eardrums.

People aren't dancing; they're just lining the walls like black padding. Everyone's dressed in black. I feel out of place in my powder blue pullover. Connor, of course, looks totally hot in a black leather jacket. Maybe I should take advantage of his vulnerability over being rejected by Radhika and ask him to prom.

Silly boy, I chide myself. *You only just lust after Connor, remember? Radhika is your true love.*

We stand behind a tall round table for a while, and then Connor yells at me, "Are they singing about devil worship?"

I shrug. I can't understand one word of the lyrics.

A waiter appears and Owen waves him off. A bunch of people greet Owen, and he chats up everyone, making them laugh. He's a pretty popular guy. A different dude in his own element.

I wish he'd include us in his conversations. Or introduce me, at least. He obviously doesn't feel comfortable associating with a bro. Especially a queer one.

This band is like retro goth. The whole atmosphere is goth. Older people, more into that culture when it was the rage. I don't think a hard-core goth band will fly at Roosevelt High.

Owen yells in my ear. "What do you think?"

I holler back, "Not so much."

He hitches his head toward the door. "We're outta here."

More people fist-bump Owen on our way out. It takes forever to leave. As we climb into the taxi, I suction my ears with my palms, hoping to realign my eardrums and muffle the ringing. I stretch my jaw to pop my ears as Owen pulls into traffic.

"The regular band broke up. Those guys suck," Owen says.

"Major suckage," Connor and I say at the same time. We both laugh.

Owen asks, "Do you want to hear DJs, too?"

"Not really," I say. "We pretty much all agreed we want a live band."

"We'll try Trex," Owen says. "See who's playing." A man steps off the curb to flag down the cab. Owen zooms by. "Can't he see I'm off-duty?" Owen growls.

Owen's sacrificing fares?

We stop at a red light and Owen swivels around to face me. He looks at Connor. He looks at me, then at Connor.

I say what I'm thinking: "I can't figure out what's in this for you. Schlepping me around. Pretending we're not related."

Owen doesn't answer.

It's a mean thing to say, but it comes out anyway: "I guess that's how bros roll."

Radhika is waiting on a patio chair outside her condo when I swerve to the curb. It's a nippy day and she's wearing her pink hoodie and black skinny jeans. She's tall and refined. She has this grace about her.

I get out, trot around the Caddie, and open the front door for her.

As she slides in, she crunches her knees to her chest and gazes ahead, like she doesn't want to engage in inconsequential chatter. Which is fine with me, because I have only one thing on my mind.

We're almost at Azure's and still my mouth won't open. I drive past Azure's street on purpose.

Radhika looks at me. "You missed the turn."

"Did I?" I smack my head. "Brain clot." I brake at a stop sign and turn to Radhika. "Will you go to prom with me?"

She freezes like an ice sculpture. Slowly, she lowers her legs. "Did you just ask me to prom?"

I nod a hundred times. A car behind me honks. My foot hits the accelerator and we jerk forward. Then I gain control of my reflexes and pull to the curb to park.

Radhika's staring at me. Those dark, bottomless eyes. She lowers them and looks away.

OMG. You know when you realize you just made the worst mistake of your life? This is that moment.

I click on my signal to merge into traffic and take the next street to circle back to Azure's.

"Luke..."

"Hey, it was a long shot," I say. "Don't worry about it."

As we enter Azure's driveway, she hurries out of the house. She opens the front and back doors of the Caddie and waits for Radhika to join her in the backseat.

Radhika says, "I'll ride up here today."

"Can you smell me from that far away?" Azure asks. She scoots in and shuts the door. "Our water heater went out and I didn't even get a shower. I know, I stink like a used Odor-Eater."

Neither Radhika nor I say a word.

Azure goes, "Brrr. Turn up the heat, Luke. It feels like it's going to snow."

I slow at the end of her driveway, then take a left toward school. I'd turned the radio off so I could ask Radhika The Question.

"Is this Day of Silence?" Azure says. "Oh my God. Did I forget it was Day of Silence?"

"No," I say. I want to add, *It's Day of Humiliation.*

Radhika twists her head to speak to Azure in the backseat. "Luke asked me to prom."

In the rearview mirror, I see Azure's eyes bulge.

"I'm really sorry, Luke," Radhika says.

"Like I said, it was a long shot."

Radhika crosses her arms, like she wishes she could disappear into herself. I know the feeling.

Azure's mute.

Damn. Dammit. In a way, I'm relieved that it's over with. Still, now I'll be going to my senior prom alone.

We ride the rest of the way to school in total silence. Awkward. I check Azure out in the mirror and she's shooting me a death glare. What? What'd I say?

As soon as we get to school, Azure flies out the back door and runs off. I figure Radhika will follow, but she lingers. "I don't know what to say, Luke."

"Don't say anything. We're still good, right? Still buds?"

Her eyes pool with tears. She says quickly, "I need to check something out in the library." She takes off.

I punch the hood. I've screwed everything up. Now nothing will ever be the same between us.

As I stagger down the hall, everyone's smiling or saying "Hi, Luke" or asking about the play. It's like this dull buzz in the background. Suddenly I'm ambushed from the right and slammed into a locker. "I hate you!" Azure screams in my face. "How *could* you?"

"What?"

Her eyes burn with fiery rage. Just when I think she's going to hurt me in a very physical way, she stomps off.

What the holy hell?

AZURE

Mr. Rosen begins the meeting by asking Luke to read the minutes. I can't even look at Luke, I hate him so much.

"Azure?"

At the sound of my name, I jolt out of my rage-induced blackout. "What?"

"Do we have the survey up to estimate attendance?" Mr. Rosen says to me.

"Yes. I haven't looked at the numbers yet." Actually, I did look, and they were dismal. Only twenty-six people said they were coming. It's early, though, and everyone always signs up for stuff at the last minute.

Luke, my frenemy, says, "Connor and I found two bands who'll play for our price."

"What is our price?" Shauna asks.

"Five hundred," Luke answers.

"When did we decide that?"

"It's the least amount they'll take," he says.

Connor adds, "It seems reasonable to me."

Shauna shrugs. "I called around to photographers, and the cheapest one I could find was three hundred and fifty. That's eight hundred and fifty more dollars we have to raise."

Geez, I think. People better donate the family jewels for the silent auction.

Connor mumbles, "The two bands are Devolve Bliss and Putrid Wixen."

"What kinds of bands are those?" Shauna frowns.

Luke and Connor exchange sideways glances and knowing smiles. I wonder what they know that we don't. Not that I care. They're both losers.

"Do we get to hear them?" I ask.

"Sure. We have their CDs," Connor says. He pulls two CDs from his pack.

Luke inserts the first one in his computer, saying, "This is Devolve Bliss."

We listen for about two minutes, until I say, "They're awful."

Shauna goes, "I agree."

Luke pops out the CD. "This is Putrid Wixen."

We listen to them and, although I hate to admit it, they have a unique sound. It's not screaming metal and heavy guitars, and the lead vocalist is a girl.

"I like them better," Shauna says. "Except for their name."

"'What's in a name?'" Luke recites. "'That which we call a rose by any other name would smell as sweet.'"

We all look at him.

"*Romeo and Juliet*," he explains.

I want to punch him in the face. Make those bruises permanent.

"Go ahead and book them," I say. "Unless anyone has an objection."

I glance at Radhika, who's doing her eye-avoidance thing again. If she felt bad about rejecting Connor, she has to feel horrible about Luke. I'll throttle him, I swear.

"See if they'll do it for cheaper," Shauna says.

Luke removes the disc. "They won't. If we want them, we'll have to pay five hundred."

Shauna grumbles.

Mr. Rosen says, "I talked to our security guard here, and he says he does off-duty work to supplement his income, but it'll cost three hundred dollars."

Shauna's head hits the art table and she covers it with her arms.

Who knew you had to raise a king's ransom to put on a stupid dance? An idea strikes me out of nowhere, and I wonder why I didn't think of it sooner. "Let's wait on that," I say.

"We can't wait too long," Mr. Rosen says.

"I know. Just until Wednesday."

Mr. Rosen says, "Oh, and Radhika, thank your parents for volunteering to chaperone."

"What?" Beside me, Radhika startles.

"And Azure, your dad volunteered, too, so thank him."

"My dad?"

"Is my mom chaperoning?" Shauna asks. "Because I told her absolutely not."

Mr. Rosen checks his list. "I don't see her on here."

Shauna exhales relief. "Thank God."

Mr. Rosen adds, "We have less than two months now to put on this prom. Can we do it?"

The silence lengthens. Why is everyone staring at me? Finally, I say, "Is the Pope gay?"

That gets a giggle from Luke, but I glare him down.

Shauna says, "I don't know. I have this bad feeling that something disastrous is going to happen at the last minute."

My anger bubbles over. "Thanks. I needed that."

"I don't mean to be negative," she adds.

No. You just mean it's all on my head if the prom sucks.

It's after ten by the time I get home. I took the bus straight to work so I wouldn't have to look at my demon ex-friend's face. Dad's snoozing in front of the TV, sitting up. I wish I could sleep sitting up; I always have to lie on my stomach with my pillow punched down and my earbuds in, fantasizing about Radhika until eventually I drift off.

The only thing I've had to eat all day is a salad at lunch, and I'm famished. I try to be quiet, but as soon as I rip open a bag of Doritos, Dad calls, "Is that you, Azure?"

I wander into the living room. "Astute powers of deduction," I say. "You should apply for detective."

He yawns.

I stand before him, crunching a Dorito. "I wanted to run something by you," I say. "You're not chaperoning my prom."

He says, "Am, too."

"Are not. Because we need you on security detail."

His brow knits.

"We have to have security, and the guard at school says he'll do it, but it'll cost us three hundred dollars. Isn't that extortion? You should book him, Danno."

Dad lets out a short laugh.

"I figure since you're coming anyway, you can pat everybody down on their way in. See if you can borrow a metal detector for knives and box cutters."

"Azure…"

"So that's settled." I head for my room.

He catches up to me in the hall, snatching away the Doritos bag. I chase him back to the living room. He plops on the sofa and I grab the bag back.

"Seriously. Will you do security?"

He opens his hand for a Dorito and I give him one. "Moonlighting is frowned upon in the department."

"You're not getting paid, so it's actually not moonlighting. Is it?"

"And I wondered how you got into Yale. Forgive me for ever doubting you."

I fake-smile at him.

He wiggles his fingers for another chip and I sit next to him to share the bag. "Are you taking a special someone to prom?" he asks. "Not that it's any of my business."

"You got that right."

"I only ask as your banker," he says. "Since I know how much prom costs."

"Still none of your biz."

Letterman's on, interviewing Angelina Jolie, who I used to be in love with. Now I'm only slightly infatuated.

Dad says, "You know if you need money you can ask me."

"Okay. Give me money."

"For prom only. I assume you have a full scholarship to Yale."

I watch as Angelina moves her luscious lips. "How was your date with Annie Get Your Gun?" I ask, meaning the voluptuous Lynda.

He laughs and shakes his head. "You're a pistol."

"Glock or snub-nosed revolver?"

We empty the bag of Doritos, then I head off to bed. It's been an exhausting day, what with Luke almost destroying Radhika and me losing a third of my triumvirate. Surely Luke knows how fragile she is right now. What the hell was he thinking, asking her to prom? If he thought it'd lessen the pain of her stomping on Connor's heart, he's delusional.

A blip of guilt pops on my radar. Maybe that's exactly what he thought, as a friend. If he'd asked me, I would've told him to leave it alone. Then another possibility stakes a claim on my cerebral cortex: What if Luke asked her to prove he's bisexual? Maybe she brought it up to him the way she did with me, and he saw it as a way to show us he's an equal-opportunity asshole. If that was his reason, I'm going to crush him into fairy dust.

LUKE

I close the door of the Caddie just as a taxi pulls into the garage. I recognize the driver by his thick neck. Dobbs. Now the chili cheese dog I ate at Sonic threatens to come back up. I hurry to the house, hoping to avoid a confrontation. It works. But then I stall at the door, waiting for him to emerge from the garage to drop off his mileage record with Owen. He doesn't. Don't ask why I'm curious about what's taking so long. Or why I'd purposely make myself a target. Or why I saunter back to see what he's doing.

The taxi door is open as I approach. I see that Dobbs has one leg sticking out. He's bent over, doing something underneath the taxi's odometer. I clear my throat and he thrusts his head up, banging it on the rearview mirror.

"What the fuck?" he says.

My question exactly.

He's holding a small screwdriver, which he slips into

his pocket before lunging out of the cab at me. "Back off, faggot." He pokes me in the chest. I wince because it hurts my bruised ribs.

Dobbs slams the taxi door and swaggers off. He gets into his Jeep Grand Cherokee and roars away.

Hmm. I open the door and check the cab's odometer, making a mental note of the mileage.

It bugs me all the way to the house. Not that Dobbs didn't leave his mileage record; Owen has a system with his trusted drivers to bill them once a month. Something else isn't right.

Owen's out on a run and his radio's squawking. I hear him calling one of his drivers to pick up a fare at an assisted-living facility in Montbello. He keeps his books by hand and they're a mess. I told him once I'd help him computerize his files, but heaven forbid I'd be involved in his business. The fares for yesterday and today are still waiting to be entered in his record book, and I see that Dobbs just took an airport run.

He's made thirteen DIA runs this week, counting this one. I know the mileage there and back, thanks to Mercy Her. Dobbs's numbers don't add up. I sit down to calculate what the total should be and what the odometer readings are. Sixty-eight miles are missing. Dobbs is pocketing fares.

Busted. Owen needs to know that his wingman is robbing him blind.

I can't seem to get into my play, and my lack of focus rubs off on the cast and crew. Everything's going wrong. The

Mothballs miss their cue; Mario forgets a stanza in the first act; T.J. can't remember the two lines of dialogue he does have. Finally, I say, "Let's call it a wrap."

A presence looms behind me as I'm getting ready to leave. I turn and see that it's Ryan. "I don't have the sets done yet," he says, "but they're coming along."

"That's good. You have time."

"Also…" he stalls.

I shoulder my man bag, waiting for him to continue.

He sticks his hands into his back pockets. "I had an idea for the closet. As it closes."

I thought we'd worked that out by having a door onstage that I'd slowly close, but I say, "Let's hear it."

He scrapes his foot across the floor. "I was just imagining…since we're going with black-and-white sets…if it wouldn't be more, like, experiential to darken the stage and have people dressed in black come in and manually move two freestanding walls closer and closer together. You'd be between the walls."

I think about it, conjuring the scene in my mind. "Wouldn't the audience be able to see what's happening? I mean, even if the lights are out, they're going to catch the movement."

"Yeah, I know. But it'd be sort of symbolic that society has a role in keeping you in the closet. If you think it's dumb—"

"I think it's genius." I can see it now, how it fits into the theme and everything. "Maybe I'll even get Mario to compose a number."

"It'd be more moving, or haunting, if it was done in silence," Ryan says. He adds hastily, "Not that I'm trying to write your play."

"No." I nod. "You're right. Silence can be powerful."

His eyes meet mine. I notice for the first time they're the color of soft moss. He smiles and backs away, picking up his backpack and jacket from the floor and dashing off. As I head out, I realize that the play was feeling stale. Or over-rehearsed. A new element may be just what it needs to add that spark.

"Luke," Radhika calls from the back of the theater. She gets up and heads my way. At the sight of her, my stomach goes into a tailspin.

"I never answered your question. We are still good." She smiles and all my bones turn to jelly. I'm overjoyed that my idiocy hasn't affected our friendship, even though I wish we could be so much more.

"Hey, Radhika," Gabe says, coming up alongside her, "did you understand the limit with the Riemann integral? I'm so lost in AP Calc."

"I think so," Radhika says.

"Can we talk tonight and go over it?"

Haley Zeligman appears out of nowhere. Linking an arm through Gabe's, she homes in on Radhika with laser eyes. "I've been waiting for, like, half an hour. Why are you so late?"

Gabe says, "Sorry. I guess rehearsal ran long."

Haley turns her glare on me.

Yikes. I step out of the line of fire.

"Maybe you could call me after dinner." He writes his number on a sheet of script and hands it to Radhika. Haley about yanks his arm out of the socket.

Everyone can hear her giving him the royal smackdown as they leave.

Radhika waits for me while I answer a question for the lighting crew. Mario's still there, riffing on his keyboard. I tell him about Ryan's idea for the closet.

"Dope," he says. "I'll cogitate on it."

As we walk toward the exit, I ask Radhika, "Do you know why Azure's pissed at me?"

She bites her lip. "Because you asked me to prom."

"Is there a law against that?"

Radhika's voice thins. "I think you need to talk to Azure."

I would, if she were speaking to me.

Earlier I was going to ask Azure what she thought about me asking Radhika to prom, whether Radhika would go with me. But I guess I was afraid of her answer. Now I'm sorry I didn't ask, because I made a fool of myself.

Radhika's quiet on the way home, introspective or something. She can be that way and it feels perfectly normal. But today it just feels weird. When we get to her house, I'm almost glad to see her go.

AZURE

I tune in to my nano, trying to do homework. I don't want to believe it, but the more I think about Luke's motive, the more I'm convinced I'm right, because being a bisexual guy is what makes him cool and special. I just can't believe he used Radhika, our best friend, in such a meaningless way.

Jerk.

Men are jerks.

I grab my cell to call and tell him what I think, then throw the phone down because I don't even want to hear his voice. Instead, I get up and log in to my laptop. As I'm waiting for it to boot up, I read my self-affirmation: "Share your deepest self with your truest friends."

Funny. Yesterday I would've considered Luke to be one of my truest friends. Now I'm thankful I didn't share my deepest self with him. I'm not sure why I didn't. Maybe I was afraid he'd run right to Radhika and tell her, and I want to be the one who does it, in my own way and in my own time. Maybe I thought he'd minimize my feelings, like I was just a horndog, the way he is.

I link to Prom Central and see that fifty-three people have now responded to the prom attendance question. The ones who've answered are either Definitely Coming or Most Likely Coming. I didn't include Absolutely Not Coming because I don't want people to even consider that as an option.

I retrieve my cell and upload the pictures I took in the formalwear room. There is a decent selection of suits and tuxes, except for the ugly baby-blue one. Luke would love it. I write captions for the thumbnails, including prices, and let people know where they can buy the clothes. I tell them their purchases will benefit Kids with Cancer. Then I add, "Formalwear is not required to come to prom."

I link to Facebook and find two messages. The first is from Luke: "Why do you want to kill me? What'd I do?" I ignore him.

The second message is a surprise. It's from Shauna.

Hi Azure,

I was wondering if Connor said anything to you about who he's asking to prom. A friend of mine (read into that) wants him to ask her, but she doesn't know how to drop hints. Do you think this friend should just ask him? And what do you think he'll say?

I sit there staring at the screen, almost laughing out loud at the absurdity. Of course, it's not funny for Shauna.

She added a PS:

PS: Maybe you could ask him what he thinks of me? I know it's juvenile, but the reason I joined the prom com is because I heard Connor was on it. I really, really like him. I think I've been a valuable member, don't you?

What is this, extortion? She's been a pain in the butt.

I don't even know how to answer her. I haven't picked up one vibe that he's into her at all. No doubt he's got a lineup of potential prom dates now, since every girl in school would give her right arm to be his accessory. Ironic that he asks the one girl who has absolutely no interest in him.

A third message arrives as I'm checking my wall. I return to my messages and see that it's from Radhika. My pulse races. She wrote:

Azure,

I'm quitting prom com. Sorry to let you down.

♥

Radhika

I call her, but her cell goes to voice mail.

Shit. I have to be at work in fifteen minutes, so I rush out the door, redialing her number as I race to the light-rail station.

After the three thousandth call, she finally answers. "What do you mean you're quitting prom com?" I yell. So many cars are passing and horns honking, people talking on their cells and construction workers drilling through concrete, that it's impossible to communicate.

"I was wrong to let you talk me into it."

"Why? You've contributed a lot."

"Like what? I attend the meetings. Basically, I take up space."

"You wrote the program to match people to singles and groups."

"It took all of twenty minutes," she says.

I panic. She can't quit. "We're so close to the end. I need you to help with the silent auction." My train rolls into the stop and the doors whoosh open. People hustling out almost knock me over. "My train's here," I tell Radhika. "Don't quit. You'll let everyone down." *Most of all me.*

"Thanks for the guilt trip." She disconnects.

I didn't mean for it to sound that way. I want to call to apologize, but there's no cell reception in the train. Radhika probably figured out why Luke asked her to prom. My stomach clenches. What if she said yes? I never even considered the possibility she might've said yes. She never told me she liked him that way, and I know she would have. Wouldn't she? Did she ask me if Luke was bi because she has feelings for him? I find that hard to believe. Impossible to believe. I don't want to believe it. The more likely scenario is that she felt obligated to say yes, since he's her BFF.

As soon as I get off the train, I dial her number. Voice mail.

I call Luke.

"Hey," he answers. "'Sup?"

"What did Radhika say when you asked her to prom?"

"That's for me to know and you to guess."

"Don't be a douche tool. What'd she say?"

"What do you think she said?"

I raise my voice, "Just tell me!"

He sighs. "She said no. Didn't you see my trail of tears? The stake through my wounded heart?"

"Shut up. You don't really like her, so why did you ask her?"

He pauses. "What makes you think I don't like her?"

"Because you can't. You only want people to believe you're bi, when you know you're really not."

"Excuse me?"

He heard me. I get to the thrift shop and pause outside the door. "Now she wants to quit prom com."

Luke goes, "She can't do that."

"I know! Everything's screwed up, and it's all your fault. You and Connor. She probably feels like she hurt Connor's feelings so bad he'll never forgive her. And in your case, she never wants to see you again."

"That's not true. When did she tell you that?" he asks.

I'm so pissed. Even if it were true, I wouldn't answer.

Luke says, "Did it ever occur to you that I might be in love with Radhika?"

"What?" I shift my cell from one ear to the other in case I heard him wrong. "You're lying."

"No, I'm not. Is it crazy, or what? After all these years."

I blink snowflakes off my eyelashes and stare blindly ahead. "You never told me."

"I was going to."

"When?"

"Earlier. Before I ruined both my and Radhika's lives by asking my best friend to prom. Not that you aren't my BFF, too."

I hang up and head inside. A roaring fills my head.

My cell rings immediately. Luke. I don't answer. He calls again.

"Azure, is that you?" Louisa comes out from the back. "Would you mind sorting through the donations we got in today?"

"No problem." My voice sounds muffled, far away.

My cell rings again. I stuff it in my purse as Louisa returns to the back room. While I'm sorting, my cell keeps ringing. Text messages. I know who they're from. Finally, I can't stand it.

I read the first one:

I'm sorry I didn't spill my guts. Maybe if I had, I could've saved everyone all this torment. And I mean that.

I remember my affirmation to share my true self, and a pang of guilt stabs me.

Should I? Can I?

No. My feelings for Radhika are too intimate. What if she turns *me* down, too?

Louisa wanders by and sees me with my cell in my hand. I haven't been texting, but I haven't been sorting, either.

"I'm sorry," I tell Louisa. "I'll work an extra hour for no pay."

She doesn't reply, and I wonder if I'll be a full-time volunteer after tonight.

Neither Radhika nor Luke speaks the whole way to school, and the tension drives me berserk. I just want to start jabbering about the weather or something, anything. As we roll into the parking lot, I say to Radhika, "About prom—"

"If one more person asks me to prom, I'm going to scream. I don't mean you, Luke. Or Connor, either."

Luke swivels his head around. In unison, we both say, "Who else asked you?"

Radhika grabs her bag. "I don't want to talk about it." She opens the door and scoots out, while Luke and I gape at each other.

"Who could it be?" I ask.

"No idea."

Luke snags my arm as I'm hustling to catch up to Radhika. "I figured something out last night," he says. "You're in love with her, too. Why else would you call me a liar? Why would you care if I asked her? And Connor, too?"

My face flares. "You're wrong."

"You think I don't know you. But I do. Just tell me the truth," he says.

The words stick in my throat. My mouth feels like it's coated with chalk dust. "Please, Luke. Don't tell her."

"Oh. Em. Gee," he says. "Both of us?"

"I'll hate you forever if you breathe a word."

"Don't you think she knows? She's not blind or dumb."

"*You* didn't know." *At least, not until now.*

"Yeah, but I *am* blind and dumb."

"You're not dumb. And you're not blind, either."

"Luke, the omniscient, sees all. Except what's right in front of his face."

"How do you know you love her?" I ask. Because I doubt very much he feels the same things I do.

"Let's see. Sweaty palms. Pounding pulse. Goose bumps whenever she's around. Fluttery stomach. Hard-on..."

"Okay." I stop him. Same physical reaction, minus the hard-on.

"Plus, love is something you just know."

I can't argue with that.

Radhika's entered the building and disappeared. Luke whispers, "Ask her to prom. Maybe she's been waiting for you to do it."

"You heard her," I say. "She doesn't want anyone else to ask."

"She doesn't want the *wrong* person to ask."

I think about that. A surge of hope races through me. She *did* give me that valentine.

We hear the bell and hurry inside, where Radhika's waiting for us. "I told my parents at dinner about the silent auction and asked Mom if she had anything to donate. She said she'd go through the garage. Then she asked who I was going to prom with, and that's when I completely lost it. I told them I'm not going to prom and I'm not going to Yale, either—and that I am joining the Peace Corps."

"What?" Luke and I say together. I add, "You have to go to prom."

Luke elbows me.

Radhika's eyes fill with tears. I snake my arm around her waist. "What happened when you told them"—I gulp down the catch in my throat—"about the Peace Corps?"

"They just looked at me. I got up from the table and went to my room. They didn't say a word; they didn't even stick their heads in to say good night. But I could hear Mom crying in her room later. Then this morning Dad's waiting in the living room for me to come down. He says, 'Sit.' Then he goes, 'How important is this prom to you?' I say, 'Extremely important. It's the most important thing in my life.'"

My spirits lift.

"Which is a total lie," she adds, "but I know it means the world to you two."

My heart sinks again.

The last bell blares and we're almost trampled from behind. Luke culls us from the herd.

"What did your dad say?" Luke asks.

Radhika gazes off over Luke's shoulder, then meets

my eyes and Luke's. "He said he'd finance our prom if I promised to go to Yale."

"No." I shake my head. "That's wrong."

"So, anyway, the prom is saved. Have a good time." Radhika pivots and speeds off toward her locker. I call after her: "Radhika!"

A hall monitor stops me and Luke and says, "Do you have a pass?"

Luke mutters, "Yeah. I pass gas."

The hall monitor writes us up.

As we're standing there, waiting for our pink slips, I say to Luke, "We can't let Radhika's dad do that. We have to raise the money ourselves."

"You think?" Luke asks sarcastically.

"Shut up." I snatch the pink slip out of the monitor's hand and hurry to put distance between me and Mr. Omniscience.

LUKE

"Houston, we have a problem," Mr. Rosen says as he walks into the art studio. "Mr. Gerardi is getting calls from parents complaining about our"—he makes air quotes—"'alternative prom.'"

"Why?" Azure asks. "What's wrong with it? It's"—she air-quotes back—"'alternative.' They should look up the word."

"Where's Radhika?" Connor asks.

Azure scowls at me, like it's my fault Radhika's dropping out of the committee and not going to prom.

"She had a test today," I lie.

Mr. Gerardi appears at the door and invites himself in. He pulls out a chair next to Mr. Rosen. "I guess you heard."

"Who cares what the parents think?" Azure says. "It's our prom."

Mr. Gerardi sets a folder on the table and opens it. "Piercing and tattooing? Paintball wars? Gambling?"

"Who said we were gambling?" Shauna asks.

Mr. Gerardi reads the list he must've printed off from Prom Central. "What's 'gaming competition'?"

"It's Wii games," I explain. "Although I play a wicked hand of Texas hold 'em."

Mr. Gerardi sighs. "When I asked you to plan a nontraditional prom, I didn't think you'd extend the boundaries beyond good taste." He looks directly at Mr. Rosen.

Azure says, "I don't remember you giving us boundaries. You were open to the idea of expanding the meaning of prom, which means including everyone's interests. We did a monkey survey...."

"I have a copy of the survey." He holds up the stapled report. "You know a lot of this is just joking around. Tattooing and piercing? Pony rides? Are you really going to sell weed?"

I raise my hand. "It was free weed, if I remember."

Mr. Gerardi drills his eyes through my skull. "The PTSA is meeting tonight at seven to discuss your plans for prom. Be there." He gets up and leaves.

Mr. Rosen says, "Hang tight." He follows Gerardi out.

We all look at one another and start grousing. "What's it to them what we do?" Azure says. "They don't have to come."

"Yeah," I say. "This is not your mother's prom."

"Or your father's," Connor says.

I press my hands together. "Our Father, Who art in heaven…"

Connor's the only one who laughs.

Mr. Rosen comes back in. "No getting out of it. We all have to go." He shoulders his backpack and leaves again. Azure stands and says, "We're going to stick together, aren't we?" She's addressing Shauna more than anyone else. Shauna's eyes are fixed on the table. She raises them and sees all of us staring at her.

"I didn't rat us out," she says.

Under her breath, I hear Azure hiss, "Sure."

The good thing about the PTSA meeting is that attendance is sparse. I don't know if that's how it always is or if calling a hasty meeting doesn't give mothers time to cancel their spa treatments. I count only two men in the audience. One of them is Azure's dad. He looks totally hot in his cop uniform.

Here's how it goes down:

The PTSA president (Shauna's mom) reads from our announcement page on Prom Central: "Seniors, this'll be the COOLEST PROM EVER IN THE HISTORY OF MAN-AND WOMANKIND." I told Shauna to write that. She listed the activities:

Live band (Putrid Wixen)
Karaoke
Drag show
Disco dancers
Spotlight dances
Street dancing (hip-hop, krunking, popping, locking, thrashing, etc.)

Gaming competition (bring your own portable Wii)
Poetry slam
Car show
Piercing and tattoo artist on-site (not included in the
cost of prom)

Did we all agree on this? Maybe Shauna thought, since no one opposed, that she was outvoted.

Shauna's mom continues to read: "Location: Ramada Inn Central. Formalwear is optional. Vote now for your royal court (gender-free nominees are welcome): king, queen, princesses, princes. Tickets are only twenty-five dollars." Mrs. Creighton looks up. "Who decided all this?"

None of us volunteers a word. I know Azure thinks that means solidarity, but I'm just scared shitless.

Mr. Gerardi moves to the mike. He says he supports our alternative prom, but adds that he wasn't aware of the full list of activities. Of course, he could've checked it out online anytime. Mr. Rosen sits in the front row with us. Like he has our backs. I'm pretty good at reading people, and even though the PTSA officers are smiling down on us, it's more like, *You poor, misguided youth.*

The students on the PTSA board don't say anything. I'm not sure they're real people. They might just be blow-up dolls stuck in seats to represent the *S* in PTSA.

Parents from the audience are allotted time to speak for or against the prom. Azure's dad is for us, of course, but he does say, "I'm not sure it's legal to have the tattooing and piercing. And you guys might require a license for the car show."

I see Azure seethe as he takes his seat. He shrugs his shoulders, like, *What?*

The next person up is Mrs. Dal. I spin my head around to see if Radhika's in the audience. She's sitting in the back row, next to her father. Her head is bowed. Then, shock of all shocks, I see Owen leaning against the door frame at the back of the gym. What's he doing here?

Radhika's mom says, "I think the students should be able to put on whatever kind of prom they'd like. I find it admirable that they'd want to find a way to include everyone in this very important event of their high school lives."

I think, *That'll send Radhika over the edge.* But when I look at her, she seems unaffected. Or paralyzed.

A bunch of radical parents rail against us. Azure looks ready to implode.

After everyone's done, the board asks us to wait outside for its decision.

In the hall, I see Owen streaking out the front door, yanking his taxi cap onto his head. Azure walks over to talk to Radhika, but her parents whisk her away.

"What do you think'll happen?" I ask Mr. Rosen.

He says, "I have no idea. This is my first year teaching, and my first committee."

Just then the door opens and Shauna's mother says, "You can come back in now."

That was fast. My stomach feels sort of queasy. The

board asks us to sit again and we all slide into our seats. "We do compliment you on trying to include more of the students in the high school prom," Mrs. Creighton begins. "But we also believe prom should carry on a sense of tradition here at Roosevelt. So, to compromise, you can have your alternative prom."

"Yay!" Azure jumps up and cheers.

"Except..." Mrs. Creighton holds up a hand.

Azure freezes.

"Without the drag show, car show, tattooing and piercing, street dancing, and poetry slam."

I go through our list in my head. What does that leave? Karaoke. Wii games. Big woot.

"That's not fair," Azure protests loudly.

"If you have a problem with our decision, take it up with Mr. Gerardi. File a formal complaint. We'll consider it at our next meeting, after spring break."

"But that'll be too late," Azure whines.

Mrs. Creighton adds, "And this band, Putrid Wixen? We'll need copies of the lyrics of any original songs." She gavels the table and the echo reverberates around the gym.

I feel shell-shocked. Azure storms out of the room, cursing like a cop.

"What'd they say?" Owen asks when I get home after the PTSA debacle.

"About what you'd think. We're back to a traditional prom, pretty much. Oh, but we can have karaoke and Kung Fu Panda Wii."

"Figures," he says under his breath.

"How'd you even know about the meeting?" I ask him.

"Mom and Dad get the PTSA newsletter and forward it to me."

"And you read it?"

"Only in the toilet," he goes.

I throw my man bag on my bed and untie my shoes.

"That guy you took around to the clubs…" Owen's trailed me to my room. "Is he your boyfriend?"

It takes me a moment. "Connor? Hell, no. He's just a friend. Speaking of…"

I yank my V-neck over my head. "Dobbs is jacking with your taxi odometers. I don't know how, but he's cheating you on fares."

Owen leaves and I traipse after him through the hall to the kitchen. He opens the fridge and retrieves a can of Coke.

"If you don't believe me, check the books."

Owen whirls. "Stay out of my books. And stay out of my business. Period."

"He's cheating you. You have to fire him."

Owen comes at me like a rabid gorilla. "What did I say?" he roars.

I back up fast, slipping on a pizza box and falling on my ass. I pick myself up. Whatever. Far be it from me to save his major suckage of a company.

It's an unusually warm day, this early day in March. All Azure can do is rant gar-blah-bage about the PTSA decision, while poor Radhika and I have to sit there and suffer. I want to say, *Just deal with it.*

Ever since Radhika turned me down, I don't have much investment in the prom. Especially since she's not even going. I won't get one dance with her. I suppose I'll go with the Diversity Club, since it is my senior year.

For lunch, I decide to buy a bag of baby carrots and a sandwich from the machine and eat outside. While I'm sprawled lengthwise on the hood of the Caddie in the school parking lot, this deep voice says behind me, "I've been looking for you."

I choke, literally. When I bend forward, Connor thumps my back until the chunk of carrot is dislodged. Could I be any less cool?

"Smokin' wheels," he says. "When are you going to let me take a test drive?"

"Say the word." I readjust my Ray-Bans on my nose.

"Word." Connor cricks a lip. "Tell me again how you got this Seville—because didn't you have a Kia at the beginning of the year?"

Connor remembers what I drove?

"Owen, my brother, owns a car service. At least he will until it goes under. Gypsy cabs and limos."

"Cool. Was that his cab he was driving when we went clubbing?"

We didn't really go clubbing. Not in my definition of the word. If Connor says we did, though, we did.

"One of several."

Connor says, "Maybe he can provide transportation for the prom. How many limos does he have?"

"Five stretch and six town cars. Prom season pretty much keeps his business in the black. That's when he knows for sure the big bucks are coming in." He'd probably make more if his drivers were honest. I wonder how many more of his "friends" are screwing him royally.

Connor shifts his feet, looking uneasy. What does he want? He confuses me. Sometimes I think he's coming on to me. Then I have to slap myself because he's all manly man.

"Scooch," he says.

I do and he launches himself up on the hood next to me.

OMG. I can smell his über-athletic sweat.

He squints because the early afternoon sun is bright and I parked facing into it. "You want my shades?" I ask him.

"No, thanks. I'll take a carrot, though."

I practically throw the bag at him.

"I have this dilemma." He crunches into a carrot. "I thought if anyone knows how to handle women, it's you."

I snort. "Oh, yeah. That's totally my area of expertise."

"At least you could tell me how to do or say something to someone without hurting her feelings."

I let out a puff of air. "Dude, you might want to check my track record on that."

He shields his eyes to gaze at me. "You'd never hurt anyone on purpose, though."

"And you would?"

"No. Not deliberately. But I might accidentally. Shit. I don't know. I hate this." He looks away and crunches his carrot.

"What's your dilemma, bad boy?"

He sighs. "There's someone who wants to go to prom with me, and I'd rather swim in a vat of battery acid."

I almost say out loud, *Don't do it! Don't scar that pretty-boy face.* Instead I go, "Here's a thought: Don't ask her."

"She already asked me. She wrote me this long gmail about how much she likes me and wants to go out with me and how she'd really, really love it if I asked her to prom."

I glance at him and see that his expression is pure misery. I draw from my own experience and say to him, "Tell her you asked someone else. Or someone already asked you."

"I did ask someone else." He crunches a carrot, chews and swallows.

Even though he can't see my eyes behind my Ray-Bans, I widen them, like I'm all surprised. "Way to go." I hold up a hand to high-five him.

"I asked Radhika. She said no."

"Whoa. I'm sorry." I lower my hand.

Connor says, "I've been in love with Radhika Dal since we were in kindergarten, and she's only ever seen me as a friend. At some point I'm going to have to get over her and move on."

"First grade might've been a good time."

AZURE

Both our Wednesday and Friday meetings are canceled because Mr. Rosen is sick. Which is just as well, because I'm still fuming.

On Friday Mr. Gerardi is waiting for me outside my third-period class. I'm not speaking to him. He says, "Miss Wells tells me the theater department's room is packed full of donations for the silent auction, so you're going to have to find another room that locks. You could use the music room, if you want."

Still not talking to him.

"And I think you have enough donations. You should make an announcement before the end of the day that people can stop bringing things in."

I shower him with death rays.

He must get the message because he says, "I'm sorry about the PTSA. An alternative prom was still a good idea."

He whaps my thigh and the tingles force out a short giggle.

"Tell me about it," I say. "I feel for you. Wanting someone you can't have."

"Why? Do *you*?" He faces me and a blush rises up my neck. I snatch the bag back from him and grab a handful of carrots to shove in my mouth.

"Wait. Is Radhika gay? Is that why…?" He smacks his head. "I'm such an idiot."

"I wouldn't say 'idiot.'" *And I wouldn't say Radhika was gay, either. I don't know where Azure got that idea.*

He keeps thunking his head and I want to clench his wrist so he doesn't cause brain damage. Finally, he stops and heaves a sigh. "If I ask someone else now, do you think Shauna will find out?"

I try not to cough my guts out. "Shauna? That's who asked you?"

Connor scrunches up his face. "She's so full of herself and irritating. Girls like that bug the hell out of me."

Shauna Creighton likes Connor Spears? Wait'll I tell Azure.

"You could always ask me," I blurt out. Then I die a million deaths. Where are the carrots?

Connor grins. He puts a hand on my shoulder and says, "Sorry. I'm not into dudes."

We both laugh. Him, because it's funny. Me, because I'm pathetic. I'd lust after a zombie if it showed the faintest interest.

There's one carrot left in the bag and I hand it to

Connor. He reaches in and snaps off half in his mouth, handing me the rest.

"Girls know everything," I tell him. "Or eventually they find out."

"How do they do that?"

"The social grid."

He leans back on the windshield, his arms behind his head. I want to reach over and rest my hand on his leg. Pat it sympathetically. Feel his muscles. Azure's right—I *am* a horndog. "Who are you going with?" he asks.

"Radhika," I say.

His jaw drops.

"Not really. She turned me down, too."

He blinks. "Seriously? You asked her?"

"Stupid is as stupid does."

"Wow." He keeps blinking. "I didn't know you liked her that way."

"Yeah, I should've called Perez Hilton to make it public knowledge. Someone besides us asked her, too. Do you know who?"

His eyebrows arch. "Girl or guy?"

Now he has me wondering. "No clue."

We exhale in unison. Connor closes his eyes and I watch him in my peripheral vision. He's such a god.

He asks, "So, who *are* you going with?"

"Probably the Diversity Club."

"Maybe I'll just go with them, too. That'd solve my problem. I could tell Shauna I'm going with someone else, and it wouldn't be a lie."

"You'd better not sign up online or she'll see."

"Right." Connor smiles so broad, his dazzling white teeth glint in the sun. "Thanks, Luke." He holds out his palm and I slap it. "I knew I could count on you."

He hops down and saunters off, while I recite in a whisper, "How do I love thee? Let me count the waves."

If he thinks that'll soften me up, he doesn't know my melting point.

I have to make a pit stop before lunch, and since the cafeteria is close to the theater room, I drop by to see if Miss Wells is there so I can check out how many donations we have. I don't see her, but I stop and gasp. Near the costume-room door, a mountain of trash bags rises almost to the ceiling. It's like all the hoarders in the world cleaned out their houses, attics, basements, and garages.

The silent auction is next week, and even with everyone working full-time, we'll never sort through all this stuff.

I slide into my chair at the lunch table across from Radhika and say, "Have you seen how much crap people have donated for the auction?"

She stabs a cherry tomato in her salad. "My mother donated jewelry and a set of collectible brass elephants."

I grimace. "I didn't mean it was all junk. I'm sure there's some really valuable stuff in there. But it'll take forever to sort." She doesn't volunteer to help, which surprises me. "I'll ask Mr. Gerardi if we can drag everything to the gym and start getting it in some kind of order."

She still doesn't...

"I can't," she says. "I'm way behind in the college seminar now, and it's going to take me the rest of the semester to catch up."

"Radhika—"

"What?" she barks.

Geez. "It's okay. We're just not using your father's money."

She looks at me, or through me.

"I mean it. If we sell all this stuff, we should have more than enough to fund the prom. Not that I even care anymore." Which is almost true. Without her there, who cares? Except there's a part of me that refuses to give up.

"I'll see you later." Radhika lifts her tray and leaves abruptly. I wonder what I said, or didn't say, or should've said or done. She seems so defeated. I'll show her that we can do this, that she's free to chase her dream of joining the Peace Corps. And I'll convince her that she *has* to go to prom, even if it's not with me.

I hate giving up the Saturdays when Dad's off and we play handball at the rec center. We always stop for lunch at Large Marge's for Philly cheesesteaks, and he tells me stories about growing up with five brothers, which must've been a blast. I swear some of the shit they did was illegal. I guess it never got on his permanent record, since they let him into the police academy.

I could wake him up and make him go to the rec center early before I have to leave for school to sort donations, or I could let him sleep in. When I open his bedroom door, he's curled up, purring like a kitten. I don't have the heart to drag him out of dreamland. Instead, I log on to my computer and check Google docs. Only Shauna and Luke responded to my Help! Alert last night about sorting today. Shauna said she'd ask the decorations committee to help, too, since they're requesting $1,500 of the budget. I wrote, "What for? All we need are balloons." And she wrote back, "We need more than that. They have to buy favors, too." I was tempted to write, *Forget the stupid favors*, but I didn't want her on my case again. Under Shauna's message, Connor wrote that the reservations at the Ramada were confirmed. Yay! That's one item we can check off.

After six hours of sorting, we still have dozens of garbage bags left. I hear Luke say, "OMG. Someone donated their underwear." He holds up a pair of yellowed jocks.

People do that at the thrift store, too. It's gross. But Louisa takes the newer-looking boxers and panties home and washes them.

"I'm only keeping the thongs," Luke adds.

"Just toss the underwear," I tell him.

He says, "Not on your life. These thongs are just my size."

I'm too tired to laugh at his jokes. I open a kitchen trash bag and empty it onto the gym floor. Jeans and shirts, some old CDs, junk jewelry. Then I see an object that makes my heart crash against my rib cage. I pick it up by the chain, and the silver heart spins in a circle. On the back is an engraving I had made: TO DESI, NOW AND FOREVER.

I gave this to her on our six-month anniversary. I'm surprised when tears well in my eyes. I blink them away and swallow a stuttered sob. I think it's the fatigue and the fact that Radhika isn't here and this whole fiasco with prom. Why did I ever agree to get involved? I'm not a leader, and I never will be.

I place the necklace in the bin for jewelry and finish

sorting the stuff that was in the bag. A lot of these items are familiar to me, and I can't handle it. Shoving the rest of the donations back into the bag, I throw it on the mound and stand. "I don't know about anyone else, but I'm wiped," I tell them. "If anyone can make it in tomorrow, that'd be great. Otherwise, we can finish next week. Let's lock up the auction items in the music room and put the rest of this crap back in the theater."

Shauna accompanies me to the music room with her stack of bins filled with old stuffed animals and children's toys. She says, "He's going with someone else."

It takes a minute for my brain to click in. Even then, it's sluggish. "Who?"

"Connor. I finally just asked him to prom, and he texted me that he was going with someone else."

He texted her? That's so rude. My respect for Connor just plunged below zero. I'm glad Radhika turned him down.

"Do you know who?" Shauna asks.

"No," I say. I don't know and I don't care. We both set down our bins and Shauna gives me this look like she doesn't believe me. "He could've told you in person, at least."

She blinks back tears. Wonderful. Now she's going to get all weepy, and I'll have to comfort her. "I know people think I'm the one who told the PTSA about what we were doing for prom, but I'm not," she says. "My mom kept asking, and I told her it was prom. As in P-R-O-M, and we were doing things a little different to get people to come.

232

That's all I said." A tear slides down one cheek, then a second tear slides down the other.

If it was anyone but Shauna, I'd hug her.

Shauna swipes her nose on her sleeve. "I really do support this prom. It could've been anyone who told their parents. Everybody has access to Prom Central."

Which, I realize, is true. Any of the prommies could've run to their mommies.

"I don't think we should change anything we planned to do," Shauna says. "I know we have to take all those activities off Prom Central, but that doesn't mean we can't still do them. I've been thinking about it, and we can put up a closed Facebook page. We've come so far," she says. "We can't stop now."

Am I hearing these words from Shauna Creighton's lips? She makes me feel fired up again.

"At our Monday meeting, let's talk to Mr. Rosen about it. I know he's on our side," I say.

Shauna heads for the door. "I'll be in to help sort after church tomorrow." As she exits, I watch her go, thinking, *Whatever my affirmation for today was, I'm rewriting it to read: "Once you get past the dark side of a person, you might just find the light."*

As I drag into the house, I interrupt Dad and a woman in the kitchen, laughing. I stop in my tracks and say, "Excuse me." Is this Lynda? It has to be. I duck my head and scurry across the living room toward the hallway.

"Azure," Dad calls. "Come back."

"Forget I'm here," I say. "I was just leaving."

Dad stands at the end of the hall. "Come back here. I want you to meet Lynda."

Sure, her profile photo was far away and blurry, but she has to weigh at least twenty pounds more than her picture showed. Make that thirty pounds. I'm livid. She misrepresented herself to my dad, and he's so naïve about women that he bought it.

I don't even take my jacket off; I just storm back to the kitchen and stand there with my arms crossed.

She extends her hand to shake. "Your dad's told me a lot about you," she says.

I have to take her hand, but I give her my wimpiest shake. I look her up and down. "All lies."

"Even the good stuff?"

I eye Dad. He can't possibly be into this woman. He's a cop. He's trained to see through people.

He says, "I've asked Lynda to go to prom with me, and she's accepted." He beams at her.

I'm going to be sick. I answer, "Groovy," as Mr. Rosen would say.

"Maybe we can go shopping for dresses." Lynda smiles at me.

Thanks, I think. *I don't shop at dressbarn.*

"Lynda's cooking up paella," Dad says.

Which is why it smells fishy in here.

"You're welcome to stay, of course," Lynda says.

"I'm going out."

Dad's eyes widen. "On a date?"

He whaps my thigh and the tingles force out a short giggle.

"Tell me about it," I say. "I feel for you. Wanting someone you can't have."

"Why? Do *you*?" He faces me and a blush rises up my neck. I snatch the bag back from him and grab a handful of carrots to shove in my mouth.

"Wait. Is Radhika gay? Is that why…?" He smacks his head. "I'm such an idiot."

"I wouldn't say 'idiot.'" *And I wouldn't say Radhika was gay, either. I don't know where Azure got that idea.*

He keeps thunking his head and I want to clench his wrist so he doesn't cause brain damage. Finally, he stops and heaves a sigh. "If I ask someone else now, do you think Shauna will find out?"

I try not to cough my guts out. "Shauna? That's who asked you?"

Connor scrunches up his face. "She's so full of herself and irritating. Girls like that bug the hell out of me."

Shauna Creighton likes Connor Spears? Wait'll I tell Azure.

"You could always ask me," I blurt out. Then I die a million deaths. Where are the carrots?

Connor grins. He puts a hand on my shoulder and says, "Sorry. I'm not into dudes."

We both laugh. Him, because it's funny. Me, because I'm pathetic. I'd lust after a zombie if it showed the faintest interest.

There's one carrot left in the bag and I hand it to

Connor. He reaches in and snaps off half in his mouth, handing me the rest.

"Girls know everything," I tell him. "Or eventually they find out."

"How do they do that?"

"The social grid."

He leans back on the windshield, his arms behind his head. I want to reach over and rest my hand on his leg. Pat it sympathetically. Feel his muscles. Azure's right—I *am* a horndog. "Who are you going with?" he asks.

"Radhika," I say.

His jaw drops.

"Not really. She turned me down, too."

He blinks. "Seriously? You asked her?"

"Stupid is as stupid does."

"Wow." He keeps blinking. "I didn't know you liked her that way."

"Yeah, I should've called Perez Hilton to make it public knowledge. Someone besides us asked her, too. Do you know who?"

His eyebrows arch. "Girl or guy?"

Now he has me wondering. "No clue."

We exhale in unison. Connor closes his eyes and I watch him in my peripheral vision. He's such a god.

He asks, "So, who *are* you going with?"

"Probably the Diversity Club."

"Maybe I'll just go with them, too. That'd solve my problem. I could tell Shauna I'm going with someone else, and it wouldn't be a lie."

"You'd better not sign up online or she'll see."

"Right." Connor smiles so broad, his dazzling white teeth glint in the sun. "Thanks, Luke." He holds out his palm and I slap it. "I knew I could count on you."

He hops down and saunters off, while I recite in a whisper, "How do I love thee? Let me count the waves."

AZURE

Both our Wednesday and Friday meetings are canceled because Mr. Rosen is sick. Which is just as well, because I'm still fuming.

On Friday Mr. Gerardi is waiting for me outside my third-period class. I'm not speaking to him. He says, "Miss Wells tells me the theater department's room is packed full of donations for the silent auction, so you're going to have to find another room that locks. You could use the music room, if you want."

Still not talking to him.

"And I think you have enough donations. You should make an announcement before the end of the day that people can stop bringing things in."

I shower him with death rays.

He must get the message because he says, "I'm sorry about the PTSA. An alternative prom was still a good idea."

If he thinks that'll soften me up, he doesn't know my melting point.

I have to make a pit stop before lunch, and since the cafeteria is close to the theater room, I drop by to see if Miss Wells is there so I can check out how many donations we have. I don't see her, but I stop and gasp. Near the costume-room door, a mountain of trash bags rises almost to the ceiling. It's like all the hoarders in the world cleaned out their houses, attics, basements, and garages.

The silent auction is next week, and even with everyone working full-time, we'll never sort through all this stuff.

I slide into my chair at the lunch table across from Radhika and say, "Have you seen how much crap people have donated for the auction?"

She stabs a cherry tomato in her salad. "My mother donated jewelry and a set of collectible brass elephants."

I grimace. "I didn't mean it was all junk. I'm sure there's some really valuable stuff in there. But it'll take forever to sort." She doesn't volunteer to help, which surprises me. "I'll ask Mr. Gerardi if we can drag everything to the gym and start getting it in some kind of order."

She still doesn't...

"I can't," she says. "I'm way behind in the college seminar now, and it's going to take me the rest of the semester to catch up."

"Radhika—"

"What?" she barks.

Geez. "It's okay. We're just not using your father's money."

She looks at me, or through me.

"I mean it. If we sell all this stuff, we should have more than enough to fund the prom. Not that I even care anymore." Which is almost true. Without her there, who cares? Except there's a part of me that refuses to give up.

"I'll see you later." Radhika lifts her tray and leaves abruptly. I wonder what I said, or didn't say, or should've said or done. She seems so defeated. I'll show her that we can do this, that she's free to chase her dream of joining the Peace Corps. And I'll convince her that she *has* to go to prom, even if it's not with me.

I hate giving up the Saturdays when Dad's off and we play handball at the rec center. We always stop for lunch at Large Marge's for Philly cheesesteaks, and he tells me stories about growing up with five brothers, which must've been a blast. I swear some of the shit they did was illegal. I guess it never got on his permanent record, since they let him into the police academy.

I could wake him up and make him go to the rec center early before I have to leave for school to sort donations, or I could let him sleep in. When I open his bedroom door, he's curled up, purring like a kitten. I don't have the heart to drag him out of dreamland. Instead, I log on to my computer and check Google docs. Only Shauna and Luke responded to my Help! Alert last night about sorting today. Shauna said she'd ask the decorations committee to help, too, since they're requesting $1,500 of the budget. I wrote, "What for? All we need are balloons." And she wrote back, "We need more than that. They have to buy favors, too." I was tempted to write, *Forget the stupid favors*, but I didn't want her on my case again. Under Shauna's message, Connor wrote that the reservations at the Ramada were confirmed. Yay! That's one item we can check off.

After six hours of sorting, we still have dozens of garbage bags left. I hear Luke say, "OMG. Someone donated their underwear." He holds up a pair of yellowed jocks.

People do that at the thrift store, too. It's gross. But Louisa takes the newer-looking boxers and panties home and washes them.

"I'm only keeping the thongs," Luke adds.

"Just toss the underwear," I tell him.

He says, "Not on your life. These thongs are just my size."

I'm too tired to laugh at his jokes. I open a kitchen trash bag and empty it onto the gym floor. Jeans and shirts, some old CDs, junk jewelry. Then I see an object that makes my heart crash against my rib cage. I pick it up by the chain, and the silver heart spins in a circle. On the back is an engraving I had made: TO DESI, NOW AND FOREVER.

I gave this to her on our six-month anniversary. I'm surprised when tears well in my eyes. I blink them away and swallow a stuttered sob. I think it's the fatigue and the fact that Radhika isn't here and this whole fiasco with prom. Why did I ever agree to get involved? I'm not a leader, and I never will be.

I place the necklace in the bin for jewelry and finish

sorting the stuff that was in the bag. A lot of these items are familiar to me, and I can't handle it. Shoving the rest of the donations back into the bag, I throw it on the mound and stand. "I don't know about anyone else, but I'm wiped," I tell them. "If anyone can make it in tomorrow, that'd be great. Otherwise, we can finish next week. Let's lock up the auction items in the music room and put the rest of this crap back in the theater."

Shauna accompanies me to the music room with her stack of bins filled with old stuffed animals and children's toys. She says, "He's going with someone else."

It takes a minute for my brain to click in. Even then, it's sluggish. "Who?"

"Connor. I finally just asked him to prom, and he texted me that he was going with someone else."

He texted her? That's so rude. My respect for Connor just plunged below zero. I'm glad Radhika turned him down.

"Do you know who?" Shauna asks.

"No," I say. I don't know and I don't care. We both set down our bins and Shauna gives me this look like she doesn't believe me. "He could've told you in person, at least."

She blinks back tears. Wonderful. Now she's going to get all weepy, and I'll have to comfort her. "I know people think I'm the one who told the PTSA about what we were doing for prom, but I'm not," she says. "My mom kept asking, and I told her it was prom. As in P-R-O-M, and we were doing things a little different to get people to come.

That's all I said." A tear slides down one cheek, then a second tear slides down the other.

If it was anyone but Shauna, I'd hug her.

Shauna swipes her nose on her sleeve. "I really do support this prom. It could've been anyone who told their parents. Everybody has access to Prom Central."

Which, I realize, is true. Any of the prommies could've run to their mommies.

"I don't think we should change anything we planned to do," Shauna says. "I know we have to take all those activities off Prom Central, but that doesn't mean we can't still do them. I've been thinking about it, and we can put up a closed Facebook page. We've come so far," she says. "We can't stop now."

Am I hearing these words from Shauna Creighton's lips? She makes me feel fired up again.

"At our Monday meeting, let's talk to Mr. Rosen about it. I know he's on our side," I say.

Shauna heads for the door. "I'll be in to help sort after church tomorrow." As she exits, I watch her go, thinking, *Whatever my affirmation for today was, I'm rewriting it to read: "Once you get past the dark side of a person, you might just find the light."*

As I drag into the house, I interrupt Dad and a woman in the kitchen, laughing. I stop in my tracks and say, "Excuse me." Is this Lynda? It has to be. I duck my head and scurry across the living room toward the hallway.

"Azure," Dad calls. "Come back."

"Forget I'm here," I say. "I was just leaving."

Dad stands at the end of the hall. "Come back here. I want you to meet Lynda."

Sure, her profile photo was far away and blurry, but she has to weigh at least twenty pounds more than her picture showed. Make that thirty pounds. I'm livid. She misrepresented herself to my dad, and he's so naïve about women that he bought it.

I don't even take my jacket off; I just storm back to the kitchen and stand there with my arms crossed.

She extends her hand to shake. "Your dad's told me a lot about you," she says.

I have to take her hand, but I give her my wimpiest shake. I look her up and down. "All lies."

"Even the good stuff?"

I eye Dad. He can't possibly be into this woman. He's a cop. He's trained to see through people.

He says, "I've asked Lynda to go to prom with me, and she's accepted." He beams at her.

I'm going to be sick. I answer, "Groovy," as Mr. Rosen would say.

"Maybe we can go shopping for dresses." Lynda smiles at me.

Thanks, I think. *I don't shop at dressbarn.*

"Lynda's cooking up paella," Dad says.

Which is why it smells fishy in here.

"You're welcome to stay, of course," Lynda says.

"I'm going out."

Dad's eyes widen. "On a date?"

I mock his shock. "It's not unprecedented." I leave them there and head out to parts unknown, wishing I'd just told the truth so I could hang in my room and decompress to music. I call Radhika. Voice mail. I call Luke. Busy. For the first time in my life, I go to the movies all by myself.

Luke swings by to pick me up on Monday. "Radhika's not riding with us anymore," he says, answering my unspoken question. "She's reenrolled in that early-hour seminar."

She's buckling under her father's threat. "We can't let her father do this," I say to Luke. "We *have* to pay for this prom. It'll be cheaper now that we won't need a license for the car show, and we'll probably be forced to use a DJ after the PTSA hears Putrid Wixen. By the way, it wasn't Shauna who narced on us."

He lifts his eyebrows, like, *Oh, really.*

"She wants this alternative prom as much as we do. We were talking on Saturday, and she's thought of a way we might be able to go ahead with everything we planned."

"Is it legal?" he asks.

"Legal, yes. Ethical, questionable."

"I don't want to spend the rest of my senior year in detention," he says.

"So you're ready to just give up?"

He shrugs. "Who really cares about krunking and a poetry slam?"

I can't believe him. "What about the drag show?"

"We can do that at Rainbow Alley whenever we want."

Unbelievable. Why is he even on this committee? He

starts to get out of the car, but I yank him back in by his sweater sleeve.

"Hey," he snaps. "Don't stretch the cashmere."

I stare at him, wondering who he is, really. I always thought he was on my side, my confidant. If not my best friend, then my second-to-best friend.

"Oh, hey." His eyes gleam. "Did Shauna tell you she asked Connor to prom?"

"As a matter of fact, she did."

He rolls his eyes. "That girl is so clueless. He asked me how to say no without hurting her feelings."

So he was the one who told Connor to text Shauna that he was going with someone else? I slug him so hard on the arm I hope it leaves a welt.

"Ow! That really hurt."

"Good." I swing my door open. Now Shauna's heart is broken. If prom is supposed to be such a blissful event in everyone's life, why is it only causing pain?

There's an extra person at prom com, and it isn't anyone we want to see. Mrs. Flacco snarls, "You're Azure, right?"

"Uh, yeah."

"Well, don't just stand there. Take a seat." Everybody else is already here. Mrs. Flacco says, "We're missing a person. I won't abide people being late, even if this is an extracurricular activity."

I turn to Mrs. Flacco and say (even though I hate to confirm it), "Radhika is dropping out."

"No!" Shauna cries. "She can't. We need her."

"She has a, um, conflict in her schedule."

Connor says, "What is it?"

I want to snap at him, *None of your business.*

Mrs. Flacco says, "Let's get started. First of all, I'm supposed to pass out this letter from Mr. Rosen." She opens a folder and takes out several sheets of paper. "Read it quickly." She hands them all to me. I take the top one and pass the rest to Luke.

Dear Azure, Luke, Connor, Shauna, and Radhika,

My sincerest apologies for the situation you now find yourselves in on the prom planning committee. I take full responsibility for allowing the alternative prom ideas to get out of hand. I've been asked to resign my position as faculty advisor...

I gasp.

...but I'll do everything in my power to make sure your prom goes off without a hitch. I know what a special day it is for everyone, so I do hope you can encourage as many people as possible to attend. I believe in your goal of inclusivity, and I believe in you.

It's been a joy to work with you, and I wish you all the best.

Phil Rosen

Shauna's in tears. Then she's sobbing uncontrollably. Next to me, Luke murmurs, "Traitor."

Connor's eyes are downcast. I doubt Shauna's crying so hard about Mr. Rosen leaving.

"Who are the officers?" Mrs. Flacco asks. "I don't see that in any of Mr. Rosen's notes." She flips through his folder. "These notes are a mess."

No one answers. "Shauna, for heaven's sake. Pull yourself together. You of all people should've been aware that the prom you were planning was a sham."

"It wasn't her fault," I jump in. "We were all in this together."

Mrs. Flacco doesn't say, *Then you're all to blame*, but the look on her face does.

"Who's the president?" she asks.

At first, no one volunteers any information. She doesn't scare me — much. "We don't have officers," I tell her. "We just discuss what we want to do, and agree or disagree. And we did a school survey."

"Yes, that ridiculous survey."

My blood begins a slow boil.

"Has anyone been keeping notes, at least?" she demands.

Luke's hand shoots into the air. "I have, I have."

She narrows her eyes at him. "I'd like a copy."

"Do you have a printer on you?" he asks.

She shoots him a steely glare. "If you could print them out and put them in my box tomorrow, that'd be sufficient."

"Done," Luke says.

"Also, I see that the prohibited activities are still listed on Prom Central. Who's maintaining the website?"

"Shauna is," Luke says.

He should shut up. The less Mrs. Flacco knows, the better.

"And how are you set financially? Mr. Rosen's records... according to what he has here, you're still short more than fifteen hundred dollars."

"Only, like, a thousand," I say. Maybe more now, what with the decorations committee draining the whole budget. "And we'll have that by the end of our silent auction this week."

"You plan to make a thousand dollars with a silent auction?" She shakes her head.

"We'll get there," I tell her. "We might have to hold two auctions, but we have plenty of donations."

She closes the folder and sits for a moment, looking at us. "I'm very disappointed," she says. "Especially in you, Shauna. But I don't blame you. You needed a knowledgeable and intelligent adult to guide you, and you didn't have one. I'm very sorry you're in this position. Shauna, if you'll correct the website tonight, I'd appreciate it. And Luke, get me those notes. We need to work on organizing the auction."

"It's already organized," I say. "I know how to run a silent auction."

"So you have the tally sheets for each item, and the bidders' numbers printed?"

"Um, not yet," I tell her. I sort of forgot.

"And you do know the printing expense will have to be deducted from your earnings," she says.

"I planned to print everything at home, so there won't be any cost."

She makes a noise, like *harrumph*, or something. Like she can't believe I had the brains to think of that.

She says to Luke, "Did you keep notes from *this* meeting?"

He covers his mouth and goes, "Oops."

Mrs. Flacco scoots back her chair. "Meeting adjourned."

LUKE

Azure's partway right. I should be more devoted to the alternative prom. But I also know a lost cause when I see one. Flacco stepping in as advisor is major suckage. But maybe if she sees what a fabulous secretary I've been, she'll raise my Civil Liberties grade a notch on her whipping belt.

As I'm running the meeting notes through spell-check and cleaning them up nice and tidy, I log on to Prom Central and confirm what our prom's been reduced to.

What's this? I refresh the screen to make sure I'm not seeing things. On Prom Central there's an ad for free limo service. Free. Limo. Service.

I call the number, and it's an answering machine. Stan's Super Sedan. I don't leave a message. Who's going to use Owen's company when they can get Stan's Super Sedan for free?

I send a note to Shauna on Google docs to move A-1

Car Service to the top of the transportation section. I tell her to write underneath: "Best service in town."

That sounds like a hooker.

I change it to: "Best value in town."

That sounds like a plumber.

"Door-to-door service."

A given.

"We make your prom special because you're A-Number-One with us."

Gag. But I leave it. Then I have a thought. To Shauna, I write, "Say, 'Free champagne and roses.'"

Instead of bottled water, I'll spring for fizzy apple juice and place a rose on the backseat.

Owen comes in, whistling, and I punch off my computer. "What are you so happy about?"

He pulls out a chair at the kitchen table and sits, tilting back and resting his feet on another chair. He twines his fingers behind his head. "Life is good. By the way, I had Black Panther stripped and painted. It's now Silver Wolf."

I wince. "How much do I owe you?"

"Chillax, bro," Owen says. "The insurance paid."

I never know if he's telling the truth.

Owen glances over at the phone. "You've been taking prom reservations, right?"

"Erm, right." The phone hasn't rung once since I've been home. "Do you know Stan's Super Sedan?" I ask.

"That bozo?" Owen tilts back farther in his chair. "Yeah, why?"

I wonder if I should tell him. Owen's counting on prom for his big seasonal boost.

"Bozo is advertising free limo service for the prom."

Owen blinks at me, sort of unseeing, or seeing red.

"I was thinking we could include champagne and roses."

"Don't worry about it," he says.

"Or maybe you could lower your price a little."

Owen's chair slips out from under him and he goes flying. His head hits the fridge. I smother as much laughter as I can. He picks up the chair and slams it down.

"I moved A-1 to the top of the list," I tell him.

He growls, "I said don't worry about it. I know how to handle my own business, Luke." He grabs a Coke and bangs out the door.

I'm worried. What if tomorrow's headline reads BOZO FOUND IN BLOODBATH?

Even though the costumes for the Mothballs are only half done, Britny assures me her mom will have them all sewn by the time we get back from spring break. I'm not worried—much. I ask Ryan, "How are the sets coming?"

"They're finished," he says. "Do you want to put them up and take a look?"

"Hella yeah."

The stage crew pulls the painted panels from behind a curtain. They slide Act One onstage. Ryan even numbered the panels with the act and scene numbers, so they'd go up in order. Smart.

I stand back on the stage to get a look. I can't take them in all at once, since they wrap around, so I go into the auditorium to check it out.

OMG. They're awesome. The art is abstract, black-and-white, almost impressionistic. If you squint or use your imagination, you can see a cityscape with crowds of people.

A body comes up next to me, then another. Then everyone is milling around, gazing at the set. They're oohing and aahing.

"Ryan," I call.

He peeks around the edge of a panel.

"Come out onstage."

He takes his sweet time, shuffling his feet and stopping in the wings. "Do you hate them?" he asks. "Because I can do them over."

"Yeah, they suck," I say. "I can't bear to look." I cover my eyes with my arm. "Take them away."

"Luke!" Britny shoves me so hard I trip over the person next to me.

Ryan slinks off. "Ryan, I'm kidding."

He slinks back.

"They're seriously cool. You're seriously talented. Did I say 'seriously'? Can we see Act Two?"

I can almost feel him glowing from where I am. As he scrambles to take down the set, my eyes stray to the back of the auditorium, where Radhika is sitting. For the first time, Gabe's not with her. It strikes me suddenly—what if he's the one who asked her to prom?

That's not possible. He's practically engaged to Haley.

If they've broken up, it hasn't trickled down the rumor mill. I vow to ask Britny before we leave today.

"Everyone get ready for a full run-through," I tell the cast.

I go back and sit next to Radhika. " 'Sup?" I say.

"Nothing." A book is open in her lap, the numbers and graphs completely incomprehensible to me. "How's it going with prom com?" she asks.

"Rosen resigned and Flacco's the advisor. You can take it from there."

Her nose wrinkles.

"Oh, and Azure's pissed. She thinks we abandoned her," I say. The sadness in Radhika's eyes penetrates me. "It's not your fault," I tell her. "We got carried away on the winds to Oz. We'll still have a prom, and all will be right with the world."

Mario warms up with the opening number for the Mothballs. "Well, I better get my act together."

A small smile creases her lips.

It's enough to warm the cockles of my heart. Wherever those are.

AZURE

The silent auction bombs big-time. I don't know if it's because people have already left on spring break or because of the crappy weather, but I can almost count on my fingers and toes how many people show up. Mrs. Flacco blows in around 7:30, takes one look at the poor attendance, and seeks me out. I slump down in my chair at the cashier box and hide my face under my hand. She removes her leather gloves and sticks them in her pocket, then heads for the jewelry section.

"Hi," Radhika says. "How's it going?"

I can't help myself. I'm so glad she's here that I jump up and give her a hug.

"Terrible." I feel like bawling.

"Hello, Azure," Mrs. Dal says. "It looks like you have quite a selection."

"Yeah. If only we had people to bid."

Luke gets on the mike and announces that the bidding

is fast and furious, telling people to get their bids in early or lose out on all the *Antiques Roadshow* unknown treasures. I roll my eyes at Radhika.

"I think I'll go look around," Mrs. Dal says as she leaves us.

"Don't say it, and don't think it," I tell Radhika. "We're not going to ask your dad for money. If we have to hold bake sales and silent auctions until the night of prom, we'll raise the money."

She sighs. "I'm so sorry about everything. The prom you envisioned. Abandoning you."

"What? You didn't abandon us. I'm the one who forced you to join prom com."

Out of the corner of my eye, I see a couple walk through the door. It's Desirae and her girlfriend. She spies me and gives a little wave. I don't wave back.

The smell of Mrs. Flacco's wet wool coat precedes her. "Not a very good turnout," she says.

Can you go *Duh* without sneering?

"Did you intentionally leave minimum bids off the sheets?"

"What do you mean?" I ask. Radhika backs away and I want to run after her, beg her to save me. Plead with her to come to prom, with or without me.

"People are writing in bids of a quarter or fifty cents. Some of that jewelry looks valuable. You should've at least put a minimum bid of ten or twenty-five dollars on the expensive items. And everything should have a minimum of five dollars."

I forgot about minimum bids. It took all week just to get this stuff organized.

Luke announces: "The first round of bidding is complete. Please pick up your items and pay the cashier."

People retrieve their items and a line forms behind Mrs. Flacco. I say, "Excuse me," as I move around the table to collect money.

The first few sales net us almost twenty dollars, which is pretty good, I think. Then someone with an armload of stuffed animals and games wants to pay with a credit card.

Oh no. I never thought about people who'd want to pay with credit cards.

"Mrs. Flacco," I call. She comes over. "I have a credit card sale, but I don't know how to do it without a machine."

"You might've thought about that earlier," she goes. "Let me go grab a machine from the front office."

"Would you mind waiting a couple of minutes?" I ask the bidder. She steps back, but when she does, she plows into a person heading out the door and drops all her stuffies.

I race around the table to help her gather them. Radhika and Shauna both come to the rescue with bags to repack everything for her.

Mrs. Flacco returns with an ancient credit card machine that I have no idea how to work. She says, "Why don't you just let me collect money, and you go take that microphone away from Luke."

He's having a good time playing auctioneer; in fact, he's taken the initiative to auction off a bunch of the nicer

248

items in a live auction. He's blabbing nonsense, but people are gathered around him, laughing and bidding. We're probably bringing in more money with his method than with my nickel-and-dime silent auction. I glance over my shoulder and see Mrs. Flacco glaring, urging me on with a flick of her wrist, and I have no choice but to ask Luke to hand over the mike.

"It's not me," I tell him in a lowered voice.

"Sorry, folks," Luke says into the mike. "You're all being arrested for indecent proposals."

I count the money we made on the auction six times. Each time it amounts to two hundred and five dollars. That won't even pay for half a band. It's embarrassing to let everyone know, and I consider waiting until after spring break, but maybe if I put it out there, someone will come up with more fund-raising ideas.

As I'm logging on to Google docs, my cell rings. It's Shauna. "Hey," she says. "I just wanted you to know that I created a new Google docs for the prom com. A separate one, where the prom com can communicate without Mrs. Flacco knowing what we're doing." She adds, "I'll gmail everyone to let them know the file name."

"I hope this works," I say.

"It will. I went through last year's yearbook and found as many seniors as I could on Facebook. Then I invited them to join our Prom page. We already have almost two hundred people."

Wow, I think. She's gone to a lot of trouble.

She says, "We'll have to keep Prom Central live for the people who aren't on Facebook or don't join the group."

"What about Mrs. Flacco?"

"I told her my computer was broken, but that I'd take all the activities down as soon as I could. And that it might not be until after spring break."

That was a good idea, but Shauna can't keep stalling her forever.

"How much did we make on the auction?" Shauna asks.

I hate to even tell her. "Two hundred and five dollars."

For a minute, she doesn't say anything, for which I'm grateful. Then she goes, "Don't worry. We'll think of other ways to raise money."

It's weird how she seems to be the only one sharing my brain waves. I want to say I'm sorry about Connor, but she's so pumped, this doesn't seem like the best time.

"I'm creating the Google docs now, so if you want to ask people about fund-raising ideas…Or I guess it wouldn't hurt to do that in our old Google docs," she says. "Maybe Mrs. Flacco has some corporate contacts. God, I can't stand her."

"Is it her helmet hair?" I say.

Shauna laughs.

We disconnect and I wonder if, in another life, we might've been friends.

Luke leaves me a text message that he's going to Germany for spring break. He asks if I want him to bring me back some Wiener schnitzel. His text only reminds me how much it hurt Shauna when Connor rejected her via text. Sincere sentiments should never be texted or IM'd. I always thought Luke was really sensitive and caring, but now I'm questioning everything I thought I knew about him.

I call Radhika to see if she wants to hang out over break, but she says her parents are taking a trip and she's required to go. "They won't even tell me where," she adds.

"Maybe it's Disney World," I say.

"Oh, I'm sure that's it. Can you see my dad at Disney World?"

I wouldn't put it past him to bribe her with an awesome trip.

Radhika and Luke and I have always spent at least part of our spring breaks together. Things are changing too fast, and not only because of the tension between Luke and me. I wish I could just erase my feelings for Radhika and go back to where we were.

Unfortunately, I've never figured out a way to control my heart.

All I can think about is the prom without Radhika there—it'll be meaningless. Not that it was going to be this cathartic event in my life. I wasn't deluding myself—much. I just got caught up in the excitement and planning. What is prom, anyway? I don't even know the significance of the word. Is it short for *promise*? Of what? A lifetime of longing?

I schedule a bunch of extra hours at work to stay occupied. The hairpins Louisa saved for me are in the lockbox in back. I take them out and replace them in the jewelry case.

"Change your mind?" Louisa bustles by with a collection of salt and pepper shakers.

"Yeah." *Actually, it got changed for me.* "But I do need an outfit for prom."

Since Desi's girlfriend bought the blue dress I wanted, I need to find something else. I riffle through the formal-wear in back and pick out three potential dresses. My favorite is a gray velvet, knee-length dress with a black lace overlay, and I also find a felt hat with a layer of beaded lace to pull over my eyes. I need shoes, too. Or boots.

I check out the complete ensemble in the full-length mirror, and I guess it looks okay. I'd be a hundred times more enthusiastic if I could envision myself dancing with Radhika in my arms.

Wow, I hate it when I feel sorry for myself. I have a lot of things to be thankful for: my friends — most of all Radhika — my dad, and my mom, insane as she is. I say to myself in the mirror what my religion means to me: "You are a beautiful creature of God. Now get out there and kick butt."

Dad had to work Saturday, too, so we delayed our hand-ball game until Sunday, after I got home from church. It feels good to work off all my stress. After our game, Dad and I decide to go grocery shopping. "Lynda not only cooks, she's a gourmet cook," he tells me as we stock up on his favorite frozen Hungry-Man Sports Grill entrees: Grilled Southwest Style Chicken and Grilled Bourbon Steak Strips. Like the meat in any of those meals ever saw a real grill.

"I can tell," I say under my breath.

He frowns. "What does that mean?"

It means I wonder if she's exaggerating about that, too. "How much do you know about her?" I ask him. "For instance, is she a gold digger looking for a husband to support her and her two kids?"

Dad's frown turns into a laugh.

"What?"

"On my salary, she'd be digging for fool's gold."

Exactly. "I mean, what are her real motives? She looks completely different from her picture." I feel Dad's narrowed eyes burn through me.

He shuts the freezer door and pushes the cart forward. We don't talk again until we get to the salty-snacks aisle, where I plan to select widely.

I toss in a bag of sour cream and onion Ruffles and some cheese popcorn. Dad adds his usual corn nuts and sunflower seeds to eat at work. "I thought better of you than that," he says. "Of all the people I know, for you to judge someone by their looks…"

"I'm not." My face flares because I totally am. But I say anyway, "Give me a little more credit than that."

He stares at me as if he can see into my cold, cold heart. "Credit is something you have to earn," he says.

Thankfully, he turns and heads off toward the register. I feel like the judgmental jerk I am. But I want him to know I have his best interests at heart.

"Dad." I come up beside him in line. "Just do me one favor: Go out with Cloud. You owe it to yourself to take advantage of every opportunity."

He doesn't speak. Great. Now he's going to pout and get all pissy on me.

We pack our groceries in our recyclable bags and carry them out. I can't let Dad make a decision he might regret for the rest of his life. What if Cloud is The One? I cover my face and pretend to cry.

Dad's face falls. "Azure…"

"Forget it." I climb into the truck and buckle my seat belt.

He sits next to me for a minute before cranking the ignition. Exhaling deeply, he says, "Okay. If it'll make you happy, I'll go out with Cloud."

I smile to myself. Men are so easy.

Dad didn't waste any time. He opens the door as I'm wrapped in a blanket, watching repeats of *RuPaul's Drag Race*. The faint scent of L'Homme swirls around him as he enters the living room. "Lynda?" I ask.

"Actually, I took your threat to heart and called Cloud."

I sit up. "I didn't threaten you." Much. "How'd it go?"

He heads for the kitchen and I unfurl my mummified body to follow. He opens the fridge, takes out a bottle of Bud, and twists off the cap. "Dad." I slide onto a counter stool, watching him take a long swig, his Adam's apple bobbing. "Come on. How was she?"

Dad lowers the beer to his side. "I'll never know. When she told me her special rate for online clients was fifty bucks, I arrested her."

My jaw goes slack.

Dad lifts his beer to his lips and says, "Not a bad rate for a pro."

LUKE

I glance up from unpacking my duffel after spring break to see Owen standing in the doorway. His arms are loosely crossed. "So, how are they?" he asks.

"Same old, same old. You should've come. 'It vas springtime een Joymany,'" I sing. I toss my empty duffel in the closet.

"I have a business to run. And besides, I don't remember receiving my invitation via satellite." He wanders off.

If he'd expressed the smallest desire to go to Germany, I know Mom and Dad would've sprung for the airfare. Some people are so stubborn.

I remove my Roaring Twenties dress from its hanger and wriggle into it. I zip up the back, then pull the blond wig over my head. "They grilled me for all the sordid details of your life," I call to Owen. Uncapping a tube of red lipstick, I stand at my full-length mirror to spread it on.

Owen reappears.

"I told them you couldn't come because of rehab. And that the terms of your parole forbid you to travel outside the country."

Owen doesn't respond, but he doesn't leave, either.

I catch the look on his face in the mirror. "What?"

"What do you mean, what? What are you wearing?"

"You like?" I adjust my wig a bit, pin it in place, and push up my boobies.

"You're not going out in public like that."

"Actually, I am. I'm wearing this to prom." A pang of sorrow shoots through me. I wish we were having the drag show. I'd win, hands down.

"You're not going to prom in that." Owen storms into my room. He yanks on the wig, ripping it off my head.

I grab the wig back and say, "This is for the drag show at Rainbow Alley tonight. I'm wearing a tux for prom."

Owen throws the wig on my bed and vanishes again.

I call to him, "A tux with sequins."

Through the living room, he calls, "You're a freak. You know that, right?"

I toss my feather boa over my shoulder. "Takes one to know one."

I realize I haven't rented my tux yet, and prom is in two weeks. It's early, four o'clock. The drag show doesn't start until eight. I strip off my drag gear, leaving the makeup on, and scavenge around for the phone book. There's one tux-rental shop near The LGBTQ Center. I tear out the page in the phone book and take off.

The rental place is on Broadway, squished between a used bookstore and a Persian restaurant. There's no parking in front. I turn in to the alley, where there are a few reserved slots open. The shop is crammed with guys and girls checking out the dressed mannequins and getting fitted. There must be a wedding or bar mitzvah, because all these little kids are running around. I recognize a couple of guys from Roosevelt. Their girlfriends are with them, helping to match cummerbunds and bow ties with their dresses.

Prommies, as Azure would call them.

Mollie's here, which means Haley might be, too. I forgot to get the skinny from Britny on Gabe and Haley, so I call out, "Hey, Mollie." I give her a wave. She turns her back on me.

Whoa. What's that about? I approach her and place a hand on her shoulder.

"Don't talk to me," she says, shoving me away. She stalks toward the exit.

What'd I do to *her*? Oh, to be hardwired into the social grid.

Suddenly, I see my tuxedo, my vision, on a mannequin near the back of the store.

"May I help you?" a woman asks behind me.

"That one," I tell her, pointing. "Can you put it on hold for me?"

She says, "We can't hold it. But I don't think you have to worry about anyone else wanting it."

Without the alternative prom, I'm guessing she's right.

"I'll take it," I say.

*　　*　　*

I have to honk three times before Azure comes sauntering out of the house. She gets in, buckles her seat belt, and says, "I'm only riding with you because I don't have correct bus fare."

What is her problem? The word *beeotch* comes to mind. I still don't know where, when, or how I pissed her off.

We ride in silence for a while until Azure turns to me. "Did Radhika tell you where she went for spring break?"

"Yeah," I say.

"Disgusting," Azure goes.

Actually, Radhika didn't tell me. I only said that to make Azure jealous. Now I'm dying of curiosity.

"Do they think that'll change Radhika's mind?" Azure says.

"I know. How could they? She hasn't, has she?" I have no idea what we're talking about.

"Of course not," Azure snaps. "She's not weak, like you."

Now I *do* know what we're talking about. "Look, I'm two hundred and twenty-two percent behind you on this alternative prom. But we can't do everything you want. You heard Mr. Gerardi. And Flacco scares me. She looks at me and I go wee-wee."

"You're such a wuss," Azure says under her breath.

"I don't want to wear Depends to school. They give me diaper rash."

She goes, "If we figured out a way to do it, would you be in or out?"

"In, of course. If I didn't have to repeat my senior year."

A smile curls Azure's lips. "Shauna has a plan. Wait'll you hear it. There's more to that girl than meets the eye."

I gasp. "Is she a lesbo?"

Azure goes to slug me, but unfurls her fist before it makes contact.

"Just stick around after the meeting," she says.

I'm first to arrive in Studio 2B, with my notes sorted and stapled for Flacco. Shauna and Azure arrive together. They sit next to each other. If I didn't see it with my own eyes...

Connor rushes in, breathing hard. "Am I late?"

I think he must have the Fear of Flacco within him.

Mrs. Flacco bustles in and sets her folder on the table. "Here are the notes," I say, passing them to her.

She takes them, not even reading them or admiring the font I chose and how I italicized the heated debates. "I see you haven't removed the offending activities from Prom Central, Shauna."

"I still don't have my computer up," she says.

"Use one in the library. I want it cleared out by tomorrow."

Shauna's lips purse.

I raise my hand. "I printed out the notes," I remind her.

Flacco asks Azure, "How much money did the silent auction bring in?"

Azure says, "I don't know exactly. Over two hundred dollars."

"Is it two hundred or three hundred?" Flacco asks. "Although it doesn't matter, because you still can't pay the band or the photographer."

"We don't really need a professional photographer," Shauna says. "Azure was right. We could ask someone from the photography club to do it."

"Absolutely not," Flacco says. "Do you want your prom photos to be amateurish?"

That sounds familiar.

"Also, since you haven't provided me with the song lyrics from this band—what is it called?" She flips through the pages of Mr. Rosen's notes. "Putrid Wixen." She makes a sick face. "You'll need to cancel the band and find a DJ."

"We're working on getting the lyrics to you." Azure cuts a look at me and I nod vigorously. Azure's voice hardens: "We still have time to raise money."

"How? And when?"

"We can have another silent auction. There's still mountains of stuff to sell."

"And we can do bake sales every day," Shauna adds. "My mother's president of the PTSA, and I'm sure she won't mind sending out an e-mail blast asking members to bake cookies and cupcakes."

Flacco says what we all know: "You have two weeks."

"I'll get with Mr. Gerardi today and see when we can have the silent auction," Azure says. "Just leave everything up to us."

"No," Flacco says. "You'll pass every decision through me from now on. Luke, are you taking notes?"

In my desire to please—and live—I forgot again. I say, "Photographic memory," and tap my head. "Hey, I'd be happy to use my superpower to draw prom pictures. Then we wouldn't need a photographer at all."

Connor snickers.

If Flacco had a hatchet, heads would roll. Make that one head: mine.

"Connor," she says, "since you're not contributing at all, why don't you look for a DJ? Keep it cheap."

Pink rises up his neck.

"We want a live band," he mumbles.

"Well, you can't afford a band, so you might as well shop around for a DJ."

Connor's jawbone flexes.

"Has anyone ordered programs yet? Have you figured that into your cost?"

Static fills the room.

Flacco adds, "I'll look back and see what they cost last year. I know it was more than five hundred dollars."

Azure gasps audibly.

"If there's nothing else…?" Flacco says, pushing to her feet.

I grab my man bag and shoulder it. Across the table, Azure mimes to me to wait, and I plunk it back down. Shauna gets up and trails Flacco to the door. She shuts it behind her. "I might have to take down our activities temporarily, but I'll transfer them to the Facebook page. Then, a few days before prom, I'll put them back on Prom Central. No one will ever know."

Except everyone, I think.

This plan has more holes than SpaghettiOs.

AZURE

I call Radhika after school and she actually answers. I ask if Luke and I can stop by. As I glance across the front seat at Luke, I see that he's still got the same expression on his face that he assumed when Shauna revealed her plan.

"What?" I say.

He keeps his eyes on the road.

"You're in, aren't you?"

"What if we get caught?" he asks. "What if Flacco figures out what we're doing?"

"She won't. She's not that bright."

"I don't know...."

"Are you in or out?"

"In, unless..."

"Unless what?" I snap.

"What happens after the prom? When she finds out what we've done?"

"By then it'll be over. We're going to have the prom we want because it's *our* prom."

Radhika opens her front door and hugs me hard. With Luke, she seems kind of awkward, but she gives him a quick hug, too. "I'm so glad to see you," she says. "I missed you guys so much during break."

"Me, too," I tell her.

"Me three," Luke says.

"I was just making a PBJ. Do you want one?"

"Sure," Luke and I both say. I wish he'd stop repeating me. I wish I would've had him drop me off, so I could fill Radhika in on our plan and try to persuade her to come to prom with me. As a friend only. But with Luke here... What if he let it slip...?

I don't hear or see any sign of Radhika's mother. As if reading my mind, Radhika says, "My mom's at pilates." She crosses her eyes at us and we both laugh. I slit-eye Luke to stop copying me.

Luke and I both begin to make sandwiches, but I muscle him out of the way. "Quit it," he says.

"You quit it."

"What's with you two?" Radhika asks. She takes the butter knife, which I'm holding at an attack angle at Luke's chest.

"Nothing," we both mutter.

"How was Germany?" Radhika asks Luke, taking her sandwich to the table.

"*Wunderbar*," he says. "If I don't get into art school, I'm definitely going back."

Luke actually waits for me to finish spreading my jelly and cutting my sandwich before reclaiming the knife. When we're all sitting at the table, I ask Radhika, "What was it like?"

She shrugs. "Pretty. Gorgeous, actually."

Luke says, "What was what like?"

I click my tongue at him. "You know."

"We got a tour of the campus," Radhika says. "There's a lot of history there."

"What campus?" Luke asks, taking a chomp of his sandwich.

"The campus," I repeat.

Radhika says, "My parents dragged me to New Haven over spring break to visit Yale."

"What?" Luke's eyes widen.

What a liar. She never told him.

"Sneaky bastards," he goes.

Which is what I thought when Radhika told me.

"You're not changing your mind about going to Yale, are you?" I ask her.

Radhika takes a bite of sandwich. "I'd get away from my parents, at least. How's the prom coming? Have you raised enough money?"

"Yeah, we have plenty. We don't need a penny from your dad." I eye Luke just in case he was going to contradict me. He's licking jelly off the sides of his sandwich.

The conversation comes to a standstill, and we all nibble our sandwiches as slowly as possible, avoiding eye contact. It's like this cliché: There's an elephant in the room, something that isn't being talked about, and in this case Dumbo's name is Prom. I can't stand having it loom over us, so I tell Radhika, "We have a plan to put on our alternative prom, just like we were going to. Actually, it was Shauna's idea."

"Really?" Radhika says. "Tell me."

I explain about moving everything to a Facebook page, then moving it back a few days before prom.

Radhika looks intrigued. "Or you could block out Mrs. Flacco's faculty ID from Prom Central. In fact, you could create a shadow Prom Central, with different activities. The one Mrs. Flacco sees would be stripped down, and the one the students access would be the real Prom Central."

"We could do that?" I say.

Radhika replies, "You'd need Mrs. Flacco's faculty ID to misdirect her. I don't know how you'd get that."

Now my synapses start firing. "She probably has her ID card in her purse. Maybe..." I look at Luke.

"Don't look at me," he says. "There's no telling what's in her purse. Weapons of mass destruction." He chokes and goes, "Do you have any milk?"

As Radhika gets up to retrieve a carton of milk and three glasses, I say, "All we have to do is find her ID card and write down the number."

Radhika sets the milk and glasses on the table and I pour. "You're a playwright, Luke," I say. "Write us a script."

"To steal her ID," he says. "I'm so sure."

"We wouldn't be stealing it. Just getting the number."

"Without her knowing." He shakes his head.

"Yeah. Like a diversionary tactic. Grab her card, copy it, then put it right back."

Luke's eyes glaze over, which means his creativity has kicked in. This is the kind of stuff he lives for.

We all finish our sandwiches and glasses of milk at the same time. "Only one problem," I say, thinking aloud. "I'm not sure anyone on Prom Com knows how to set up a shadow file."

Radhika says, "I'll do it. On one condition."

"Anything," Luke and I say together.

"What?" I add.

Radhika goes, "You let me back on the committee."

That must mean she's dropping the seminar and not going to Yale! And maybe, just maybe...

"OMG," Luke says. "Yes, yes, and hella yes."

"You were never off," I tell her. "We were keeping your seat warm."

She smiles at me. "Has Mr. Rosen said anything at all to anyone?"

"He wrote us a letter apologizing for letting us get carried away," I reply. "But he said that he supports us still. I have your copy of the letter in my backpack. Just a sec." I dash to the foyer, where Luke and I dropped off our bags, then hurry back and hand her the letter.

She reads the letter and her face falls. "None of this was his fault," she says.

"I know," I say. "He's cool." I feel bad for Mr. Rosen. I hope getting fired from the committee doesn't affect his salary, or lack thereof.

Once we get going, it feels like someone led the elephant out of the room because we talk about other things, like Luke's play and my dad's online dating. Then the garage door whirs open and Radhika says, "My mom's home. I better get back to studying." She hugs us both good-bye, and Luke and I head out to the Caddie. Then I think of something and tell Luke, "I'll be right back."

I race to Radhika's door. I forgot: The self-affirmation I've been saving all spring break is in the front pocket of my backpack, and I pull it out. I stuff it into Radhika's hand and wait for her to read it. The smile she gives me is worth PBJs for breakfast, lunch, and dinner. The affirmation reads: "The choices you make today may affect the lives of everyone you love."

There's applause when Radhika enters the art room. I added a note in our Google docs that she was returning to the committee, and outlined our plan for the shadow Prom Central, so everyone is really happy to see her. Luke actually came up with a devious ploy to get Mrs. Flacco's ID, and everyone responded, "YAY!" Naturally, he put himself in the starring role.

When Radhika sits next to me, Mrs. Flacco snipes, "We're having a meeting in here."

"I know," Radhika says. "The prom com. I had to drop out temporarily, but now I'm back. If that's okay with you."

Flacco exhales a weary breath. "I don't suppose one more person could do any more damage."

Geez, what is it with her? Teachers love Radhika. Everyone loves Radhika.

Under the table, Radhika squeezes my hand, and my love for her comes rushing through me like a river.

"Where's Luke?" Mrs. Flacco asks. "Why can't people get here on time? It's no wonder this committee has accomplished nothing."

I seethe and Radhika squeezes my hand harder. Today's self-affirmation is actually appropriate: "Anger is an unproductive emotion. Channel it into action."

Luke comes tearing into the room like a whirlwind, his messenger bag slamming into an easel, then smacking Mrs. Flacco in the head. "OMG," he says. "I'm so sorry. I'm sorry." With both hands he pats down her hair, which doesn't move a millimeter, and while he's apologizing, he snags her carryall from the chair back. It thuds to the floor and Luke goes, "OMG. I'm sorry." He crouches down, apologizing some more, and Mrs. Flacco doesn't even have time to react as Luke overturns the bag, dumping its contents. With his back to her, he riffles through her stuff until he finds her wallet.

I watch all of this, trying not to laugh.

"Will you stop it!" Mrs. Flacco pushes him away, then scoots back her chair and squats down to shovel her belongings back into her bag. "For heaven's sake."

The fire alarm blares.

We all spook, and I look around to see that Connor has disappeared. Right on cue.

"Leave it," Mrs. Flacco orders Luke. "Everyone out of the building."

As I'm grabbing my backpack, Luke passes Mrs. Flacco's wallet to me and I stick it in my pack.

We gather in a group outside the gym to wait for the fire trucks. "I have to text my mom," Shauna says. All of us text one another so we don't have to converse with Mrs. Flacco.

Mr. Gerardi hustles around the corner of the building with two firefighters. "Did any of you see if someone set off the alarm?"

We glance sideways at one another, feigning innocence.

Luke says, "We were in the art room."

Mr. Gerardi calls to a student in the parking lot, "Hold up there."

Once the all clear is given, I say, "I need to make a pit stop on the way back." I duck into the restroom, while everyone else files back into Studio 2B.

As quickly as possible, I flip through the pictures in Flacco's wallet. Aw, cute baby. Does she have grandchildren? Poor kids. She has a ton of credit cards. Finally, tucked behind her driver's license, I find her faculty ID card. I start to write the number on my palm, then realize she might see it. Instead, I scrounge for paper in my pack, and find an old English essay.

When I return to the studio, Luke's still shoveling items back into Mrs. Flacco's bag, then pulling them back out, stalling for time. "I'm really sorry," he says again, holding up a ginormous bottle of Excedrin. She snatches it away from him. I pass behind Luke and hand off the wallet. He just manages to stick it in a side pocket of Mrs. Flacco's carryall as she yanks it away from him.

I sit and covertly give everyone the thumbs-up.

I call Radhika, and the first thing she says is, "The shadow file is up and running."

"Already?" She's a computer geek — in a good way.

"I added a note in the real Prom Central asking people to please not tell their parents about the alternative prom. I explained how we wanted to make the prom inclusive, so everyone would feel welcome and wanted. I don't know if it'll help. We'll have to wait and see."

This wasn't the reason I called Radhika.

She fills the quiet by asking, "When's the next auction?"

Crap. I forgot to ask Mr. Gerardi. "I'll know tomorrow."

"I saw that Shauna wrote in Google docs that her mom didn't want to impose on the PTSA for another bake sale," Radhika says. "Shauna said…well, you'll have to read what she thought about that." Radhika lets out a small laugh.

Great, I think. I'm definitely putting high minimum prices on each of the auction items.

I open my mouth and finally the words come out: "Radhika, about prom —"

"Azure, I don't want to talk about it."

"But you have to go." Desperation makes my voice crack. "Come with me as my friend, at least, so I don't have to go alone."

There's a prolonged pause. In a halting voice, she says, "Why did you have to say that?" Then, as if she's swallowed a lump in her throat, she adds, "There's nothing you could say or do that could make me change my mind. And you're wrong about my choice. It has no effect on anyone."

LUKE

A flock of vultures descends on me in the theater. It's coming down to the wire and the costumes still aren't complete. The lighting and sound crews want to know when we'll be doing another full run-through for their final checks. And someone asks, "What kind of hair and makeup do you want for the Mothballs?"

"Mothballish," I say. "Where's Gabe?"

"I assume he's jumping off a building."

"Why?"

"Didn't you hear?" Britny says. "Gabe and Haley broke up."

"OMG! Details, girl."

Britny says, "I can't. I promised Haley. And I'm surprised you don't know why."

What does that mean? Maybe she'll go with me.

And stomp on my heart again. Never mind.

"Do you want the Mothballs to all look alike, or can they have different hair and makeup?" Britny asks.

I'm still back on Gabe and Haley. Gabe comes rushing in, muttering, "Sorry I'm late." He doesn't look so hot, like he's got a terminal case of bed head.

People are hustling around, but something's missing. Music. "Where's Mario?"

Britny replies, "He went snowboarding over spring break and broke his arm."

I start hyperventilating. My chest aches from what I'm sure is an imminent heart attack. All the other stuff I can handle; in fact, I thrive on the adrenaline rush of performance anxiety, the last-minute jitters. But I have no backup plan for my keyboardist being out of commission.

My cell rings and it's a text from Azure:

Get over to the art studio. We're in deep shit.

This can't be happening.

I clap my hands. "People. Listen up." I wait until the din dies down. "Everything's going to be fab. Let's do a walk-through today without the music. I have to leave for just a sec, but I'll be right back. T.J., stand in for me."

His face brightens. "Will do."

"Gabe, can you stand in for T.J.?"

Gabe gives me a glazed look and mumbles, "I don't think so."

Swell. "Ryan," I shout at him. "You take over for T.J."

"Me?"

274

"Awesome. Thanks. I promise I'll be back."

There's a buzz of commotion while everyone takes their places. If they knew how panicked I felt at this moment, they'd be racing for the nearest exit. But a writer, producer, choreographer, director, and star must remain calm at all times. Thank God for antiperspirant.

I'm out of breath when I sprint into the studio and skid to a stop. Flacco snarls, "So nice of you to join us."

I slide in next to Radhika, where I feel safe. I scan the room. Everyone's head is down.

Flacco snipes, "I'd like to know whose idea it was to block me from Prom Central and think you could get away with it."

How'd she find out?

Azure says, "Nobody blocked you. Maybe it was just a computer glitch."

"And maybe *this* copy of Prom Central is fraudulent." She slaps down a printed version of our real, restored file.

I start breathing hard again, wishing I had an inhaler even though I don't have asthma.

Mr. Gerardi lumbers into the room. The expression on his face makes him look like a bear on the prowl. "What's going on?" he booms.

Flacco juts her chin at us. "Ask them."

Silence.

"Well?" Mr. Gerardi asks.

Azure speaks up. "You told me to put on an alternative prom, and that's what we're doing."

"A toned-down alternative prom," Mr. Gerardi says.

"They lied." Flacco's voice is like a whip. "They plan to go ahead with their original prom, even after they were told it was unacceptable. Here, look at this." She flaps the printout at Mr. Gerardi.

Mr. Gerardi scans the sheet and hands it back to Flacco. "You have to remove the items specified by the PTSA."

"Why?" Azure cries. "It's *our* prom. You said so."

"It's the school's prom, and you're making a mockery of it," Flacco fairly shrieks.

Mr. Gerardi folds his fullback-gone-flabby frame into a chair. "Tell me how many people have bought tickets."

Shauna's keeping track of that. She says, "Sixty-two. But a lot more people on the survey said they're coming, and almost everyone buys tickets at the front door. I know a bunch more people will come as soon as they see all the fun activities we have planned."

Flacco says, "It won't matter if the whole school comes. You won't break even with the ticket price at twenty-five dollars."

Mr. Gerardi asks, "Who lowered the price to twenty-five dollars? It's usually seventy-five, isn't it?"

I look around the table. Azure answers, "We all agreed that more people would come if the price was lower. I mean, come on. Who can afford seventy-five dollars for a dance?"

"People who plan ahead for prom," Flacco snaps.

Right. Like we open a savings account in kindergarten. With a glare, Flacco continues, "I'd still like to know how I'm getting one version of the prom online and every-one else is getting another."

None of us would ever rat out Radhika. But knowing her, she'd throw herself under the bus for us. "I did it," Shauna says. "I created two files."

"No. I did," Azure goes.

"I did it," Connor says.

"Enough." Mr. Gerardi holds up a hand.

I hate being left out. "I'm the only one with a netbook; I did it."

"They didn't do it. I did," Radhika says. "They're just trying to protect me. It was all my idea."

"You?" Mr. Gerardi says, sounding shocked.

"But we all agreed to it," Connor speaks up. "It wasn't just Radhika."

Flacco says, "But how did you manage? Unless—"

I'm close enough to feel the tinder ignite under her.

"You had to know my faculty ID."

That's my cue. I stand and say, "I have to get back to play practice."

Flacco and Mr. Gerardi shout, "Sit down!"

I flop back into my chair.

"You stole it," Flacco says. She riffles through her bag.

"We didn't steal anything," Azure says. "We might have copied it down...."

"When?" No one answers her and she screeches, "*When?*"

Connor mumbles, "During the fire drill."

Mrs. Flacco's face turns purple. "You should all be expelled! Expel them!" She aims a witchy finger at us.

"Let me get this straight." Mr. Gerardi crosses his arms on the table. "You stole Mrs. Flacco's ID —"

"Borrowed," Azure says.

"Then you set up a fake website to deceive her. Is that the gist of it?"

None of us can deny the truth. Images flash through my mind. I wonder how I'll look in a prison-orange jumpsuit.

Mr. Gerardi pushes back from the table and gets up. "I'll speak with you all momentarily. Mrs. Flacco, please come with me."

She stomps out like the nazi she is.

I clunk my head on the table. "Kill me now."

Shauna says, "What can they do?"

"Expel us," Connor replies. "I'm sorry, but if an expulsion is on my record, I'll lose my soccer scholarship."

"BFD," Azure says.

Connor scowls at her. "It may not mean anything to you, but it's my whole future."

Out in the hall I hear Flacco and Mr. Gerardi debating. Make that her shouting at him. The door opens and Mr. Gerardi enters. Alone. He says, "I'm canceling the prom."

AZURE

The words echo in my head, and not Mr. Gerardi's: *There's nothing you could say or do that could make me change my mind.*

That's a definite no from Radhika. I curl up on the sofa and smother my face in a pillow. The tears begin in my gut and erupt like a volcano. All this time I thought I had a chance. Stupid.

I feel arms snaking around me, and then Dad's holding me against him. He presses my head against his chest and goes, "Shh. It's all right."

"No, it's not." I wail like a baby.

He lets me cry it out. I hope to God Lynda isn't with him, but then I think, *Screw it if she is.*

"Girl troubles?" he asks.

I sniffle and he reaches for a tissue on the coffee table. "How'd you know?" I blow my nose.

"The only time you ever cry is when your heart gets broken."

That makes me cry even harder.

He holds and rocks me until I get myself under control. Enough to breathe again, at least. Lynda isn't here, so I ask, "What do you want for dinner? I can make you a gourmet grilled cheese sandwich."

He smiles. "How about I order a pizza?"

He calls Domino's while I blow my nose a hundred more times. While Dad is changing out of his blues, I sit at the counter, thinking about everything *but* Radhika. Or trying to. I've ruined our senior year. Not only are we not getting an alternative prom, we're not going to have any prom at all. If I hadn't been so hell-bent on adding all those ridiculous activities to a dance, none of this would've happened.

Dad comes in dressed in his sweats. "They canceled the prom today," I tell him.

"What? They can't do that."

"They can and did."

He pulls up a stool next to me. "What are you going to do about it?"

"Get stoned."

He gives me a look.

"Not like that. When people find out it was my idea to have an alternative prom, which resulted in no prom at all, they're going to stone me to death."

"Azure…"

"I mean it."

For some reason, I remember a lesson from the civil rights movement. "Is it legal to have a sit-in? Or a walkout?"

"Where?" he asks.

"At school."

"I don't see why not. As long as it's peaceful. Tell me more about why your prom got canceled."

I was afraid he'd ask that. I explain about "borrowing" Mrs. Flacco's ID. "I know we were wrong to trick her, but we couldn't think of any other way."

The pizza arrives and we sit in the living room, eating and watching TV. I wonder if anyone would walk out. I mean, it's only the stupid prom. But then, people will do anything to get out of class.

A prom protest. It might be a first in history. I'd go down as either the dumbest person on the planet or an iconic figure at Roosevelt High.

It's supposed to be in the low seventies, so I wear shorts and a tee. "Radhika had a dentist appointment this morning," Luke says first thing.

Why didn't she call me? Unless she thinks the protest is a terrible idea and she doesn't want any part of it. Or me. "I wrote to the committee on Google docs, but no one wrote back," I tell Luke.

"Maybe that's a sign you shouldn't do this," he says.

"Does that mean you're not coming?"

He doesn't reply.

Without his and Radhika's support, I feel naked and insecure.

"Guess what I found out?" he says. "Gabe and Haley broke up."

I could give a rat's ass.

"Guess what else?" he says. "Gabe's been hanging around Radhika before play practice, and calling her at night. Supposedly about homework. I think he's the other person who asked her to prom. And from the way he looks, she turned him down, too. You still have a chance."

Tears well in my eyes, but I choke them back. "She's not going. You heard her. And anyway, there won't be a prom if this protest fails. The walkout is planned for noon on the front lawn, so will you text and tweet everyone you know? Tell them to keep it a secret, as much as possible."

He exhales a long sigh, like I'm asking him for the sun and the moon and most of the planets. Or like this is for my own personal gain. Which, okay, I guess it is. But it's not only for me. It's for the entire senior class. Doesn't he get that?

As I'm loading up my books for my morning classes, I call Shauna. I'm surprised she didn't respond to my Google docs message, but then she probably blames me, too, for getting the prom canceled. Is a protest with only one person still a protest?

My stomach churns cottage cheese all morning; then, about five minutes to twelve, I excuse myself from class early, sprint to the restroom, and barf. It actually makes me feel better. As I splash cold water on my face, I hear thunderous footsteps in the hall, and when I exit, I'm almost trampled to death. It's weird, like a herd of zombies marching to a silent call, because no one is speaking or smiling or anything. I get sucked in and carried away by the crowd.

The sight outside is eerie. The whole student body is gathered on the lawn, just standing there, gazing at the front door. Concrete steps lead up to a curved outdoor entrance, where I stop and stand. Alone.

I swallow hard. "Hey, everyone," I call. My voice trembles. I cup my hands over my mouth. "I guess you heard the prom was canceled."

There's no reaction. All at once a bullhorn is thrust in my hand and Connor's standing to my right. "Thought you might need this," he says. "We have to get it back to Coach's office before he figures out who took it."

He gives me a crooked smile. It's hard to be mad at him right now.

I hold the bullhorn up to my mouth and nothing happens. Connor shows me the On button. "In case you hadn't heard," my voice booms, "your prom was canceled. But I guess you know that, since you're here."

Rumbling *boos* arise from the crowd.

Radhika and Luke materialize beside me. I want to hug her, and him, too. "That's right." I feel my confidence grow. "*Your* prom." I turn to Radhika. "Do you want to take over?" *Please*, I pray.

"You're doing great," she says. "Hurry, though. The wolves are closing in." I glance back and a bunch of faculty are storming out the door. Mrs. Flacco is leading the pack.

I press the On button again. "All we wanted to do was give you guys a prom that represented you. We wanted to include everyone, not just the popular people, or the ones who could afford to go."

"Yeah!" someone yells from the back.

"So we added activities, like karaoke and a poetry slam and a drag show and Wii competition. Things you voted for."

Now a lot of people are chatting among themselves. The same person in back yells, "Yeah!"

Mrs. Flacco grabs the bullhorn out of my hand. "Go back to class," she orders. "You're all suspended."

Connor sucks in a gasp, and I think Luke's about to faint.

"You don't have the authority to suspend us," Radhika says.

Is she right? I can practically feel steam rising off Mrs. Flacco. Someone snatches the bullhorn away from Mrs. Flacco and hands it back to me.

It's Shauna. She tosses me a smile.

Mrs. Flacco stalks back into the building. The other faculty members mill around, waiting to see what happens, I guess.

My voice echoes as I call out, "Do you want a prom?"

"Yeah!" more than one voice calls.

"Are we going to let them cancel our prom?"

"No!" people shout.

"It's *our* prom," I say. "If we want it, we need to let our voices be heard."

Luke leans into the bullhorn and starts chanting, "We want our prom. We want our prom." Everyone picks up the chorus, and fists punch the air.

All the voices ringing in unison sound as beautiful as a Sunday choir. Out of the corner of my eye, I see a lady in heels marching up the sidewalk. Shauna clutches my arm, saying, "Oh my God, hide me."

It's Mrs. Creighton. We shield Shauna between us as her mother hustles by and into the building.

Shauna says, "What's she doing here? I swear I didn't say anything."

I believe her. The chanting goes on for another few minutes, until Mr. Gerardi comes out. He stares at me for a prolonged moment, then extends his hand. I give him the bullhorn.

"Everyone return to class or lunch or wherever you were."

There's grumbling, and I see most people waiting for our—my—lead. I cup my hands around my mouth and holler, "This isn't over." Then I have a brainstorm. "Everyone sit."

Almost simultaneously, the whole school sits on the front lawn.

Mr. Gerardi turns a fiery glare on me. "To my office. All of you."

As we follow Mr. Gerardi in, Luke does a flippant dance move that makes people laugh.

Inside, phones are ringing off the hook. All three secretaries are fielding calls, and I see Shauna's mom in Mr. Gerardi's office. When we walk in, she yells at him, "I paid two hundred and fifty dollars for my daughter's dress, on sale, and I can't return it!"

Mr. Gerardi says, "I understand your problem, Mrs. Creighton."

"No, I don't think you do. Prom is a once-in-a-lifetime event, and you're stealing the memory from Shauna. From all these kids."

Shauna glances at me, wide-eyed.

Every light on Mr. Gerardi's phone is flashing, and the secretaries are saying, "I'll let Mr. Gerardi know how you feel." One adds, "Sir, there's no need to use that kind of language with me."

Mr. Gerardi's eyes meet mine and I cross my arms. He motions us all inside his office and shuts the door. Shauna's mom snakes an arm around Shauna's waist, pulling her in close.

Mr. Gerardi says, "As you can see, I've been getting calls about the prom from angry parents all morning."

"Not to mention how mad the students are," I say.

Mr. Gerardi tips up his blinds to view the sea of students out on the grass.

Luke goes, "One word: angry mob."

Mr. Gerardi turns back to us and says, "I've reconsidered. You can have a prom."

"Yes!" we all cheer.

"But it'll have to be a traditional prom."

I don't know where the courage comes from, but I say, "No deal."

The room goes quiet.

"It's our prom, on our terms. We want karaoke, a drag

show, a poetry slam, and everything else we planned for the alternative prom."

"Azure..." he says.

"Okay, maybe not the car show, since we'd have to get a license. It'll be night, anyway. I'm willing to compromise on the tatting and piercing, too. But that's all."

With the bunch of us crammed in here, it's hot. Or maybe it's the intimidation factor, because Mr. Gerardi pulls a hankie out of his pocket to dab at the sweat beads on his forehead. "You win," he says. "Have your prom."

Just then Mrs. Flacco opens the door and bursts into the room. "What's going on?"

"One more thing," I say. "We want Mr. Rosen back."

LUKE

The triumph turns Azure into a lesbian avenger. God help us.

"We still have to raise money for the music, photographer, programs, and whatever else," she says as we head out to end the sit-in. "We'll need an approximate count for food and drinks. I don't even know how to vote on royalty."

"Leave that to me," Shauna tells her. "By the way, you were awesome in there."

Everyone claps Azure on the back. I go to give her a squeeze around the shoulders, but she shakes me off. "What are you waiting for?" she asks. "We have nine days!"

Mr. Rosen is lingering in the foyer after the final straggler comes in from outside. "Hey, Mr. Rosen," I say. "We got Flacco fired and you back on board. O Captain! My Captain!" I salute.

He looks at each one of us. "I appreciate your vote of

confidence," he says, "but I don't have time. I'm really sorry."

Does that mean he's not coming back? We're going to be stuck with Flacco to the end?

Traitor. How could he leave us with her?

Speaking of witch, Shauna's mom bustles out of Mr. Gerardi's office. She slows to a stop and says, "You still don't have enough money to put on this prom. You'd better work fast." Then she flies off on her broomstick.

Radhika asks, "How much do we need?"

Azure and I say together, "Nothing."

Azure adds, "We've got it covered. We'll make it."

Radhika gives her a knowing look.

Azure says, "I just need to ask Mr. Gerardi if we can hold the silent auction tomorrow night. See you guys later."

Mr. Rosen, who's still standing there, says to Shauna, "Can you stop by after your lunch period and see me?"

"What about?" she asks. I don't hear his answer because I'm mentally erasing him from my favorite-teachers list. Plus, the *click-click-click*ing of Mrs. Creighton's high heels all the way to the front door is distracting. I can see where Shauna gets her fierce.

I fully expect to be physically and verbally accosted at rehearsal when I announce that I've written a new scene. It's near the end of Act Two, where I go back into the closet. If I'd never come out in the first place, I might've gotten the girl of my dreams to go to prom with me.

Which is wishful thinking, I know. If Radhika was into me, she would've said yes. Still, the scene is relevant. I know a lot of people who've regretted coming out. It's like a pit stop in the process. It doesn't usually last long because, in the end, what you gain by coming out is so much more than what you lose.

But Ryan's right. There's a time when you wonder if it's worth the heartache.

Before I meet the firing squad, I see Mario onstage in his shoulder-to-hand cast. He raises his arm like Frankenstein. Without music, my musical…isn't. Yesterday, when I logged on to Facebook, I checked the *Closets Are for Mothballs* page and not one single cast member had left a comment on the wall recommending another keyboardist. In fact, no one had IM'd or texted me since I skipped out of the last rehearsal. If they're quitting, I hope they have the decency to tell the writer, director, choreographer, producer, and star.

I figure I'll delay the bloodshed by sneaking in the back door of the theater. It's dark except for the lights onstage. Music reverbs, but it's not from an electronic keyboard. Mario's playing some kind of horn. Not a sax or clarinet, because he only has the one good hand. I'm not that familiar with all the orchestral instruments. Is it an English horn?

I slither behind the set to listen. The horn sounds cool—kind of mellow and bittersweet. The way I feel.

People ask one another where I am. I crouch deeper in the shadows.

"Let's just start," Ryan says. "T.J., would you play Luke?"

He can't possibly do me justice. The Mothballs dance the opening number, then T.J. walks out from stage left. "Ten," he says. "That's how old I was when I knew I was different." The scene takes place in a classroom. One desk. "Sitting behind Zach Zimmerman, I'd doodle in my science notebook LO + ZZ = LUV. One day my notebook got swiped and I heard these girls snickering. 'Hey, Luke. Is ZZ Zack or Zena?' Yes, lucky for me, Zach had a sister named Zena. I loved her, too."

I smile. It's a true story.

T.J. begins the Zach and Zena song and I clap a hand over my mouth. OMG. He has a gorgeous voice. I had no idea — maybe because I gave him only one silly song, which a mime could do.

The musidramedy continues. T.J. knows every line and every song, and he's good. His comic timing is impeccable. He even makes me laugh. I hate to say it, but T.J.'s better than I am.

The Mothballs dance out of the closet in a chorus line, high-kicking and singing, "Closets are for mothballs." It's hilarious. Mario's switched to a trumpet to herald their arrival.

T.J. bursts out of the closet to the "Hallelujah" chorus. What a scream.

When T.J. gets to the part where he comes out to my parents, I'm mesmerized. "Mom, Dad, I have to tell you something," T.J. says.

I feel the anxiety in the pit of my stomach all over again. How clammy my hands were at that moment. How dry my mouth felt.

"Are you flunking out?" Britny, aka Mom, asks. She even sounds like my mom.

"No," T.J. says. "I'm bisexual."

The silence is drawn out. I hold my breath until Mom says, "Are you sure?"

T.J. says, "Positive."

Mom says, "You know we'll always love you, no matter what."

Gabe, aka Dad, goes, "But you still like girls, right?"

There's no line here; only a nod.

Dad's spotlighted with me, I hope, and I hear him say, "Then there's hope for you yet."

A tear slides down my cheek and suddenly I'm hiccuping. Onstage, T.J. will be hanging his head while the spotlight fades. There's more to come, more humor to lighten the second act. But I'm so moved by the performance I can't stop myself from standing and applauding. I start around the set, clapping all the way.

"That was…" I flap my hand to dry my tears. "You guys." And I realize something: I wrote this musidramedy to engage the audience in my life, but it's not only my life. It's all our lives, every bisexual or gay or lesbian or transgender person who's had to come out. My whole purpose was to share with the world how hard it is.

"That was a powerful performance," I tell T.J. "You're officially the lead."

"What?" he cries. "Oh my God." He covers his face with his hands.

"Mario, love how you improvised, dude. You're a genius." He gives me a peace sign with the free fingers sticking out of his cast.

"Mothballs, what can I say? You guys are the Rockettes."

They squeal.

"Are we going to be ready for next Friday night?"

I don't hear any nays. Everyone seems psyched.

A wave of pride washes over me and I think, *I wrote, produced, directed, and choreographed an entire school production. If my acting career doesn't pan out...*

It will. My future flashes before my eyes. I'm accepting a Tony, a Grammy, and an Oscar, all in the same year. Look out, world.

AZURE

Why does the worst weather day of the week always blow in right before my silent auctions? The snow begins in the morning, and by noon there are drifts up to the window-sills in the cafeteria. Mr. Gerardi's voice booms over the loudspeaker: "We'll be closing at one today. Buses will be here by twelve forty-five."

"Noooo," I say to Radhika. "That means we won't get anyone to come tonight."

She says, "You should probably cancel it."

If we can't raise a thousand dollars or more... There's no way I'm going to ask Radhika to let her father fund our prom. Especially if she's not even coming.

She must be reading my mind, because she says, "Be reasonable, Azure. It's nothing to him. A drop in the bucket."

"But it's everything to you," I say. "It's your future."

She shakes her head and replies in a soft voice, "It doesn't matter."

"It does to me." *I love you*, I want to say. *I won't destroy your life.*

The snow continues to fall all Friday afternoon, and the weather forecasters are predicting one of those Colorado spring snowstorms that can dump two or three feet of heavy, wet snow on the city. Louisa calls to tell me she's closing the thrift shop and not to come in tomorrow.

I hate feeling shut in, even though I don't know where I'd go.

Dad comes home around six, stomping his wet feet in the foyer. "Whew," he says. "What a mess. Traffic accidents everywhere. Turn on the news, will you?" He grabs a Bud and two Twinkies from the cupboard. Tossing a Twinkie to me, he pads into the living room.

I switch from MTV to Fox. The meteorologist, who is totally hot, is saying we're going to get at least another five to ten inches in Denver, on top of the two feet that have already fallen at DIA. "Stay off the roads so emergency vehicles can get through," she says.

Dad perches beside me, yanking off his wet socks and propping his feet on the coffee table.

"Ew," I say. "What makes you think I want to look at your toe hair?"

"Sexy, isn't it?"

I let out a puff of air. "To Cloud, maybe."

He gives me a noogie. We watch as the poor weather

reporters are forced to stand out in the blizzard and tell people how dangerous the driving is. I say to Dad, "You can thank me now for never wanting to drive."

"What about driving me to drink?" He takes a swig.

"You're doing that on your own."

We watch for a while and I pull the comforter tighter around me, just listening to the snow pelt against the windows.

"What do you plan to do next year?" he asks.

I turn to him. "Why? Are you afraid I'll stay or go?"

He holds my eyes. "I'm not sure."

At least he's honest. He's gazing at me so intently I have to look away. "I haven't decided. Go to college, I guess. Or join the police academy."

He chokes and beer bubbles out of his nose. "No," he says in a cough. "Absolutely not."

"Why not? Don't you think I can protect and serve?"

He sets his beer on the table. "Azure, you have the will and ability to do anything you want. I just don't..." He gets all serious. "I'd be too worried about you."

"Like I'm not worried about you? Every time you step out that door, I worry you won't be coming back."

He frowns. "Sweetie." He tries to loop an arm around me, but I lean away.

"Don't 'sweetie' me. I mean it, Dad. Why can't you be an accountant or something?"

He says, "I suck at math."

"Is that where I inherited it from?"

My cell rings and I push up from the sofa to go find it

in my room. It's Radhika. I kick my door closed and say, "Hi," as I sprawl on the bed.

"Are you watching the news?" she says.

"Um, I was."

"Go turn it on."

"It's all about the weather. Blah, blah, snow, snow."

"Turn to channel nine," she says.

I return to the living room and sit, snatch the remote off the coffee table, and click over to channel nine. It's a breaking news story.

"Firefighters are blaming the weight of the snow for the roof's collapse. Fortunately, no one was injured, although three events were scheduled in the meeting and ballrooms this evening."

I sit on the edge of the sofa and ask Dad, "Where is that?"

"Some hotel," he says.

"The Ramada is currently looking to relocate all the guests to nearby hotels. Needless to say, repairs will be extensive."

My stomach drops through the floor. In my ear, Radhika says what I already know: "That's our prom hotel."

My cell beeps; I have another call. My eyes are glued to the screen, where half of the hotel is rubble. "Azure, are you there?" Radhika says. I hear her voice, but it's coming from outer space. This can't be happening. Not now.

Mrs. Flacco writes in the old Google docs file, "Call around to other hotels. There are always last-minute cancellations."

I spend most of Saturday on the phone. There's one available ballroom, and it's twenty-five hundred dollars. We could reserve it—at Radhika's future expense. I refuse to even mention it to the others. By that evening, no one's found anything, and in our new Google docs file, Shauna writes that Mrs. Flacco had a long list of hotels last year, but she probably wouldn't lift a pinkie to help us.

As I'm lying in bed, listening to the wind rattle my window, I have a sudden epiphany. It's almost midnight, but I get up and log on to Facebook. Radhika's not there. Neither is Luke, which is surprising; he lives online.

On a whim, I search for Mr. Rosen. Eventually I find a Phillip Rosen who teaches at Roosevelt. I message him and hope he reads his Facebook tomorrow. Seriously, why be on Facebook if you don't read it two or three times a day?

The first thing I do when I wake up on Sunday is check my computer. Mr. Rosen has written me back with the information I need. He adds, "There's an outside chance, I suppose. If you want me to call, I will."

I write him a message: "That's okay. I'll do it." I'm kind of mad at him for being unavailable to us after he got fired and I got him reinstated. But whatever. I write, "I hope you get your deposit back from the Ramada. We're going to need it."

In our new Google docs file, I tell everyone what I'm thinking: "Remember the pavilion? Mr. Rosen said it's a historic landmark, so what if we call the foundation and tell them we'll clean up all the tagging so they won't have to? We can remove the plywood and sweep the inside. Or we can paint the plywood with murals. We'll get it all ready for them to open by May."

No one writes back immediately, so I log off and call the number Mr. Rosen gave me for the Highlands foundation.

The president, whose name I can't make out because of her whispery voice, sounds like she's about ninety years old. She keeps repeating, "Speak up, dear." I feel like I'm shouting as I explain our idea to use the pavilion for our prom.

At the end of my spiel, she doesn't say anything. I wonder if she's fallen asleep. Or... died?

"Hello?" I yell.

"I can't make that decision," she says. "It's up to the foundation committee."

Committees. Why do I suddenly loathe committees?

"Let's see," the president says. "Our next meeting is April twenty-eighth."

"But our prom is April sixteenth," I tell her.

"Oh. Then that won't work, will it?"

Duh.

"I'm very sorry," she says.

I sense that she's about to hang up. "Wait. Can't you hold a special meeting?" *Like, tomorrow?* I think.

"Oh, my," she says. "That'd be breaking with tradition. We've always met once a month for as long as I've been on the foundation committee."

Which must be a hundred years. "Just this once, could

you meet early? We'd need to know as soon as possible so we'd have time to clean up all the graffiti and decorate for prom. It'd be such a gorgeous place to have it," I add.

She's quiet for a moment, then says, "You know, in my day there used to be an actual ballroom next to the carousel. Dances were held every Saturday night. 'Dancing Under the Stars,' it was called." I hear the nostalgia in her voice. "It was romantic and wonderful. You're right—the pavilion would be a lovely location for a prom."

"I know," I say. "So much better than some stuffy, smelly hotel room."

She hesitates again. *Please, please, please*, I pray.

She says, "Let me contact the committee and see if we can call an emergency meeting. Why don't you give me your name and phone number, and I'll let you know."

After I hang up, I squeal and jump around on the bed because I have a feeling the foundation is going to say yes. How could they not?

As I bounce in a circle, I see Dad standing in the doorway.

"I knew the day would come," he says, entering my room and extending his palm. "Hand it over."

I break my bounce with bent knees. "What?"

"Whatever you're on."

I click my tongue. "It's a natural high."

He goes, "Hoo boy. No more Twinkies for you."

LUKE

Azure's back to being Chatty Cathy on the way to school, telling us all about calling the pavilion president and how prom's going to be so ultracool under the stars. I say what I'm thinking, which is, "What if it snows another ten inches?"

"I thought of that," she says. "We'll just paint the plywood on the inside. You can do murals or something."

"I can, huh? I'm a little busy with my musidramedy."

"Well, there are other artists in the school," she says.

Which totally offends me.

I was worried about the roads today. It was a fast-moving storm, though, and the sun came out yesterday afternoon. Half the snow is already melted.

Azure seems so happy I get the feeling she's talked Radhika into coming to prom. Maybe even with her. Although wouldn't she have told me? That's pretty monumental news. Maybe Azure's going to keep everything to herself now, since we've sort of lost our connection. And Radhika — where does she stand? Only one way to find out. "So, Radhika," I say, "I'm glad you decided to come to prom after all."

Radhika says, "Who told you that?"

In the rearview mirror, I see Azure seething at me. Radhika turns to gaze out the side window. Under my breath, for Azure's benefit, I go, "Bawk, bawk."

The first thing Flacco asks at the prom com meeting is: "Has anyone found another hotel?"

No one speaks up. Azure checks her cell, like maybe she missed a call.

"If we don't have a location, there's no use going any further," Flacco says.

"Wait a minute," Azure speaks up. "I talked to the president of the Highlands foundation to see if we could use their pavilion."

"What pavilion?" Flacco asks.

Azure describes the pavilion and how it was one of our initial finds.

"Is it indoors?" Flacco asks.

"Yes and no," Azure says.

"Either it is or it isn't," Flacco says.

Azure has to explain about the plywood.

"You want to have your prom in a cement building with plywood sides? Is it heated?"

Azure glances around the room. No one has an answer. "If it's not, we could always rent heaters."

"That sounds like a fire hazard," Flacco says.

Azure continues, "But if the weather's nice, we can take down the plywood, and it'll be amazing."

"It'll be cold," Flacco counters. "We just had a major blizzard. Do you want girls to have to wear their winter coats with their prom dresses?"

"Or pants," Azure says.

Flacco repeats, "Pants? To prom?"

Tight-lipped, Azure says, "We don't know what the weather's going to be like. This is Colorado."

Flacco bounces the tip of her pen on the table. "What do the rest of you say? You don't seem very in favor of this idea."

No one replies. Azure looks ready to strangle someone, starting with me. Finally, Shauna says, "I loved the pavilion. But I am worried about the weather. And it's not big enough to put tables inside to sit and have cake, plus dance and set up the band. We might need to rent tents and chairs for outside."

"How much will that cost?" Azure asks.

"My sister rented outdoor tents and chairs for her wedding last summer," Connor says. "You don't want to know what it cost."

That shuts everyone up.

Flacco asks Azure, "How much is it to rent the pavilion?"

Azure swallows hard. "I don't know. I mean, I haven't exactly gotten permission to use it yet."

Flacco's face changes from irritated to indignant. "Then why are you wasting our time?"

I feel Azure shrivel—and she doesn't wither easily.

On the way home, I learn that Azure knows curse words I've never even heard. I want to cover poor Radhika's ears. Azure's cell rings and she digs it out of her backpack. "It's Shauna," she says.

She listens, then says, "Thanks. I appreciate your support. Okay. I'll let you know if and when the foundation calls." She disconnects. "They're never going to call." Just then Azure's cell bleats again. She still has it in her hand so she flips it open after one ring. "This is Azure," she says. To us, she mouths, *It's them.* She listens. We're at Radhika's gate and I roll down the window to key in the security code.

Azure goes, "Uh-huh. Okay. Thank you." Her face and voice are unreadable. As I pull up to Radhika's condo, Azure disconnects.

At the top of her lungs, she screams, "We got it!"

"How much?" Radhika asks.

Azure smiles from ear to ear. "Free!"

Dress rehearsal is an utter disaster. I'd be worried if it wasn't. At least the Mothball costumes are all sewn and the sets are done. But the Mothballs aren't in tune and can't sing loud enough over Mario's horns. We try adjusting the stage mikes, which seems to help. But then the Mothballs keep tripping over one another because they can't see over their balls. Whoever's working the spotlight must be a stand-in because when T.J. enters stage left, the spotlight illuminates stage right. This is supposed to be a comedy, but it's turning into a parody.

"It's okay," I tell everyone. "Dress rehearsals are supposed to suck. You get out all the bad karma before the real performance."

They look as freaked as I feel as we finish the run-through.

Owen's getting out of a cab as I pull up at the house. He waits for me at the front door. "The whole fleet is going to need detailing before your prom. Can you help me drive the limos to the detailing shop on Friday night?"

I just stare at him. Doesn't he know Friday is my play?

"What?" he says.

"Let me in." I try to squeeze by him, but he blocks my way.

"I thought you wanted to help with the business. This is what I need help with."

"Do you mind?" I push him aside.

I hate him. He's so lame. Not that I'd want him to come to my musidramedy. Not that he should care about what's important in my life.

That's how bros roll: in opposite directions.

AZURE

I stop at the faculty lounge before our meeting to see if Mr. Rosen's there. He's not, but as I'm heading for the art wing, I see him coming toward me. "Mr. Rosen," I call, hustling toward him. "We got the pavilion."

"Excellent," he says. "I'm proud of you. I'm proud of all of you."

"All we have to do is clean the graffiti, and the foundation will pay for utility costs. Isn't that cool?"

"It is. I knew you could do it."

He walks with me toward Studio 2B; we both stop just outside the door. "I was wondering," I ask, "if you'd gotten your deposit back from the Ramada? Because we still need a thousand dollars for the band and the photographer."

He grimaces. "I haven't. They called and said they'd refund the money as soon as their insurance pays. I don't know when that'll be. Probably not by Saturday."

My heart sinks.

Mrs. Flacco sticks her head out and snaps, "Are you coming, Azure? I need to leave early to supervise detention." Like a turtle, she pulls her head back in.

"That's my cue," Mr. Rosen says, taking off.

What a coward, I think.

When I relay the good news about the pavilion to the committee, they all cheer. "Is everyone willing to help get the pavilion in shape?" I ask. "Because I can't do it by myself. How do you remove tagging, anyway?"

"Usually you just paint over it," Connor says.

"I don't think they'll like that," I say. "The pavilion is concrete."

"Then we might have to rent a power washer and get some special graffiti-removal chemical," Connor goes.

"How much does that cost?"

He shrugs. "We're still short by, what? A thousand dollars?"

"Not that much," I say. "Only, like, nine hundred." Big diff.

"Unless we want to rent tables and chairs," Shauna says. "And we really should."

Why is it all about the money?

Up to this point, Mrs. Flacco hasn't said a word. I'm sure she's thinking what I am: you're out of money, out of time, and out of luck. Give it up. Instead, she stands. "I don't know how you did it, but a large contribution came in today that'll pay for everything you want. Just let me know the amount." She bustles out, leaving a trail of hairspray fumes behind her.

I turn slowly to Radhika, who's watching Mrs. Flacco's retreat like everyone else. Obviously avoiding my eyes.

Why, Radhika? I want to say.

But I don't have to ask. We've been friends long enough that I know how her heart works. She'd sacrifice everything for other people's happiness.

"If no one has anything to do right now, can we take a drive to the pavilion to check it out again?" I ask.

Shauna says, "I have to call…you know who." She pulls out her cell.

Connor goes, "I have my car, so I'll meet you there."

Radhika says quietly, "I can't. My mother asked me to come home right after school."

She's making that up.

I meet Luke's eyes and know he's thinking the same thing I am: She doesn't want a public confrontation about the money, and I guess I can't blame her.

"Do you want me to drop you off?" Luke asks Radhika.

"No. I'll call my mother. She won't mind picking me up here."

"It's no problem.…"

She gathers her stuff and leaves. I want to run after her so bad.

On the way to the pavilion, Shauna says, "I'm taking the prom program to the printer tonight. How many copies should I have them print? I know we've sold three hundred and some tickets."

"Is that all?"

"It's more people than attended last year," she says.

I'm disappointed. I really expected more. "Have them print a thousand," I tell her. "Just in case."

Shauna arches her eyebrows at me.

"Positive thinking," I go. I don't add, *To pull this off in four days, we're going to need a miracle. We're going to need miracles raining down on us every day.*

Shauna says, "I'll put the pavilion's address on Prom Central. And I think we should make an announcement about it tomorrow. Luke?"

"At your service," he goes.

Connor's already at the pavilion when we arrive, peeking through the peephole. "Let's take down one of these planks to see what the inside looks like," he says.

It's nailed onto a frame and we can't even loosen it. Connor says, "I think I have some tools in my trunk. Maybe a tire iron." He returns to his car and Shauna peeps through the hole. I grab Luke by the shirtsleeve and pull him aside, out of Shauna's range of hearing. "Why did you tell Connor to text Shauna that he was going with someone else to prom?"

Luke goes, "Huh?"

"I can understand if he didn't want to go with her, but he should've told her in person. He really hurt her feelings."

Luke frowns. "I never told him to text her. I just suggested he tell her he was going with someone else."

I glare him down. I want to believe him. I want to….

"How could you even go there?" he says. "Do you think I'm that callous?"

I don't answer.

"Thanks. Thanks a lot." He stomps away from me. He whirls around and barks, "For your information, it's your fault Radhika's not coming to prom."

"Why is it my fault?"

"Because you should've asked her. You chickenshit."

"I did ask her. As a friend, even, so she wouldn't be shocked and appalled by the truth. She said there was nothing anyone could say or do to make her come."

Connor appears at my side. "Radhika's not coming to prom?"

"No!" we both raise our voices at him. Then Luke says, "Give me the tire iron."

I cover my head, expecting him to crack my skull with it. I deserve it; I never should've doubted him. He's the most sensitive guy I know when it comes to girls' feelings.

Connor says, "I asked Radhika to go to prom with me and she said no. I figured she was going with someone else."

I look over and see that Shauna's listening in on our conversation. I expect her to burst into tears, but she doesn't. She just turns away without a word.

Luke rips off the plywood in one yank. It opens up the pavilion like a doorway to heaven. I gasp.

Luke enters and goes, "OMG." The whole inside is like a swirling mural, plaster walls painted with carousel zebras and elephants and giraffes.

Connor steps inside. "It's awesome," he says.

"It is," I breathe, wandering toward the middle.

"I'm going to take some pictures and send them to

Radhika," Connor says. "Do you think that'll change her mind about coming?"

From across the pavilion floor, Shauna says, "It won't hurt to try."

Connor snaps away with his cell while the rest of us walk around the perimeter.

It's mystical and magical.

Shauna says, "We should've gone with a carousel theme."

I agree. But how could we have known?

She adds, "Oh, well. Once we get the twinkling lights and the rainbow balloons in here, it'll be cool."

"We should have a disco ball," Luke says.

We all laugh. Then the laughter dies and, in a wistful sigh, we all go, "Yeah."

"I'll see if the decorations committee has enough money left over," Shauna says. "In fact, I'll call Mollie right now." There's a park bench outside the pavilion, and Shauna goes over to sit, her cell to her ear.

My eyes drift to the ceiling of the pavilion, where the mural of carnival animals continues. It's like the Sistine Chapel. I can't help moving in a circle to take it all in.

As I'm twirling, I hear a snatch of conversation from the corner. It's Luke, ragging on Connor about texting Shauna and not manning up. Connor's hanging his head. He glances over at Shauna, out on the bench, and then heads her way.

Luke eyes me briefly, and looks away.

He's making this extra hard, and I guess I deserve it. I approach him. "I'm sorry about assuming you told

Connor to text Shauna," I say. "I'm sorry about Radhika, too. I didn't know you liked her."

"Loved her. Still do. And I didn't know you felt the same way."

We're both quiet for a minute, then Luke says, "I hope this hasn't destroyed our friendship."

Tears well in my eyes. He holds out a fist to bump and when I knock my knuckles against his, he pulls me in for a hug.

Connor comes back and says, "It's getting dark. We better put the plywood back up. The tagging's pretty bad on the west side, so I'll call and see how much it'll cost to rent a power washer. What's the most we can spend?"

I tell him, "Just assume the money's available."

My cell rings the minute I step into the house. It's Shauna. "You won't believe what happened back there," she says.

I already know, but I play along. "What?"

"Connor asked me to prom."

"What?"

"Can you believe it? First he apologized for texting me a rejection, then he said he'd like to take me after all." Shauna laughs.

I laugh, but it sounds as forced as it is.

"Of course I said no," Shauna says. "Not only because I have a date—"

"You do?" Oops. Do I sound shocked?

Shauna says, "I used Radhika's matching program, and it works!"

Wow. "Sweet," I say.

"I know. I'm so excited. It's weird. I can't believe I ever liked Connor. You know how one day you think someone is so hot, then the next day you look at him and go, *What did I ever see in you?*"

I've known that feeling in the past, for sure.

Shauna says, "I better go get our programs ordered. See you tomorrow."

LUKE

I know I should eat before the play. My stomach's too jittery, though. Besides, the only thing in the fridge is an old carton of Chinese takeout and—you guessed it—Coke. Owen's out, hopefully on a cougar run. Just as I'm leaving, my cell rings. It's Owen. I debate whether to answer or not, and decide I'm already too stressed to deal with him.

He doesn't leave a message. As I'm climbing into my Caddie, a text arrives from him:

Running late. See you there. Break a leg.

I sit and stare at the message for a long time. What was all that about detailing the limos? Did he want it to be a surprise that he was coming? I'm surprised, all right. I'm totally freaked. Yeah, I want him to acknowledge my existence. But after he sees this play he'll know the real story of my life. Then we'll have to deal with each other on a different level. Like, man to man.

Almost everyone's backstage when I get there. Mario's warming up on his horns. The Mothballs are zipping up their costumes, chittering away like cheese balls. The lighting crew is huddled in a corner, making notes on the script. I hurry over to them and say, "Remember to keep the spotlight on T.J. at all times."

I see T.J. standing next to Britny, peeking out at the audience.

I rush over to him. "Remember, if you forget your lines, I'll be stage left to cue you."

He opens his mouth, but nothing comes out. Then his face pales. His knees must go weak because he slides down the wall.

I squat in front of him. "T.J., get a grip."

"I can't do it, man." His voice is raspy. He covers his mouth, shoots to his feet, and races off toward the restroom.

OMG. Okay, okay. Plan B. What's Plan B? I'm back to playing the lead. Ryan. Ryan can step in for T.J. He did a good job the day of dress rehearsal.

"Forget what I just said," I tell the lighting crew. "Keep that spotlight on me."

"Ryan!" I shout. "Has anyone seen Ryan?"

I run around calling for Ryan and finally find him talking to the stage crew. They're all dressed in black. They'll be closing in the closet walls.

"Ryan, T.J. has stage fright, so I need you to play his part."

"I...I..." Blood fills his cheeks.

"Please." I grasp his shoulders. "I need you."

He gulps and looks at me long and hard. He shakes his head. I squeeze his upper arms and say, "You'll be fab. Just think of it like another practice." *With an auditorium full of people watching your every move and judging you,* I don't add.

He wanders off to hair and makeup seeming dazed. If he faints, I may have to play both roles. Which, I guess, would add to the humor.

Britny races up to me. "Have you seen how many people are here?" she asks. She starts flapping her arms like a baby bird. "I'm going to throw up."

Not her, too. "Do it now," I tell her. "Before we go onstage."

She sprints off. I peek around the curtain behind the set. The auditorium is standing room only. I hope Owen's in back, where he can't see or hear.

Miss Wells appears out of nowhere. "Luke," she says, "are you ready to start? It's getting late."

I gather everyone together in a group and say, "This is it. No matter how it goes—and it's going to be awesome—I want you to know, you guys rock."

The first act is flawless. People laugh where they're supposed to. I even hear a few sniffles at the end, when I come out to Mom and Dad. The second act is all about my love life. Britny's great in the role of Haley, my only GF—so far.

Then I had the LDR with Seamus, who used me. My best work in this act is in the bluesy love songs I wrote. The Mothballs are my backup singers and dancers.

The last scene is futuristic, because it hasn't happened yet. I fantasize that someday it will, though. I was hoping it'd be with Radhika, but since that's not to be, I changed the script.

Ryan recites T.J.'s line: "I never thought I'd find you."

My line: "I've been searching the universe."

Ryan: "Leaping from star to star."

Me: "Falling to Earth."

Ryan: "Questioning my worth."

Me: "There's no question about it: I love you."

Ryan stands there looking at me for a long moment. I panic. He's forgotten his line. The last line of the play.

I see him raise his right hand, then feel it scoop the back of my head. He takes a step forward and kisses me. Softly at first. Then he wraps his arms around my waist and presses his lips to mine. I lose myself in time and space. In the distance, I hear hooting and hollering. People in the audience are standing and clapping.

The spotlight extinguishes and the curtain closes. Ryan pulls away as the cast and crew come out onstage. The curtain opens and we take a bow. Someone pushes me forward and puts a bouquet of flowers in my arms.

The applause seems to last an eternity. All I care about is finding Ryan. Where is he?

The curtain closes and I dodge through the mob. "Ryan!" He's folding the set.

He stops and I take his hand. "I've heard of ad-libbing. But ad-lipping?"

He smiles shyly.

I'm not aware of the curtain opening again or the spotlight finding me. I just hold Ryan and kiss him until the roaring of the crowd is a *symphonie fantastique*.

AZURE

Location? Check.

Theme? Check.

Band? Check.

Photographer? Check.

Traditional activities? Check.

Alternative activities? Check.

What am I missing?

Taking the love of my life to my senior prom. Empty box where check should be.

Dad knocks on my door and I tell him to come in. I'm trying to decide if I should wear the hat veil up or down. *Down*, I think. He whistles.

If I could whistle, I'd return the compliment. He's dressed in a black suit with a pink shirt. Only my dad can pull off pink and look macho. "I thought you'd be wearing your uniform. You know, to frisk people on the way in."

Dad says, "Your teacher called and told me the school was going to provide security."

How did Mrs. Flacco know I'd volunteered my dad? It must've been in Luke's notes.

"Do you want a ride to the pavilion?" Dad asks.

"No," I lie. "I'm riding with Luke and his new crush." *Crush* is an understatement; they've been lip-locked since the play last night.

Dad pulls a square box from behind his back. "I know you like purple, so…" He opens it to reveal an orchid corsage. I choke back tears. He's so considerate, and I'm so miserable. He removes the corsage and tries to pin it to my dress. After the third time it falls off, I tell him, "I'll do it. Klutz."

He steps back to the door and says, "You look rad."

I make a face at him and go, "That is so eighties."

"Translation," he says. "I think you're beautiful."

If he doesn't leave, my makeup is going to be a lost cause.

"I'll see you there." Dad winks. "Save me a dance."

"Daaad."

He grins. "Just joking."

The weather was so nice all week that almost all the snow melted. I made an executive decision this morning to take down the plywood and have an open-air prom. Now the weather forecasters are predicting rain for later this evening. Great. If prom is a disaster, it'll be on my head. Again.

I sit at my desk and log on to Prom Central for transportation options. Limos are listed first. I don't care if I have a date or not; I'm taking a limo to my prom.

I know Luke's brother owns A-1 Car Service, so I call that number first. A recorded voice says: "I'm sorry. All of our cars are booked this evening, but please try us again for your future needs."

Crap. There's a free service listed — Stan's Super Sedan. I'm sure they'll be booked, too, but I try anyway. "Hello?" a man says.

"Hi. I'd like a ride to my prom."

He takes down my address and asks, "How many people?"

"Just one."

He hesitates. I know it's a waste of his time to drive one person, and I almost tell him to forget it, but he says, "I'll be there in five minutes."

Five minutes later, a stretch limo pulls into the drive. I'm glad Dad isn't here to witness what a loser his daughter is.

"Miss?" The driver holds open the back door. He's wearing a dark blue suit with a lipped cap. For an instant the light catches his face, and I see him clearly. He looks like...

"Owen?"

He does a double take. "Do I know you?"

"I'm Azure. Luke's friend?"

"Oh, right. Sorry; I didn't recognize you."

"I think we've only met a couple of times."

He removes his cap and swoops it in a gesture for me to get in.

I slide across the leather seat and smell a toxic mixture of perfume and cologne. "I thought your company was A-1," I say.

Owen takes a wide turn out to the street. "I go by a lot of names." His eyes meet mine in the rearview mirror.

Okay. Weird. Luke never told me that.

I do remember Luke telling me that Owen takes in a lot of money from proms. "Why would you do this for free?" I ask. "Limo rides must cost, what? A hundred, two hundred dollars? Unless you charge by the person, which means you'd get, like, twenty bucks from me."

He says, "There are tons of proms coming up. This is Luke's. It's the least I can do. Don't tell him, though."

"Why not? I think it's nice."

"I don't want him getting the wrong idea about me."

Like you care? Like you love him? Luke should know how cool Owen is, because life's too short to not appreciate the kindness and devotion of others—especially your own family.

I hear the prom before we exit the freeway. Owen has to wait for another limo ahead of him entering the parking lot before he can pull in. The other limo driver's window is down, and Owen calls to him, "Dobbs, when you finish your last run, there's a parking lot down the street where we can wait for after-prom pickups."

The driver gives him a thumbs-up.

The pavilion is already packed. People are dancing in couples and groups. The decorations are fantastic. The rainbow balloon arch is three times the size I imagined, and there are multicolored twinkling lights strung all the way around the pavilion, with shimmering Mylar draped between the columns.

I can't see the band from where I'm standing, so I try to inch closer to the front.

As Luke would say, Oh. Em. Gee. They're — what do you call it — dominatrixes? Dressed in black leather and chains. One has a whip, and she's snapping it.

A laugh burbles up from my core and I cover my mouth. Then I see her — Radhika! My stomach does a loop-de-loop. She's dancing with someone and, as I make my way over to her, I see that she's dressed in a yellow silk sari with bracelets and anklets. Her hair is braided and pulled back.

I put a hand on her shoulder and she spins around. Her eyes are outlined with black kohl, and she has a jewel in the middle of her forehead.

"Azure." She embraces me.

I hold her tight. "You came," I say in her ear.

"How could I not come to my own prom?" She smiles slyly. "Do you know Mario?"

Mario, from Luke's play. "Hi," I say. Actually, I yell, because the band is so loud.

The song ends and Mario says, "Do you want some cake, Radhika?"

She says, "No, thanks. Do you mind if I talk to Azure for a minute?"

He looks from me to her. "Not at all. I'll just be…eating cake." His eyes have this glassy, lovestruck look in them. I know how he feels.

The band starts up again and Radhika says in my ear, "We can't talk here. Let's go outside."

I follow her out of the pavilion to the lawn. "I wasn't going to come," she says. "I really wasn't. But then I finally just said, 'To hell with it,' and I asked him."

"'Him' being Mario?"

"Yes. And he said yes! I've been going to Luke's practices, hoping Mario would see me there and maybe ask me. I've liked him for a long time." She lowers her eyes.

"You never told me that."

"I know. I'm sorry. I was afraid you or Luke might say something to him."

Which Luke probably would have. Knowing Radhika, it would've embarrassed her to death. And okay, I might've hinted to him, too. Anything to make Radhika happy.

"You look gorgeous," I tell her.

She meets my eyes and smiles. "The other day my mom brought out this sari for me and said she'd been saving it. I knew she'd be disappointed if I didn't go to prom, after she defended it and all. Not that I cared about that so much, but I never want to live with regrets. You know?"

Do I ever.

Her eyes sparkle in the lights. Mine stray to a clump of adults at one end of the pavilion, where I see Mr. and Mrs. Dal, both dressed in traditional Indian garb.

Radhika's eyes search the tent where the chairs and tables are set up. She says, "He's nice, don't you think?"

I don't really know him all that well. "Yeah, I guess."

"He told me he's had a crush on me for a while, but

thought I was out of his league. Can you believe that?" Before I can answer, she adds, "Do you know how hard it is to like someone and keep it all inside?"

I almost laugh out loud.

"Oh, Azure. I'm so happy." She hugs me hard.

I try to look as stoked as she feels. "I'm glad you came," I say. And I mean that sincerely. "Tell your father thank you for making the prom possible."

She frowns. "What do you mean?"

"You know."

Her frown deepens. "If you mean the donation, it wasn't from him. I don't know where the money came from. I never asked him for a cent."

"Radhika..."

"What?" she says. "I wasn't about to be coerced or bribed into anything."

"But...Who? Where?"

"I'd already decided I was going to Yale. I guess I should've told you that, too."

Now I'm doubly shocked. "Uh, yeeeah. What changed your mind? The trip to the campus?"

"No. Well, yes and no. It was really what you said about how I may only get one opportunity, and I should take it. Besides, I may be of more use in the Peace Corps with a degree in engineering or something."

Mario returns with a ginormous square of cake and three forks. He offers the forks to us. "You go ahead," I tell them. "I need to, um..." *Get lost.*

I see the makeshift dressing rooms behind the band,

which must be set up for people to change before and after the drag show. I haven't seen Luke, so maybe that's where he is. Except I thought the drag show followed the announcement of the prom king and queen.

"We'll be taking a break now," the lead singer says, and people head off for the tables and chairs.

"Excuse me. May I have your attention?" Shauna speaks into the microphone onstage.

She looks pretty. She's wearing a short, spaghetti-strap, cream-colored, shimmery dress, with shoes to match. Her hair has rainbow ribbons in it. I wish I'd thought of that.

She says, "It's time to crown our prom royalty."

I hear a few *boos* from the tables. Shauna must hear them, too, because she snarls, "Oh, get over it." She cracks me up. Shauna holds an envelope with the voting results. "Just a minute," she says, then disappears backstage, returning with the band's drummer.

"This year's prom king is…" She cues the drummer, who *rat-a-tat*s the announcement. Shauna rips open the envelope and arches her eyebrows. "Luke O'Donnell."

People whistle and applaud. I don't see Luke at first—then this streak of white lightning flies up the stairs.

My eyes widen. His tuxedo is pure white and the jacket is long, like a zoot suit, with sequined lapels, over a black shirt and black tie. He looks so totally cool.

Shauna places the crown on Luke's head and he raises his arms in the air as he swaggers away.

"And now for your prom queen." Shauna cues the

drummer, who does a wild riff, twirling the drumsticks and ending with a clang on the cymbals. Shauna opens the envelope and stares at the results. She shakes her head. "Luke O'Donnell."

People shriek. Luke races back to the stage.

Shauna seems kind of reluctant to give Luke the tiara, so there's a bit of tussling. Eventually, she relinquishes the crown and sash. He bows and curtsies. Into the mike, he says, "I'm honored. And humbled."

I snort.

He makes circles with his hand. "Thank you, my liege. And now for the royal dance." He wraps his arms around himself and sways back and forth. People are either laughing or booing, but in a kind way. Luke leaps off the stage into Ryan's arms. He places the king's crown on Ryan's head.

The rest of the band returns and begins again with a slow song. I feel a tap on my shoulder. A familiar voice says, "Can you dance?"

I turn and it's Desirae. My eyes span the length of her and I let out an audible gasp. Under the dome and at night, the red dress is ravishing on her.

"You like?" She pulls out the sides and shifts from one foot to the other.

"I love," I say.

She smiles. "So would it be okay with Radhika if I danced with you?"

"Why wouldn't it be?" I ask.

She blinks. "Because she's your girlfriend?"

"Huh?"

Desi tilts her head.

"She's not my girlfriend," I say.

She looks confused. "She's not?"

"No. She never was." *And never will be*, I admit to myself. "What about *your* girlfriend?" I ask. "Will she mind?"

Desi makes a face. "What girlfriend?"

"I thought you said…That girl who hangs around with you."

"You mean my cousin, Christine?"

Her cousin? "But I thought you said you had a girlfriend."

"I never said we were still together. We broke up in September. Christine's a senior and she didn't have a date for prom, so she asked if I'd come with her."

A beat goes by and we both laugh a little. Then a lot. Desi opens her arms to dance.

The only way I know how to slow-dance is to put my arms around the person and sway to the beat. Desi rests her head on my shoulder, and her warmth spreads through me. I feel the hitch in my lower belly that I used to get with her.

"You smell good," she says. "Like vanilla."

"I ate a carton of Ben and Jerry's for dinner," I say.

She laughs softly. We don't talk again until the song ends. I don't want to let her go, and I wish Putrid Wixen would play slow songs all evening. Then I notice the necklace.

"I saw that at the silent auction," I tell her.

"I know! I've been looking for it forever. It must've gotten hooked to some other jewelry, because when I saw it at the auction, I about had a heart attack. Of course, I had to buy it back." She fingers it gently and says, "It means everything to me."

A memory floats to the surface. "The Valentine's Day card in my locker…"

A slow smile spreads across her face. "Did you like it? It took me an hour to find just the right verse online, then I was scared to death to give it to you. And I knew I shouldn't because you were with Radhika."

Crazy. Such craziness. We gaze into each other's eyes.

Desi says, "Do you believe the theory that people may be right for each other, but they meet at the wrong time in their lives and don't realize it?"

I tell her the truth: "I never thought about it."

"I have," she says. "I've thought about it a lot." The music starts again and we dance to the heavy-metal beat, but close together. Her hand touches mine and a jolt of electricity zings up my arm.

I lean in close and ask her, "Why did you and your girlfriend break up?" Then I want to clap my hand over my mouth, because what if Desi got dumped again?

But she just smiles and says in my ear, "Because she wasn't you."

LUKE

It's funny that the gamers are all dressed in tuxes. But then, everything is funny. The whole world has come alive. Ryan's holding my hand, swirling me under his arm. I feel like the carousel is going round and round. Where it stops, nobody knows.

I think that's supposed to rhyme, but I'm too light-headed to remember the verse.

"Mind if we sit for a minute?" Ryan says. "These shoes are killing me."

My feet could be bloody stumps and I wouldn't feel a thing.

As we head for the tents, I see Gabe dancing with Haley. Last night at the cast party I got the scoop: Gabe broke up with Haley to ask Radhika to the prom, and when she said no, he wanted to get back with Haley. Initially Haley was pissed, but in the end, true love won out. Connor's dancing with Mollie. He gives me a thumbs-up. I blow him a kiss. I blow everyone a kiss as we pass by.

For the millionth time, I pull out my cell and take a picture of Ryan and me. If he's getting annoyed, he doesn't say anything. He's so adorable.

I snap him from the back, too. He has a cute tush.

Azure's at the table with her old girlfriend, Desirae. They're sort of snuggling and whispering sweet nothings. What did I miss while I was blissing out?

Desirae sees me and says, "Props on winning prom king and queen."

"Thanks," I say. "And I didn't even vote for myself."

Azure blows out a puff of air.

"What's with this?" I circle my hand around the two of them.

Azure imitates my gesture around Ryan and me. "What's with this?"

'Nuf said, I guess. Ryan sits and pulls up a chair in front of him to rest his feet.

"Ryan was my secret admirer," I tell Azure. When her face remains impassive, I add, "On Valentine's Day."

She looks at Desi and they both laugh.

What? It's not a joke.

"Guess who mine was?" Azure goes.

It takes me a second, then I join in the laughter.

Shauna wanders over to our table with her date in tow. "Do you guys know Hans?"

I do, of course. He's the hunky exchange student from Sweden.

We all introduce ourselves and Shauna and Hans pull up chairs at the table. She says to me, "You'd better get ready for the drag show, Luke. It's getting late."

For the first time, I'm hesitant. What if the real me sends Ryan running? If it does, I'll know he's not The One, as Azure says. I so want him — need him — to be The One. Stomach in knots, I head backstage to get ready.

I pass Radhika, who is holding Mario's good hand. "Hey, when did this...?" I gesture at the two of them.

Radhika leans down and plants a soft kiss on my cheek. She's still gorgeous and desirable. But maybe a little less so? I hope we'll always be friends. I glance back over my shoulder and Ryan smiles such a sweet smile that it melts me into marshmallow creme.

I quickly race to the makeshift changing area behind the stage. Putting on my drag gear is a well-practiced routine.

The lead singer of Putrid Wixen hands me the mike and I announce from behind the drummer: "And now... now...now...From the Excalibur in Vegas...Vegas... Vegas...The Thunder from Down Under."

Whoops of glee rise up from the audience. Before I get in trouble, I add quickly, "Okay, we couldn't get them. But we do have our own Roosevelt Roosters." I hit Play on the boom box and this smarmy prerecorded music comes on. The entire football team, dressed in drag, struts across the stage. People cheer wildly. This is going to cost me a fortune in bribe money, but it's worth it.

The serious dragsters are up next.

I strut out to rousing applause. Cuing the music, I lip-synch "Popular" from *Wicked*. I'm followed by a gaggle of guys dressed like girls. They do a dance routine to Lady Gaga's "Born This Way." Then a girl karaokes Michael Jackson's "Man in the Mirror."

The band returns while everyone changes and I hurry back to our table. Thank God Ryan hasn't bolted.

I sit and he says, "You were awesome."

OMG. He's The One! "Maybe I'll buy you some boobies for graduation," I tell him.

He stutters, "Th-that's okay."

He'd make a fab drag queen. Those high cheekbones, those luscious lips.

"Is that your dad, Azure?" Shauna points to the cluster of adults in back, who are no doubt spiking their punch.

"Yeah," she says. "He's with his crush, Lynda. The one he met online?"

"Ooh. Do I hear wedding bells?" I say.

Azure goes, "I don't know. He's not the commitment type."

Her dad glances our way and waves. Azure ducks her head.

"Is that Flacco?" I ask. "Who's she with?" My God, she's wearing a frumpy flowered dress that looks like flocked wallpaper.

"Must be her husband," Shauna replies.

The thought that someone actually likes Flacco—maybe even loves her—gives me hope for all humankind.

Shauna stands. "I need to get the poetry slam started."

She heads for the stage and waits until Putrid Wixen has finished their song. After Shauna's announcement, a line forms near the stage. A bunch of these people are the moles, the invisible students who hide out in dark corners of the school. It's cool that we've gotten them to prom. The first person, a girl dressed in black, recites some ragey poem about the apocalypse.

Shauna comes back to the table and says, "God, my feet hurt." She slips off her shoes and wiggles her toes. "The ticket table told me that they sold more than nine hundred tickets. That's the most people who've ever come to prom in the history of Roosevelt."

We all high-five.

Azure says, "I have a question: Does anyone know who donated the money?"

I just look at her. She and I both know it was Radhika's dad.

Shauna says in a lowered voice, "I wasn't supposed to tell, but Mr. Rosen's been calling around for sponsors, like, twenty-four/seven. It's one reason I held off on printing the program—so we could get all the companies listed on back."

I twist my head around to eye Radhika. She and Mario are playing finger puppets or something.

There's a program on the table and I pick it up. I scan the sponsors. I don't see Mr. Dal's name anywhere.

"We'll have to get Mr. Rosen a present to thank him," Shauna says, "Mrs. Flacco, too."

I groan.

Shauna huffs at me. "She helped us. Whether she knew it or not."

Which makes us all roll our eyes.

A moment passes, then Ryan says, "You guys did an amazing job on this prom."

I want to kiss him. In private. All night long.

Azure says, "It didn't turn out too shabby."

I add, "I soooooooooo wish we could've gotten the Thunder from Down Under."

"Oh, stop," Shauna says. "We'll put it on the list for next year's prom com."

Ryan and I leave the group to dance what's left of the night away.

At the stroke of midnight, Flacco announces that the prom is over. The people who are still here let out a collective moan. I holler, "Conga line," and everyone grabs someone's waist. We snake around the pavilion, singing, "Conga, conga, con-ga," kicking out on the last beat. Even the chaperones and PTSA join in. I see Owen leaning against a column. "Bro. Come on," I call.

He waves us off. Some people just refuse to be included.

Owen's limos are parked, ready to transport people to the after-party. This year the party is at Family Fun, an indoor amusement park. The PTSA rented it for the night.

As the band is packing up, I race over to Azure and look for Shauna and Connor. "You guys, we need to get a group pic before the photographer leaves."

Shauna says, "Find Mr. Rosen and Mrs. Flacco. They should be included."

Ugh. Her, too? I find Mr. Rosen with his hot date and tell him to meet us under the balloon arch. Flacco is handing checks to the band and the security guard.

"We're going to get a group photo of the prom com," I tell her. "And, um, we request your presence."

She whirls on me and I flinch, like she's going to take me down.

"Why me?" she asks.

"Because you're one of us."

She narrows her eyes.

My voice shakes a little when I add, "Because it's all about inclusion."

She doesn't seem to have a snippy answer for that. She pays the guard, then follows me to the balloons.

Under the arch, we stand and kneel and bunch together to get us all in the shot. The photographer snaps us at different angles. Then I say, "Silly shots."

We make vertical and horizontal peace signs. We stick out our tongues and cross our eyes. It's hard to believe, but even Flacco makes a funny face. I go, "Hold me up," and then jump to splay myself across their outstretched arms. The photographer shows us the digital pictures and we all laugh.

As people pass by, they shout things like, "Guys! Best prom ever."

I waggle a victory sign at them. Or is it the Texas Longhorns? Whatever.

"Everyone's coming to the after-party, right?" I say.

"I want to say good-bye to my mom and dad first," Radhika replies.

"Yeah," Azure says. "I should let my dad know that a broken curfew on this night of nights will result in no penal code enforcements." She takes Desirae's hand. "Oh, Luke," she says, "tell Owen thanks for giving everyone free rides all night."

"What?" I ask. "There's no way he's doing that."

"Is too. He's both A-1 and Stan's Sedan. All rides are free."

Something's not kosher. "People were complaining to me about how expensive my brother's service was. Every carload had to come up with three hundred bucks."

Azure's jaw drops. "My ride was free. He told me all the rides were free."

I turn to see Owen talking to Dobbs. I storm over there and hear Dobbs say, "I'll take this group of booger eaters." He leads them to his limo.

"Owen," I say, "did you know one of your drivers—*at least* one of them—is charging three hundred bucks per carload?" *And I think I know who.*

Owen stares at me. Then his gaze shifts to Dobbs's limo.

Dobbs backs up to leave, but Owen smacks the hood, hard. The limo stops. Owen goes around and opens the driver's-side door. "Get out," he orders.

"Why?" Dobbs says.

"Get out!"

Dobbs cranks the ignition off and steps out.

"How many, Dobbs? How many fares did you charge?"

He glances at me, then back at Owen. "All of them. Do you know how much you're losing tonight by giving free rides? I'm saving your ass, dude. Someone has to."

"I told you the fares were free tonight," Owen says.

"Yeah, well, I need the money, even if you don't. They're just a bunch of kids. What do they know?"

Both of Owen's fists ball. I think—I hope—he's going to pound Dobbs into dog meat. In a flash, he reaches up and removes Dobbs's chauffeur's cap.

"Give me the money." Owen holds out an open palm. "Every cent you stole."

"Dude, it's not stealing. It's business."

"Is that what you call it? You've been stealing from me for years. Did you think I didn't know, Dobbs? Did you think I was stupid? Give me the goddamn money!" Owen yells.

"All right." Dobbs holds up his hands defensively. He pulls an envelope from his uniform pocket.

Owen grabs it and looks inside. He says, "*All* of it."

"That's all—"

Owen snags Dobbs's jacket and searches the inside pockets. He finds another envelope stuffed with cash. He says, "You're fired."

"Oh, come on...."

"Luke." Owen turns to me. He hands me the chauffeur's cap and the cash. "See if you can figure out who paid this a-hole and get them their money back." Then he adds, "And Dobbs's limo is yours for the night."

My eyes bulge at Ryan. Plans are already formulating in my sex-crazed brain.

I say to Owen, "Could we switch caps? Because, like, this one has Dobbs's DNA all over it. I don't want my kids to be genetic slimeballs."

Owen switches caps.

"Excuse me, maggot." I push past Dobbs and hold the passenger door open for Ryan.

Owen starts back to his own limo.

"Owen," Dobbs calls to him. "How am I supposed to get home?"

Owen says, "Call a cab."

AZURE

I wake to the sound of Dad clunking around in the kitchen, and I hear a woman's voice. The aroma of cinnamon rolls wafting up the hallway is heavenly and my stomach growls, but I decide to give Dad and Lynda a few minutes alone. It was dawn by the time I got home, and Dad had left a note on the pantry door, like he knew the first place I'd go would be in search of food.

"You were the belle of the ball," he wrote. "I hope you know you make me proud."

I wrote him back: "You make me proud, too. Just don't get offed in the line of duty."

I lie in bed, listening to the rain pounding on the window. Thankfully, the clouds didn't roll in until after the prom.

I replay every second, every moment, every feeling and emotion from last night. I have to be at work in an hour and I'll probably be late, but that's okay. I deserve to give myself time to devour this delicious slice of life.

Right before the lead singer packed up her guitar, I asked if she knew Mercy Her's "Now's the Time." She said she loved that song, and that she could probably fake it well enough. I led Desi out to the middle of the pavilion floor and said, "I believe this is our dance."

So cool, dancing in the dark, under the carousel dome.

Desi. Who'd have thought?

I roll over and the first thing I see is my tote bag of party favors. I dump it on the bed. We got a set of rainbow-colored pens with the Roosevelt High logo, a flash-drive keychain, a photo cube, a candle in a tin, and a car air freshener. Not a bad haul. On my nightstand is a stack of photos Desi and I took in the photo booth at Family Fun. Ooh, yeah. Some of these are not for Facebook.

Also in the tote is the program. Shauna did a gorgeous job on it. I'm sliding it back into the tote when I see the back page. Holy macaroni, as Mr. Rosen would say. We had, like, forty or fifty sponsors. Mr. Rosen really worked his butt off. One company on the list catches my eye: Fred Flacco's Fish and Chips. That couldn't possibly be.... There's even a twenty-percent-off coupon.

I shake my head. You never know about people.

Something Shauna said comes back to me: One day you look at a person and they're all hot, then the next day, they're cold as ice. Except in the case of Desi; with her, the complete opposite is true. Her good-night kiss lingers on my lips. Make that a good-morning kiss. The first of many to come.

My calendar is next to my bed and I rip off the page. My affirmation for April 17 makes me smile from the inside out. I'm keeping it with my prom memorabilia forever and ever. It reads: "Open your eyes to every possibility in life."

Have I been blind? More like blinded by my misplaced love for Radhika. One word swirls around in my brain: *opportunity*. I think Dad's wrong, and Radhika, too. There's a chance that opportunity knocks more than once. You should never close that door.

IT'S OUR PROM (SO DEAL WITH IT)
Questions for Discussion

1. Have you ever crushed on someone you shouldn't, such as a best friend or someone else's girlfriend or boyfriend? What did you do? Do you wish you'd handled it differently?

2. Do you think it was fair for Azure to insist that Luke and Radhika join the prom planning committee with her? Why or why not?

3. How would you describe Luke's relationship with his brother, Owen, when the book opens? How does their relationship change over the course of the novel? How do you think Owen could be more supportive of Luke?

4. Discuss Radhika's relationship with her parents. What do you think of the way Radhika deals with their high expectations? Have you ever felt a similar pressure?

5. Azure's first impressions of Shauna are negative, and vice versa. Do their opinions of each other change as they spend more time together? In what ways? Have you ever judged someone before you truly got to know him or her? What happened?

6. Azure has trouble with her dad's online dating. Why? Have you ever disapproved of something your parents did? Were you able to talk to them about it? Did you gain a deeper understanding of their needs?

7. Do you think Radhika should follow her dream and join the Peace Corps after high school or is attending college a better choice? What do you think about her final decision?

8. Do you feel the efforts of the prom committee were worthwhile? Would you have taken the risks that they took?

9. What is your opinion of the way the prom committee raised money for the prom? What would you have done in the same way? What would you have done differently? Have you ever had to raise money for a dance or school organization?

10. Would you attend an alternative prom? Why or why not?

Provocative, heart-wrenching, hopeful...

Read all of Julie Anne Peters's inspiring novels

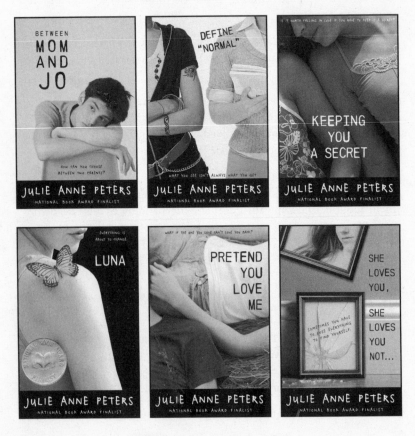